PRAISE FOR
CHARMED PARTICL

"Part immigration story, part Midwestern pastoral, Kolaya's charming debut maps the schisms of a small Illinois town that's divided over a proposal to build a Superconducting Super Collider at the local research lab.... The book is at its best and most nuanced when Kolaya turns her attention to the personal: Abhijat and Sarala's marriage, Lily and Meena's increasingly difficult friendship, and—above all—Abhijat's internal struggle to come to terms with the reality of his career."   —*Kirkus Reviews*

"This is such an accomplished debut novel.... Kolaya handles an intriguing and sympathetic cast of characters with aplomb—it's a brainy, witty page-turner, and marks the start of what I hope will be a long career for Kolaya as a novelist."   —Newcity Lit

"*Charmed Particles* is inspired by very real stories straight from today's headlines, yet managed to mesmerize me in the way of an intoxicating fairytale. Kolaya's characters are flawed, though sympathetic citizens, gazing suspiciously at one another across great chasms of misunderstanding—passionately divided. Yet in her alchemical hands we're shown what is possible when we have the courage to venture deep within our wounded hearts: sweet magic."
—Susan Power, author of *The Grass Dancer*

"*Charmed Particles* is a deftly constructed fable of modernity told in elegant, pellucid prose. Kolaya draws her characters with affectionate acuity and the whole reminds me—in its depiction of childhood precocity and earnest adult eccentricity—of one of Wes Anderson's wry wonders."   —Peter Ho Davies, author of *The Welsh Girl*

CHARMED PARTICLES

CHARMED
PARTICLES

CHRISSY
KOLAYA

DZANC
BOOKS

DZANC BOOKS

5220 Dexter Ann Arbor Rd.
Ann Arbor, MI 48103
www.dzancbooks.org

Designed by Steven Seighman

Excerpts of this book appeared, sometimes in slightly different form, in the following publications: "Unveiling the Wild: Being the Account of the Expeditions of Randolph Winchester, the Last Great Gentleman Explorer," *Chariton Review*; and "The Search for Charmed Particles," *Crab Orchard Review*.

Library of Congress Cataloging-in-Publication Data
Kolaya, Chrissy.
  Charmed particles / Chrissy Kolaya.
    pages ; cm
  ISBN 978-1-938103-17-9
  I. Title. PS3611.O5824C48 2015
  813'.6—dc23

                                    2015008017

First U.S. Edition: November 2015

Printed in the United States of America

10 9 8 7 6 5 4 3 2 1

In memory of Helen Calvert Bergman
wise reader, dear friend,
dream-come-true mother-in-law.

CHARMED
PARTICLES

CHAPTER 1

Charmed Particles

Particles containing a charm quark...have only a fleeting existence before decaying into more conventional particles.
—FREDERICK A. HARRIS

1972

ABHIJAT MITAL ACCEPTED THE POSITION AT THE NATIONAL Accelerator Research Lab with great pride. The offer itself was the realization of his greatest dream, now made concrete by the desk he would sit behind, the nameplate on his door, the drive every morning through the gates, where he would present his pass to the security guard who would, after a matter of weeks, begin to wave him through, recognizing Abhijat as one among the parade of scientists he'd been waving through those gates for years, and on that day, Abhijat would feel, at last, like he belonged.

He had written Sarala with the news that he'd accepted a position at the premier particle accelerator and research facility in the U.S., some argued in the world. The job would begin at the end of the semester, after he had fulfilled his academic commitments to the university.

In the evenings, he took the short, quiet walk from his office on campus to the small set of rooms he rented in the house of an emeritus professor of philosophy, with whom he sometimes enjoyed an evening game of chess before returning to his desk to pore over his work. As he walked, snow falling quietly around him as was common on those dark midwinter nights, he often caught himself peering into the lit-up windows of the houses he passed, imagining the life he and Sarala would make for themselves.

Sarala had pointed out that he neglected to respond to the questions in her letters, and so, in the next letter he posted, he included the following chart:

Letter Number	Question	Answer
3	Are you making progress with your research?	Yes.
4	Are the Americans friendly?	Not overmuch.
5	Do you think I will like it there, in the United States with you?	I am unable to answer this. Any response would be pure speculation, an area I prefer to avoid.

To which Sarala replied:

Yes, but if I understand your work, you are doing precisely this—speculating—in making predictions about the possible existence of new particles before they have been detected.

To which Abhijat responded (keeping to himself his delight at Sarala's pluck, as well as her surprisingly accurate grasp of his research project):

You are correct. I will here attempt a prediction. I believe it is likely that you will be happy here and with me, but that you will at times experience some degree of homesickness, as I have.

Abhijat had been working at a university in the U.S. since leaving Cambridge, where he had done his training and emerged from the group of young theoretical physicists as a quiet, serious student, one his professors had decided possessed a great deal of promise. And all that time, back in Bombay, his mother had been on the hunt for a suitable wife. Sarala had emerged as the foremost contender. The wedding had taken place on his last trip home, and soon Sarala would join him in the States to begin their new life together.

@

After the wedding, Sarala had gone to Abhijat's mother's home, a custom they kept despite Abhijat's absence. He had needed to return to the university to finish the academic year, and so the months between Sarala's wedding and her arrival in the U.S. were spent in close companionship with her new mother-in-law, who, she was surprised to find, she liked a great deal.

"You must help Abhijat find some happiness in the world," her new mother-in-law said to Sarala one night as they shared their evening meal. "Since he was a boy, he has always grasped for something just out of reach, never happy with what he has accomplished.

"You will be good for him," she added. "As for a wife, he gave no thought to it. 'Abhijat,' I told him, 'now is the time.' 'Yes, Ma,' he said, but I wonder, had I not spoken, how long he would have remained with eyes only for his articles and equations."

@

Sarala had studied business administration at university. The majority of her knowledge of American history had been gleaned from a castoff sixth-grade textbook entitled *Our Colonial Forefathers,* which Abhijat's mother had found in an English-language bookstore in Bombay, and which she had bought and presented to Sarala, hoping to help smooth the way for her new daughter-in-law in this land of foreigners.

Though Sarala had not yet realized it, her own mother had slipped a gift for her daughter's new life in with the things that were to be shipped to her new home: a small wooden box of recipes written in her own hand on square pieces of blue paper—what she imagined Sarala would need to know for a happy union and a marriage that would grow into love.

For After an Argument:

Below that, her mother's recipe for pav bhaji.

On the Days When You Have Been Short-Tempered:

Followed by her careful instruction on how to prepare aloo gobi.

When You Wish to Call into Your Life a Child:

Here, the steps for making rajma chawal, one of Sarala's favorites.

And so on.

@

Sarala occupied herself on the long series of plane rides by immersing herself in her copy of *Our Colonial Forefathers*. In it, she found a map illustrating the thirteen colonies and the westward expansion of settlers during the period. The land where she and Abhijat would live—Illinois—was marked out on the map as a vast, unexplored territory, wilderness—unknown, untamed, and uncharted terrain.

When, near the end of her last flight, the pilot came over the loudspeaker to announce that they would now begin their descent into Chicago, Sarala peered out the window through the clouds, watching for her new home to materialize. The plane circled over a wide blue body of water—Lake Michigan, she guessed—and made its way inland down a tiny grid of geometrically arranged streets, the roofs of small houses, outlines of yards, and then tiny cars becoming visible as they descended. When the wheels touched down, Sarala felt herself pulled forward in her seat, then back as the plane strained to a stop.

They rolled slowly toward the gate where Abhijat would meet her. As they approached, she looked out toward the large-paned window of the terminal, wondering if she could make him out, if he could find her face framed in the tiny round window of the plane.

@

Abhijat greeted her with a bright, warm smile as she stepped into the waiting area of the terminal, and she was reminded of their wedding ceremony months earlier. Their embrace was again like their first, and Sarala hoped they would soon grow to feel comfortable and at ease with one another.

Abhijat carried her bags and led her out to the parking garage to the beige sedan he had recently purchased. Though tired from her long hours of travel, Sarala peered out the windows as they drove, here and there Abhijat pointing out places of interest, Sarala taking in her new home—first the bright, busy maze of highways and billboards near the airport, and off in the distance the skyscrapers of the city.

As they drove west, the buildings grew low to the ground and thinned out into farmland. Sarala's eyes traced the great metal towers strung with wires that stretched across the highway, cutting a swath through the farmland, so that this new land appeared to Sarala to be all cornfields and infrastructure.

On one side of the highway rose a great green sign: NICOLET, NEXT 3 EXITS. Abhijat pointed out the landfill just off the highway, the strange glow of a flame burning off methane. Then, a little further on, the place where he had been staying—executive housing, they called it. The outside of the building looked like a hotel, but inside, the rooms included small kitchenettes that looked out over neatly made double beds.

@

Before bed, Sarala undid her long, dark rope of a braid, brushing it smooth. Abhijat watched as the hair fell around her like a veil. That night they slept side by side for only the second time.

In the morning, Sarala arranged herself on the room's foamy couch, which gave the sensation of being at once both soft and hard, and read carefully through the brochures and orientation packet the Lab had provided for Abhijat, and which he had presented to her. They were so glossy and pristine that she wondered whether he had even opened them before handing them to her.

In the photos, the Lab's facilities were green and sunlit. The cover featured a tall building that rose up over the flat expanse of grass. She peered at a photo of a white-coated man standing inside a large room: *The Collision Hall,* the caption read.

The Lab sat on a piece of fertile land which had once been farmland, and which had, before that, been undisturbed prairie. Now the Lab's expansive campus was ringed with a series of tunnels that made up the particle accelerator, in which cutting-edge experiments in high-energy particle physics were being conducted.

Abhijat and the other theoretical physicists had offices on the nineteenth floor of the twenty-story Research Tower, which looked out over the Illinois landscape, the tallest building for miles. Sarala looked at the image of the Research Tower and tried to imagine what Abhijat's office might be like.

In the center of the brochure was a section titled "Living and Working at the Lab," which included tips on opening a bank account in the U.S., how to obtain a driver's license, and an overview of common laws and regulations. There were language classes for the spouses of foreign scientists, but her English was good. What Sarala studied most carefully was the list of the Lab's social activities and organizations:

Automobile Club   Dancing Club
Badminton Club   Fitness Club
Lab Choir   Jazz Club

Martial Arts Club	Amateur Radio Club
Photo Club	Model Airplane Club
Squash Club	Gardening Club

With a pen, she carefully underlined *Dancing Club, Photo Club, Lab Choir*, imagining that together, she and Abhijat might fill their evenings with new hobbies and new friends.

@

Sarala spent her first week acclimating to the time change and taking in everything she could. In the small space of the hotel room, she and Abhijat learned each other's daily routines and habits: that Sarala liked first to carefully make the bed before preparing their morning tea; that each morning, Abhijat emerged from the bathroom freshly showered and fully dressed, his dark hair combed along a strict and unwavering part. This close intimacy of preparing to build a life together was their honeymoon.

Once Abhijat left for work, Sarala had the day to herself. In the small room, she busied herself with washing, drying, and putting away the breakfast dishes in the kitchenette and then with tidying their things, gathering the materials Abhijat had brought her from the Lab—brochures from the Nicolet Chamber of Commerce, a helpful booklet prepared by the Lab indicating where new residents might find doctors, dentists, childcare, cultural activities, etc. These Sarala gathered into a neat pile on the end table next to her side of the bed, leaving the desk uncluttered should Abhijat need it. She opened the drapes and stood before the window, which looked out over the grey pavement of the hotel parking lot. She gathered their clothes in the small plastic laundry basket she found in the closet and made her way down the long hallway to the laundry facilities.

The hallway was silent, every door closed, and Sarala wondered about the other people living behind those closed doors. "Divorce apartments," she had heard the clerk at the front desk call them. The few times she'd encountered other guests in the elevator or lobby, they had all been men. She'd thus far met no women, no children.

Still, in the halls she'd now and then caught a familiar smell. Ginger and garlic one night, coming from room 219. Green chilies and coriander, she guessed, the next evening, from 256. But overwhelmingly, the smell of America, she had decided, was the smell of nothing—carpet, cardboard, wallpaper, framed paintings of lakes and animals, bedspreads with bright floral patterns. Even the small slivers of soap wrapped in paper in the bathroom seemed to be entirely without a scent, Sarala thought, peeling open the wrapping and holding the small white rectangle up to her nose.

She prided herself on being adaptable, one of the many qualities she felt was necessary in a good wife, and so did not allow room for the question of whether she was or was not homesick.

When the laundry was dry, Sarala loaded it back into the small basket and returned to their rooms. Since her arrival, she'd grown familiar with the plotlines of a number of the soap operas that aired during the long, quiet afternoons while Abhijat was away. Her favorite was *Search for Tomorrow*, and she watched as she folded, anxious to find out whether Joanne would regain her sight in time to identify her captors.

The realtor had arranged to pick them up at the hotel to begin *house hunting*, as she called it when Abhijat phoned to make an appointment. Her car was a plush, champagne-colored Cadillac. Abhijat sat in the front seat, and Sarala, in the back, leaned forward to hear them speaking.

"Whatever neighborhood you settle on, the schools will be great," the realtor said. "District 220 schools are all top of the line. Some of the best in the state."

Abhijat made a note on the pad of paper he kept in the breast pocket of his blazer. Most of the other foreign scientists at the Lab were there temporarily—they and their families were housed on the Lab campus or, like he and Sarala, in small hotel-style efficiency apartments. However, as Abhijat was to be a permanent hire, he and Sarala would need to find a permanent home.

The realtor had a pleasant voice, Sarala thought, noting also her delicate perfume, hair the color of straw, sculpted and set, flipping up at the collar of the shirt she wore under her muted, neutral suit. Sarala ran her hand over the smooth beige velour of the seat as they drove, the realtor pointing out here and there the benefits and drawbacks of each neighborhood.

"Well, of course, you'll want to be close to the Lab," the realtor continued, "which makes Eagle's Crest an excellent choice. Just across Route 12, and one of the most exclusive neighborhoods in the community."

By the second day in the realtor's car, Sarala was certain they had been inside every home for sale in Nicolet. And how strange it had seemed to her, to be allowed to walk right into the homes of these strangers, to wander through their rooms, imagining her own future there, her clothes hanging in the closet.

At the first house, Sarala and Abhijat had stood uncomfortably in the foyer, even as the realtor strode off into the living room, assuming they would follow. Finding herself alone in the room, and looking back to find Abhijat and Sarala still standing, rooted in the entry, she'd had to explain: "It's okay to come in and look around."

Sarala knew she was supposed to be imagining her own life in each of the houses the realtor pulled up to, fiddling with the lockbox on the front door, then leading them through the rooms one by one, each house a different possible world for her and Abhijat, but Sarala found herself distracted again and again, instead trying to piece together the clues left out—family photos, a child's drawing on the refrigerator. Trying to imagine the lives of the people who lived there, for now at least.

In some houses—pristine bathroom counters, kitchen sinks that gleamed with polishing—she had the feeling no one really lived there. In others, it seemed the owners had dashed out only moments before, something of their movement suspended in the air.

"And to your left we have Heritage Village," the realtor announced, turning her head a little in acknowledgement of Sarala, who, alone in the back seat, had begun to feel a bit like a child. "It's one of the most notable living history museums in the area," the realtor continued.

Sarala looked out the window as they passed. Women in long skirts and bonnets walked among rustic buildings. In front of a rough wooden shed, a man in a leather apron tended a blazing fire.

@

What Sarala liked about Nicolet: Heritage Village. It had been what decided her as she weighed their options: school systems, property taxes, expanses of wide green lawns, and subdivisions where the streets turned in on themselves like mazes. Riding in the real estate agent's car she had sometimes forgotten entirely which suburb of Chicago she was in.

When she'd seen Heritage Village, though, she knew this was the place for them.

Here was America. Here was where they would raise Meena, the baby she could already feel growing within her, though she was months from being conceived. The America she'd read about: a place of pastures, animals grazing, frontiers stretching ever westward. Here was Paul Revere Road circling around, branching off at Independence Drive. Here was a worried Martha Washington waiting for George to cross the Delaware, Betsy Ross on her porch sewing the first American flag, log cabins from which each morning these pilgrims might set out to discover, each day, a newer America.

Back at the hotel that night, Abhijat sat at the desk beside the television making a list of pros and cons for each of the houses they had considered. On the other side of the kitchenette's half wall, Sarala folded the dishtowel and draped it over the faucet.

Eagle's Crest subdivision. Sarala wanted a house there. She loved the sound of it, and the way Eagle's Crest separated the two parts of the town—on one side, the Lab, where scientists crashed subatomic particles into each other hoping to reveal the tiniest building blocks of the universe; on the other, Heritage Village, where costumed re-enactors bent low over kettles, settling day after day this new country—the neighborhood itself like a literal threshold in time, holding apart the past and the future.

Abhijat took out a long legal pad, on which he began to draw an elaborate decision-making matrix. But Sarala had already decided. She held her tongue and waited for him to finish.

@

They made an offer on the only house available in Eagle's Crest. A gray two-story—four bedrooms, a study, three bathrooms, and a finished basement. When their offer was accepted, they celebrated with a modest dinner Sarala prepared in the kitchenette of the hotel room and which they ate on trays balanced on their knees while watching *Let's Make a Deal* on the television. The woman who stood before the prizes, revealing them to the exuberant contestants, reminded Sarala of the realtor, all hairspray and makeup and hands gesturing.

On the day of the closing, Sarala signed her name over and over again to pieces of paper she hadn't even read. Each time, she looked to Abhijat, who had already read them over carefully, totaling the figures in his head, and he would nod, yes and yes and yes, it's okay.

CHAPTER 2

Unveiling the Wild: Being an Account of the Expeditions of Randolph Winchester, the Last Great Gentleman Explorer

It is useless to tell me of civilization. Take the word of one who has tried both, there is charm in the wild life.
—WILLIAM COTTON OSWELL

1972–1974

RANDOLPH LIKED ROSE TO TRAVEL WITH HIM. IN HER SAFARI khakis she looked like Katharine Hepburn, her long chestnut hair wound into a loose bun, pith helmet shading her pale pink skin, kerchief knotted loosely around her neck.

In the early days of their marriage, Rose had accompanied Randolph on all of his assignments. He was a journalist, traveling sometimes with a photographer, but more often, as he preferred, on his own, to the far corners of the world. From these distant places, he crafted for *Popular Explorer Magazine* mesmerizing stories of the people and places he found, stories that allowed his readers—largely sedentary Midwestern folk—to imagine themselves there with him on his wild adventures. Randolph's ability to make readers feel as though they were journeying right along with him accounted for the popularity of his pieces in the magazine, where they were accompanied by striking photographs, many of which he had taken himself.

He was proud of the distances Rose had hiked in Borneo. "She's the equal of any man I know," he would say to anyone who might doubt her fitness for such an expedition.

In Arabia, they rode dromedary camels across the desert, and Randolph watched her, slim torso swaying back and forth on the animal before him, her hand reaching up to shade her eyes as she peered off into the horizon line, sand meeting sky, sun hanging overhead.

Threading their way through the narrow passes of the Alai Mountains along the Isfairan River valley along with their pack horses, Rose and Randolph spent their nights side by side in a yurt, eyes tracing the elaborate pattern of latticed framework over which a thick felt covering was stretched. It was avalanche season, and how thrilling it was to know that, as they slumbered, they might at any moment be buried under a new small mountain of snow. How thrilling then, also, to awaken in the morning, to step out of the yurt, and to see that it had not, after all, happened—not that night, at least.

In Sri Lanka, during Esala Perahera, they watched the procession of elaborately decorated elephants to honor and venerate the sacred tooth of Buddha.

In Tanzania they hiked Kilimanjaro. Rose made it only three-quarters of the way up before being stricken with altitude sickness, and Randolph spent a long night beside her as she shivered, wrapped in both of their sleeping bags.

Rose had been ashamed that she'd taken ill; it meant neither of them would summit the mountain. But their guide assured her it might happen to anyone, insisting that, were they to try the climb again, it might be Randolph who was struck down and Rose utterly unaffected—yet another of the mysteries of the world.

@

Randolph was a polymath, dabbling in everything, lucking into doing nearly all things well. As a child growing up in the English country-side, his heroes had been William Burchell, who, it was said, had set off on history's first safari after being jilted by his fiancée, and Cornwallis Harris, whose safari paintings and drawings Randolph had pored over as a boy. He'd read Rider Haggard's Allen Quatermain series again and again, conjuring wild worlds, darkest Africa, determined to live a life of adventure.

His favorite tales were those in which the natural world triumphed over hubristic attempts to ignore or pave over them entirely, as in the story of the old Muthaiga Club in Nairobi, where patronage of the golf course dropped precipitously after a player was mauled by a lion on the fairway.

Randolph's parents had been decidedly unadventurous. Careful and protective of their only son, the most adventurous thing he'd been permitted to do as a child was to attend boarding school.

His interest in adventure and exploration had begun when he had seen advertised in the back of his father's *Popular Mechanics* a strange and mysterious book—*The Secret Museum of Mankind*—for which he immediately sent away. It arrived a few weeks later, a hefty volume filled with dusky mimeograph-quality photo reproductions.

He spent his nights under the covers of his bed, flashlight in hand, poring over the book's images and captions—*Smiling Mothers and Their Wooly-Headed Brood, Men of a Tribe of Sinister Reputation, Witch Doctor of Darkest Africa and His House of Fear: With keen, cunning eyes...he sits by his primitive stock of quackeries.... Expert in hypnotism, trances, and sleights of hand, he rules the village*—imagining the day when he might venture out into such a world of mystery and exoticism.

This strange object, he underlined in a stubby pencil by light of his flashlight, *with bits of iron, small bells, rusty nails, copper coins, and other metal rubbish dangling about him, and holding a weird drum, is a Shaman priest in ceremonial garb, ready to conduct intercourse with supernatural powers.*

In the section titled *The Secret Album of Africa,* the young Randolph drew a careful question mark in the margin beside the caption reading: *The African has not the European's sensibility to pain.*

From *The Secret Museum*, he had found his way to Livingstone's accounts of his travels through the dark continent, and from there he had graduated to Thesiger's travels in Arabia, Grant's *A Walk across Africa*, and Sven Hedin's treks through the Himalayas, having already decided that this was the life for him.

©

In between his expeditions and assignments for the magazine, Randolph lectured on his adventures, traveling mainly through the small towns of the American Midwest, where he seemed strikingly exotic himself. He had met Rose at one of these lectures—a young girl itching to stretch beyond the rural farm community where she had grown, confined, into a smart and curious young woman, listening with rapt attention to his presentation. Then, after the lecture, coffee at the Cozy Café and Diner, during which she had peppered him with question after question and Randolph had fallen under the spell of Rose's bright, curious eyes.

And so at eighteen Rose had eloped with Randolph. They married aboard a steamer en route to Ceylon (she sent her parents a telegram by way of announcement), honeymooned among the Wanniyala-Aetto people, where the local women, clucking in disapproval at Rose's shocking lack of skill as a homemaker, had taught her to gather edible roots and berries, and, alarmed to find that she had never been taught to prepare pittu, a staple of any respectable meal, had taken it upon themselves to teach her.

By the end of their honeymoon, Rose was as taken with exploration as Randolph.

©

During the Imilchil Betrothal Fair in Morocco, Randolph and Rose watched, transfixed, as the young men dressed in djellabas stood unmoving, displaying their silver daggers, a sign of wealth, the young women moving past, assessing this plumage, the Middle Atlas Mountains rising up around them. At the Palace of Winds in Jaipur, they turned their faces up to the small windows lining the walls, imagining the royal concubines, kept secluded there, peering out over the city. In Madhya Pradesh, they visited the sandstone temples of Khajuraho, admiring the erotic sculptures that decorated the walls.

With each expedition, Randolph felt he was unveiling a bit of the world, coy temptress, slow to reveal her secrets. He came to life on these trips—at night, around the camp's fire, the sound of animals all around them, and later, sleeping side by side under the stars, the sound of native drums from the bush.

Two years into their travels Rose discovered she was pregnant. She told him at a Shinto temple, whispering the news into his ear over the monks' chanting.

They decided she would go home, to the small farm town outside of Chicago where she had grown up. But the small farm town had changed during Rose's absence. The National Accelerator Research Lab had arrived, transforming Nicolet, and so what Rose found when she returned was not the sleepy rural town she remembered, but a bustling, blooming suburb.

Rose bought a house in a neighborhood in the middle of what she remembered as the Anderson farm and which was now called Eagle's Crest. On one side of Eagle's Crest, there now stood Heritage Village, a living history museum where reenactors in period costumes performed the settling of the country, manifest destiny, conquering the prairie day after day for tourists and school groups. And on the other side of the neighborhood, beyond the rolling, manicured greens of the new golf club, which had been built on land that had once marked the border between the Amundson and Heggestadt farms, there now stood the imposing National Accelerator Research Lab, its twenty-story Research Tower rising up over the prairie.

The townspeople were split in their opinions regarding the purpose of the Lab. Some argued it was a secret research facility for UFOs. Some believed the scientists there were studying invisibility, the better to battle the Communists. Others swore it was a testing ground for remote viewing experimentation.

But the truth was at once more magnificent and more mundane. The Lab was a facility for the study of high-energy particle physics, where scientists employed a particle accelerator to collide protons and antiprotons, watching the detectors for signs of new, smaller particles, all the while attempting to puzzle out the mysteries of string theory, supersymmetry, gauge theories, leptons, neutrinos, and quarks.

@

In building the Lab, the government, noting the principle of eminent domain, had, as they put it in the official literature, *annexed* the surrounding land holdings, each family finding one morning on their doorstep a grim-faced government official whose job it was to break the news.

In a letter to the editor of the *Nicolet Herald-Gleaner*, one local farmer wrote that he considered it "dastardly to build such a facility on some of the richest farming soil in the world."

Rose's parents had not, like so many of their neighbors, lost their farm to the Lab. But they had seen their small rural town transform around them, swelling and sprawling as neighborhoods sprung up to accommodate both the displaced farm families and the Lab's scientists. And so, when Rose returned to Nicolet to raise Lily, this was the town she found.

Some of the former farmers still longed for their land, refusing to attend the annual picnics the Lab put on for the displaced families, during which they were invited back into their homes, many of which had been moved via trailer to a small, clustered area the Lab called "the village" and now housed offices or the families of visiting physicists.

But not all of the families had been so resolute. Once the initial shock and surprise wore off, there were those who, recognizing the declining role of small family farms and watching their taxes rise year by year, had been pleased to accept the price the government offered, had been watching for years as the land surrounding Chicago grew from farmland to suburb and had realized that, Lab or no Lab, it was only a matter of time.

@

Rose pushed Lily up and down the aisles of the grocery store. Lily, perched in her seat in the cart, offered a running commentary on what she thought they needed. A bright and precocious child, she'd begun speaking in full sentences. There had been no preliminaries, no warm-up sounds, no baby's babbling in imitation of adult language. "Look at that dilapidated building," she'd said abruptly one morning, pointing from her car seat in the back of her mother's station wagon. One day she'd been silent, regarding her mother with her wise baby eyes, and the next, she was conversant. Now she chattered on as they made their way up and down the aisles.

The woman at the checkout picked up the eggplant and the mango as they traveled down the conveyor belt, eyeing them suspiciously—a not infrequent occurrence during their shopping trips. Often, the clerk would hold up some unfamiliar produce and ask Rose what it was and how on earth one cooked with such a thing. Rose was happy to to explain, and sometimes shared one of her favorites among the many recipes she'd collected on her travels, but she suspected that these women, who regarded this strange new produce with misgivings, infrequently tried her suggestions, feeling safer, she imagined, with sensible vegetables like corn and green beans.

"It's an eggplant," Lily chimed in from her seat in the cart, making what the clerk considered to be a disconcerting level of eye contact. "You might know it instead as an aubergine."

Since her return to Nicolet, few of the faces in the store, the post office, or the library were familiar to Rose. No longer bound to family farms, many of Rose's generation had moved away, so that those left behind were mainly her parents' age.

Back at home, Lily played with her blocks on the living room floor while Rose read aloud. They were beginning Deutscher's three-volume biography of Leon Trotsky.

"The reign of Tsar Alexander II was drawing to its gloomy end," Rose began. Lily listened as she stacked her blocks, arranging them into neat configurations. "The ruler whose accession and early reforms had stirred the most sanguine hopes in Russian society, and even among émigré revolutionaries, the ruler who had, in fact, freed the Russian peasant from serfdom and had earned the title of the Emancipator, was spending his last years in a cave of despair—hunted like an animal." Lily smiled up at her mother as she read aloud.

In a strange way, Rose's return to Nicolet felt liberating. She had returned not as the Rose Webster they had all known, but instead as Rose Winchester, wife of a renowned explorer, mother of an exceptional child. There, flanked on one side by the Lab and on the other by the pioneer reenactors of Heritage Village, Rose settled down to raise their daughter.

She and Randolph were devoted, besotted, if unconventional parents. In his letters home, Randolph sent stories he'd invented and illustrated for Lily, which Rose read to her at night, mother and daughter together marking out the path of Randolph's latest expedition on the globe beside Lily's bed, her chubby toddler fingers tracing her father's travels all over the word.

Rose had been Randolph's constant and steady companion through years of travel together. And then, just like that, as though something had come over her as surely as it had when she had met and run away with Randolph, she knew that she would be happiest home in Nicolet with Lily. That Randolph would be happiest out in the world. And thus they had arranged their peculiar little family, Randolph visiting every few months, a situation much commented upon by the—especially older—ladies of Nicolet (friends of her parents, who were by then long dead, for life on a farm is hard labor, tiring on a man and a woman), who were never sure whether they should think of Rose as an abandoned woman left with a child to raise, or as one of the new feminists out to remake what they had always thought of as a perfectly functional world.

Her exploring days over, Rose packed away her good, sturdy boots, allowed her membership in the Explorers Club to lapse, and set about making a life in Nicolet.

Some had wondered—Rose's father in particular, who, before his death, had found it impossible to understand why Randolph didn't settle down with a good job at the bank or the hardware store—what point there was in Randolph's exploration, given that the world had already been well and thoroughly explored in his opinion. But Randolph rejected this idea as lacking imagination. Can you imagine, he said to Rose, de Gama or Cortés listening to those who insisted that the known world had already been mapped and charted? Surely, he believed, there was always more to know.

But Rose wasn't thinking at all about what Randolph had asked. Instead she was thinking about the ways in which their unconventional arrangement was certain to ensure that their marriage would never fade into the kind of relationships she had seen all around her growing up—all of those hardworking farmers and their wives, her own parents, who sometimes sat beside each other for entire evenings without exchanging a single word.

Hers and Randolph's, Rose felt certain, would be one of the world's grand love stories.

CHAPTER 3

The New World

1973

IT HAD TAKEN SARALA TIME TO ADJUST TO THE MIDWESTERN climate. Her first winter, she could be found in a sari and sandals, and over the ensemble the puffy down coat—purple—which Abhijat had helped her order from the Sears catalog shortly after her arrival. In addition to being insufficient protection against the icy Chicagoland winter, especially where feet were concerned, the ensemble brought looks from her fellow shoppers at the grocery store, which suggested to Sarala that it was not quite the thing.

During her first trip to the grocery store, she'd spent hours rolling the cart up and down the aisles, stopping to look at every foreign possibility. She'd found herself frozen, mesmerized, taking in the images of meals before her on the boxes that lined the supermarket shelves. Photographed on plates garnished with parsley, the food—all of it new and unfamiliar—looked enticing and delicious.

"You need a hand, honey?" A woman in a blue vest, her gray hair tightly curled, approached. VERA, her nametag read.

Sarala smiled. "What is the most traditional American dish?" For the first meal in their new home, she wanted to prepare something in honor of their adopted country.

"Well, that's a good question." Vera thought for a moment. "You've got your hot dogs and hamburgers," she said. "Pizza. No—" she corrected herself, "that's I-talian."

Finally, deciding on turkey dinner with stuffing and mashed potatoes—because that was what had been served at the first Thanksgiving, after all—she commandeered Sarala's cart, wheeling it to the frozen entrée section, and helped Sarala select the Hungry-Man Deluxe Turkey Dinner because the Stouffers were too skimpy in Vera's opinion, and, she confided, your husband will leave the table still hungry. In any household, she intimated, that was nothing if not a recipe for trouble.

⊚

Although they now lived close enough that, in good weather, he could have walked, Abhijat preferred to drive to the Lab, the radio tuned to the classical music station. Each morning he joined the slow-moving traffic of neighborhood husbands inching their way toward their places of work, a nod now and then in greeting, though this was the extent of Abhijat's interaction with his neighbors.

The sound of geese each morning meant he had arrived. They congregated in the reflecting pond just outside the Research Tower, honking loudly at the arrival of each scientist. In the parking lot, Abhijat threaded his way through rows of old cars, Volvos and Subarus in need of a wash, university bumper stickers announcing their academic pedigree. On his first day he had parked next to a car with a personalized license plate reading QUARK, and as he made his way into the building, his heart swelled with a sense of being, finally, at long last, at home in the world.

One of the proudest moments of Abhijat's life had been the day he had announced to his colleagues at the university that he would be taking a position at the Lab. For his family, even for Sarala, some degree of explanation had been necessary to help them understand the importance of such a position, but his academic colleagues understood immediately and responded just as Abhijat might have hoped: mouths agape, eyes wide, hearty handshakes and pats on his back. Among physicists, the Lab was a place they dreamed of visiting, perhaps conducting research there for a summer. They had understood what it meant to be offered such a position.

In the lobby, over the bank of elevators, two clocks displayed the time at the Lab and the time at CERN, their greatest competitor. Among the Lab's physicists, the consensus was that it was wise to begin the day imagining what those rascals in Geneva might be up to.

The theory group's offices were on the nineteenth floor, near the library, where many of the theorists spent the mornings poring over the latest journals. Abhijat had been given his choice of offices—one that looked out into the Research Tower's atrium, or one that looked out across the eastern arc of the accelerator, over which the land had been returned to its original prairie grasses. Abhijat hadn't liked the sense in those atrium offices of being on display, great floor-to-ceiling windows through which anyone in the lobby or cafeteria might watch you working, so he had selected an office looking out over the campus of the Lab toward Chicago. On clear days, as he puzzled over an equation or the proofs of his latest paper, he could make out the skyline of the city and watch planes rising and descending from the airports.

©

Sarala spent her days carefully unpacking and arranging their new lives in the house on Patriot Place, room by room—first the kitchen, then the master bedroom, then the living room, family room, and a study for Abhijat just off the foyer.

In the hallway, she hung the framed blessing her mother had sent as a housewarming gift:

> *Here may delight be thine*
> *through wealth and progeny.*
> *Give this house thy watchful care.*
> *May man and beast increase and prosper.*
> *Free from the evil eye,*
> *not lacking wedded love,*

bring good luck even to the four-footed beasts.
Live with thy husband and in old age
mayest thou still rule thy household.
Be glad of heart within thy home.
Remain here, do not depart from it,
but pass your lives together,
happy in your home,
playing with your children and grandchildren.
O generous Indra, make her fortunate!
May she have a beautiful family;
may she give her husband ten children!
May he himself be like the eleventh!

Here in the States, people always and only wanted to know if she and Abhijat had an arranged marriage. But Sarala didn't like to think of it like that. Rather, she thought of it as a thoughtful introduction made by their parents, and who better to know the best possible mate for their child? She kept a contented tally of the ways in which she and Abhijat had begun to love one another, Sarala marveling at Abhijat's dedication to his work, Abhijat admiring Sarala's social ease.

"Everyone likes to talk to you," he said to her one night, and Sarala furrowed her brow, bemused.

"But that is nothing difficult, nothing to be proud of," she said.

@

Sarala sat at the kitchen table to write a letter to her mother, the house silent as it always was in the afternoon, the clock over the sink ticking quietly. *You asked how I find it here,* she wrote. *There are, of course, many things that I miss, many things that feel strange and unfamiliar, but this is my home now, and it is of no use to dwell on a thing that might make one unhappy. Rather, I have determined to do everything I can to help us both make the best of our new home.* She'd sealed the letter and mailed it off the next morning.

In response, a few weeks later, she'd received an envelope full of the same small blue pieces of paper as in the recipe box, her mother's same feathery hand in delicate pencil strokes.

For when you miss the warmth and joy of your home, and here a recipe for vada pav.

For when newness feels no longer thrilling, but instead fatiguing, and here her recipe for suji ka halwa.

No, Sarala thought, reminding herself that one must not dwell in sadness or longing. She tucked the pieces of paper into the recipe box and pushed it to the back of the cupboard above the oven.

@

One weekend afternoon, Abhijat proposed that he give Sarala a tour of the Lab's campus. She had been delighted to accept, curious to see the place where he spent his days. As they neared the security booth, she watched Abhijat stiffen with pride as the guard recognized him and waved him through the gate. Together they drove along the curving, tree-lined drive, and when they emerged, as though from a tunnel, the twenty-story Research Tower rose up before them, mirrored in a reflecting pool dotted with geese.

Winding, smoothly paved roads cut through the tall prairie grasses growing all around the grounds. Abhijat drove around the circumference of the accelerator, first in the direction of the protons, then of the antiprotons, the sunlight reflected in the cooling pond which, Abhijat explained, had once been necessary to maintain the temperature of the first generation of magnets used in the accelerator, but was now mainly aesthetic, and, as if to illustrate this, a family of ducks made their way home across the water.

He drove along the path of the old fixed-target experiment, squat blue buildings punctuating the berm that had once housed the linear accelerator, a now nearly obsolete technology whose facilities, rusting with disuse, had been abandoned or used for storage. Abhijat pointed out the power lines stretching off into the prairie along the path of the fixed-target accelerator. "Energy in and protons out," he explained as he traced their path with his finger to the horizon line and back. The future, he explained, was in the circular accelerators, and the Lab was home to the largest, highest-energy accelerator in the world. It was what made the Lab such an important place for his work, he explained. Here, they were working on the very frontier of high-energy particle physics.

But what Sarala noticed was the herd of buffalo in the distance. "That, I'm afraid, I cannot explain," Abhijat said. "A quirk of the Lab's first director," he offered, and Sarala laughed at the idea of these enormous animals living among the scientists and their tiny, hypothetical fragments of the universe. Abhijat, smiling, began to laugh with her.

Like much of Nicolet, Abhijat explained, the Lab had been built on land that had once been farmland. In recent years, though, the Lab director had begun a project to return the land under which the tunnels ran from its geometrically arranged agricultural fields to the wild chaos of native prairie grasses. The addition of the herd of buffalo had been part of the prairie restoration project. There was speculation, though, among some local residents, that the buffalo were there less for aesthetic reasons and more as canaries in a coal mine—that their demise would be the first warning sign of something amiss at the Lab, of some nefarious plot afoot in the tunnels of the accelerator. Abhijat had only recently begun to apprehend the uncertainties many of his new neighbors harbored about what went on at the Lab.

As Abhijat and Sarala drove, he pointed out the places where the land's original farmhouses and barns had been left standing. When the Lab had acquired the land, the houses had been repurposed as offices, the barns for storage. A gambrel roof peeked out over the berm of the old fixed-target beam path. A silo stood at attention beside a red barn, silver tanks labeled *liquid nitrogen* and *argon* lined up against its outer walls.

Across the road from the detector, Abhijat showed Sarala the untouched pioneer cemetery where local settlers had been buried, including a general from the War of 1812 who had come west with his family to explore America's frontier. Sarala thought of how even the Lab—red barns against green fields against blue sky—was America as she had always pictured it.

As the sun began to set, they made their way to the Research Tower. A flock of geese waddled slowly across the road in front of the car, trumpeting their indignation.

Inside, Sarala and Abhijat rode the elevator up to the theory group's offices on the nineteenth floor. A hand-lettered sign outside the conference room read THE CONJECTORIUM. In the hallway outside Abhijat's office, Sarala admired a framed image of a collision event in which the subatomic particles created by the collision were shown spiraling off in all directions, each path delineated in a different color so that the image looked, to her, like a strange blooming flower.

Abhijat's office was a small room with floor-to-ceiling chalkboard walls covered in equations. Sarala didn't know what the constellations of numbers and symbols meant, but they filled her with a sense of awe. She thought of the advice her mother-in-law had given her about helping Abhijat find happiness in the world. How, she wondered, could she compete with the importance of this work? Perhaps his mother was mistaken, and it would be his work that would bring him happiness and contentment.

Across the hall, Abhijat pointed out the office of Dr. Gerald Cardiff, his closest friend at the Lab (by which he meant not that they shared personal troubles or the details of their lives outside of the Lab, but that they regularly shared a table in the cafeteria at lunch, and that it was understood that Abhijat, when stranded by a difficult idea, was welcome to wander into Gerald's office where, together, they might hash the issue out).

When she first arrived in Nicolet, Sarala had imagined that she and Abhijat would, together, join one of the Lab's many clubs, a good way to get to know one another and meet others, but she had soon found that Abhijat, as well as his other colleagues, made little time for such diversions. The clubs were well advertised but sparsely attended. A good idea, if only in theory.

As Sarala came to more thoroughly know and understand Abhijat, she saw how he had created for himself a disciplined life. For Abhijat, it was a discipline born of constant reaching, whereby each time he achieved one of the many goals he set for himself, he responded not with celebration and satisfaction at his own accomplishment, but by thinking, *Yes, but there is more to be done.* A place in the top graduate program in his field—*yes, but still the matter of prestigious fellowships.* A teaching position at a well-regarded university—*yes, but even better would be a place at the National Accelerator Research Lab.* And having accomplished that? *Yes, but there were always papers to be written, prizes to be won, a career to attend to, a legacy to build.* Deep within him was the fear that if he allowed himself a moment to enjoy the successes he'd worked for, it would mean the end of them. That he might find the resting on his laurels so comfortable, so seductive, that he would never again accomplish anything of note. And then where would that leave him? No, he had decided—that was the sure road to an unremarkable career. Not what he imagined and planned for himself.

Knowing so little about what it took to make a career as a successful theoretical particle physicist, Sarala was unsure whether she should regard Abhijat's constant striving as something to be concerned about, as his mother had suggested, or as something to be proud of, as was Sarala's inclination. Though she didn't apply the same set of standards to herself, she resolved to do her best to help Abhijat accomplish his ever-shifting goals.

@

Abhijat had been surprised and impressed by the easy way with which Sarala embraced the challenges and differences of their new home, but he wondered if underneath her enthusiasm there might lie some of the homesickness he had himself experienced.

"It's thoughtful of you to think of this," Sarala said when he asked, "but I am adaptable. There is no reason you should worry about me. There is plenty for me to discover here. Plenty of ways to occupy my time. And you have enough with which to occupy your mind."

"Yes," he responded, taking her hand, "but I have chosen—and chosen well, I think—to occupy my mind with your happiness, too."

Sarala looked down, embarrassed.

At the window of his office, Abhijat and Sarala stood looking out over the prairie, the skyline and lights of Chicago off in the distance. Together, framed by his office window, they watched the sun sinking into the prairie, the horizon gone gold and glowing for just a moment before twilight.

@

The next morning on the way to the Lab, recalling their conversation, Abhijat thought unexpectedly of the book he'd read in preparation for his own relocation to the United States. At Cambridge, he'd borrowed from the library a well-used copy of Alexis de Tocqueville's *Democracy in America* and had pored over it, hopeful and expectant.

Remembering this, and feeling thoughtful and solicitous of his new beautiful wife (as well as having recently noted what was, in his opinion, the less-than-edifying reading material with which she had returned from her first trip to the Nicolet Public Library—a mix of paperback Westerns and romance novels), he planned to stop at a bookstore on his way home that evening.

He presented Sarala with his gift over dinner, explaining that he had found the book invaluable in helping him to understand his new country when he first arrived, and that he thought she would likely find volume two, in which de Tocqueville addressed such topics as "In What Spirit the Americans Cultivate the Arts," "How Democracy Renders the Social Intercourse of Americans Free and

Easy," and "Some Reflections on American Manners," most useful. He had inscribed the dark indigo paper of the flyleaf—

FOR MY BEAUTIFUL AND BELOVED WIFE

AS SHE LEARNS HER WAY IN OUR NEW HOME.

Sarala had done her best to read enthusiastically, and, in fact, she did find the chapter titled "The Young Woman in the Character of the Wife" of interest; but, truth be told, she did not find the book terribly helpful in navigating contemporary suburban Chicago, and so she put de Tocqueville on the shelf in the living room and returned to her own selections, though she was careful now not to leave the books she had borrowed from the library where Abhijat might find them and note her choice of reading material.

CHAPTER 4

Notes on the Discovery of America

1974

MEENA ARRIVED DURING THEIR SECOND YEAR IN NICOLET. During the months when her stomach swelled with the growing baby, Sarala enjoyed the way, with this round, welcoming belly, anyone might stop to talk to her, asking, "When is your baby due?" and "Do you think it's a girl or boy?" and "What will you name her?" when she confided that she knew, most certainly, that it would be a girl.

Sarala's childhood home had been a rowdy, busy household in which she might toddle from aunt to grandmother to mother; in which uncles, her father, and grandfather were always coming and going; in which there were always cousins for playmates. She wondered what it would be like for her child to grow up in the quiet and solitude of their new home.

Abhijat and Sarala's mothers, who had liked each other from the start, congratulated themselves on a successful and fruitful match, and traveled together to be there for the birth and for several weeks afterward. When the mothers arrived, they were surprised not only by the quiet of the large empty house but by how far everything in Nicolet was from everything else. They found it amusing how one rode in a car nearly everywhere one went.

Sarala's mother began cooking almost as soon as she arrived, filling the house with smells that transported Sarala to her girlhood home. Abhijat's mother had set about the cleaning, both of them insisting that Sarala take to her bed and rest. Sarala obeyed, but from her bedroom she could hear the mothers talking happily to one another as they worked, and she longed to join them. At dinner, with the mothers chattering away, Sarala felt happier than she had in quite a long time.

The mothers, though, seemed concerned. Had they not met and befriended any other Indian families, Sarala's mother asked, loading plates into the dishwasher after Abhijat had retired to his study as he did nearly every night.

"It's complicated," Sarala said. Most of the other Indians at the Lab were visiting scientists, she explained, there for only a few months at a time. And, given how little time Abhijat had for socializing, she'd found it difficult to connect with them. Sarala noticed a look of concern pass over the mothers' faces.

@

When Meena finally arrived, the house bustled in a way that felt familiar, one grandmother tending to the baby and one in the kitchen cooking what seemed to Sarala enough food to feed them until Meena was herself a grandmother.

The grandmothers stayed with them for several weeks, and when they left, Sarala was surprised by how quickly, even with the new baby, the house returned to its imposing silence. In the afternoons when Meena slept, and at night when Sarala woke to nurse her, the house stood large, still, and silent around them.

When the winter finally began to melt away, Sarala loaded Meena into her stroller and ventured out into the neighborhood. Sarala loved the way, with her baby smile and soft cooing, Meena drew the attention of the neighbors as Sarala pushed her along the sidewalks in her stroller. The leaves on the slim trees newly planted along the subdivision's streets unfurled slowly as bright blades of grass began to stand proudly at attention in every yard. In the driveways, husbands tinkered with lawnmowers in preparation for the summer, wheeling snow blowers into the back of their garages, and in the yards, wives planted rows of bright blooming flowers along walkways.

Sarala's favorite moments on these walks were when one of the neighbors, seeing Meena and Sarala coming, stopped to admire her daughter, to exchange baby conversation with her, to compliment her thick dark hair—"Who had ever seen such beautiful hair on such a tiny baby?"—further suggesting to Sarala that what she and Abhijat had on their hands was the world's first and only perfect baby.

@

In fall, Sarala watched the leaves changing with a kind of wonder, new each day, as she stepped outside to find what colors the trees might have turned overnight, and it was with sadness that she watched them fall from the trees just after the first frost. They gathered on the grass, and in the evenings or on crisp, sunny weekend days, the neighborhood husbands raked the leaves together into piles, bagging them up and hauling the fat, shiny black plastic bags out to the curb.

Sarala and Abhijat's lawn, however, remained covered in leaves. Sarala knew this was not the sort of thing Abhijat was likely to notice, so she made her first visit to the hardware store, where the clerk, a kindly old man who admired Meena's perfect, tiny fingers, sold her a rake and bags for the leaves.

Back home, having arranged Meena on a blanket on the grass surrounded by her favorite playthings, Sarala set about tackling the leaves herself, the baby watching her with her wise, deep brown eyes.

It seemed to Sarala that the neighborhood husbands spent nearly the entire weekend outdoors, working on their homes and yards, tinkering in their driveways, screen doors slamming as they came in and out of their houses all day, shading their eyes from the sun, some new tool in hand. But Abhijat was not like these husbands. He spent his weekends, like any other workday, at the Lab, and Sarala did not feel it was her place to ask him to change. These other husbands, she guessed, did not have jobs as demanding as Abhijat's.

@

Sarala had been delighted when Meena began to speak. She now had someone to talk with through the long, silent days that had, if she were being truthful with herself, begun to feel a bit lonely.

In the morning, after Abhijat left for work, Sarala poured milk into the last bit of his tea, added a spoonful of sugar, and let Meena finish it, her small hands wrapped around the teacup. Afternoons, she loaded Meena and her stroller into the car and visited the shopping mall, pushing Meena proudly before her to be admired by the older ladies who power-walked there together. In the J.C. Penney, Sarala bought small items to decorate their home—a burgundy ceramic vase full of always-blooming artificial flowers, a toothbrush holder with matching cup and soapdish for the powder room—that was what the realtor had called the small half-bath on the first floor, though Sarala had yet to find a satisfactory explanation for why it should be called that.

On rainy days, they visited the library and together selected books to borrow, Sarala lately favoring inspirational biographies of business leaders and the paperback romance novels whose front covers featured images of heroes and heroines in shiny foil, which the librarians kept in a rotating rack near the checkout desk. Meena favored sturdy board books with pictures of farm animals in bright primary colors, and Sarala was taken by how much the farms in Meena's books resembled the farmhouses and barns left standing on the Lab's campus.

On sunny days, they made the rounds of Nicolet's parks, and sometimes, on special days, Sarala took Meena to the place in town she loved most—Heritage Village.

Sarala's favorite exhibit was America's Frontier. She loved the pioneer home, a simple one-room log cabin where a woman in a long dress and a white cap leaned over the hearth stirring a cast-iron pot, tended the fire, or churned butter in the yard near the barn. Sarala loved peeking inside the Conestoga wagon next to the log cabin and imagining what from her home she might bring with her were she to set off for such a new, unknown world.

Meena loved the blacksmith shop—the rough wood rafters of the shed hung with horseshoes and lanterns, carriage wheels lined up against the stone walls, the warm building noisy with clanging as a man in a leather apron hammered away at the red-hot piece of metal he'd pulled from the fire, the banging of his hammer carrying out over the day's bright blue sky. She squealed in delight at the noise, clapping her tiny hands each time a blast of air from the bellows caused the fire in the hearth to leap up. Next to the bellows sat a barrel of water, and when the blacksmith pulled the metal from the fire, its tip glowing yellow-orange and cooling, as he hammered, back to a black-grey, he finished by dipping the tip into the water, the metal cooling with a *fitz* sound, smoke snaking up into the rafters.

Occasionally they encountered school-aged children on field trips. Often they crossed paths with other mothers and their children, most of them older than Meena. But Sarala loved Heritage Village best on quiet days when, aside from the costumed villagers, she and Meena were the only ones there. Then, it was easy to feel part of the illusion, part of this imagined past.

The first time she had come, not realizing that she could simply wander the grounds as she liked, Sarala had signed up for the Time Traveler Tour. She and Meena, paired with a group of mothers and children, were led through the grounds by a costumed tour guide who, after explaining that they were to imagine they had been transported back in time to colonial America, asked, "Before we begin our exploration, does anyone have any questions?"

One little boy's hand shot into the air immediately, as though he had been waiting for just this moment.

"Jacob, what is your question?" his mother hissed at him.

He looked back at her and whispered, "Where are the chickens?"

The mother looked exasperated. "If I hear about chickens one more time. This is not a farm, Jacob."

But another child had beaten him to it. "Do you have any live animals from the time period here?" a little girl called out.

The guide smiled at her, looking, Sarala thought, as though this was a question she answered frequently. "I'm afraid not. No animals. But if you'll all follow me, we'll begin our tour at the schoolhouse."

The group followed her down the pathway toward the white clapboard building, Sarala holding Meena's small hand as they walked.

Inside the one-room schoolhouse, they passed a row of benches and coat hooks in the entryway and came into a square room filled with desks arranged around a large grey metal stove, the teacher's long desk at the front of the room under a wall-length chalkboard. "Schoolhouses of the period were not like schools today," the guide began, encouraging them all to take seats in the wrought iron and wood desks arranged in neat rows.

Sarala sat down sideways in one of the child-sized desks, Meena resting on her knees. The tour guide took on a schoolmarm's imperious tone and began to read out a list of the school rules, which had been chalked out on the blackboard:

Children should be seen and not heard.
Speak only when spoken to.
Idleness is sinful.
A fine hand indicates a fine mind.
Busy hands maketh a quiet mouth.

The children in the tour group snuck looks at the adults in the room, wondering how far they were willing to play along with this game of pretend. Along the wall, Sarala noticed wooden signs that read:

Idle girl
Idle boy
Tongue Wagger
Bite-Finger Baby

These, the guide explained, had been hung by the teacher around the necks of disobedient students.

Sarala looked down at Meena on her lap and wondered what her child's education here in the States would be like. Surely quite different from her own, from Abhijat's.

Later, Sarala would learn that she and Meena could wander the grounds on their own, peeking into the buildings that interested them, interacting with the villagers stationed in the tall, red-brick mansion at the top of the hill, in the post office, or in the sawmill. Wandering the grounds this way, Sarala could imagine what Nicolet must have looked like in the years before the arrival of the Lab, though here and there the illusion was broken by the power lines strung along the streets that bordered the grounds or the sound of the football team practicing off in the distance where Heritage Village abutted the high school.

And so, together, Sarala and Meena discovered America, Abhijat in his office surrounded by chalkboard walls on which he had scratched out equations that might predict the existence of some heretofore unknown part of the universe so tiny that Sarala had to ask him again and again for some way to conceive of it, to hold this smallness in her mind.

"The proton," he explained, "is to a mosquito as a mosquito is to Mercury's orbit around the sun." And then she reminded herself that the particles he worked on were even smaller than a proton.

What Sarala understood was that what Abhijat and the other theoretical physicists worked with was possibility, and beneath it, nothing concrete. She imagined his workdays, his head cradled in his hand, looking up, out the window, perhaps, out over the prairie, imagining the physical world into being.

She wondered if thinking about such tiny particles all day caused him to see the world they lived in as ungainly, inelegant.

@

Sarala felt it was her job to make their home life, herself, and Meena as unobtrusive to Abhijat as possible so that he might occupy his mind with greater matters. She was proud of his work, read carefully through each article he published, understanding here and there only a bit of it. The fact that she—herself a smart woman, she knew—could understand so little of it was the source of a strange sort of pride for Sarala.

In letters home to the grandmothers, Sarala recorded Meena's latest accomplishments: toddling across the living room unassisted, successful recitation from beginning to end of the alphabet, each new word she acquired—as well as Abhijat's: a paper in the latest issue of a journal she understood from Abhijat's enthusiasm to be important, a presentation at a prestigious conference. And in this careful recording, it escaped Sarala's attention that she never once included news of her own.

And when might you and Abhijat begin thinking about another child? her mother had written. *I don't know,* Sarala replied, leaving out any mention of the series of charts, graphs, and spreadsheets Abhijat had presented to her, as though to an audience at a conference, shortly after Meena was born, each one outlining the benefits of one rather than a houseful of children.

Together they'd thought long and hard about their decision. For Sarala, it had been difficult to argue with such persuasive data, and it pleased her to know that their decision meant they could devote themselves to Meena. She had a sense that it would be best to evade questions on the subject for as long as possible, but she had also begun to think about how she might explain their decision to the grandmothers, who would, she suspected, certainly be disappointed. She had been working on the following for when she could avoid the question no longer: that blessed with a beautiful child, healthy and of an easy temperament, Sarala and Abhijat had decided that one was enough. That one child, rather than many, meant they would be able to dedicate themselves and their resources to her, ensuring that what would march out before her would be a fine future, full of opportunity and possibility.

©

One afternoon, Abhijat invited Sarala and Meena to have lunch with him in the Lab's cafeteria. It was a beautiful day, sunny and warm, so Sarala loaded Meena into her stroller and walked through the neighborhood, across the busy Burlington Road, waiting first at the light, then making their way over the crosswalk and along the paths of the Lab grounds. Beside the pathways, the mowed lawn sprung up suddenly into wild prairie grasses, which blew in the warm wind like a soft brown ocean. When the trees rose up around them, they walked under the shady canopy of leaves until they emerged at the reflecting pond, the Research Tower rising up over the water and prairie grasses.

They made their way up to the entrance, Sarala negotiating the stroller and the glass doors. Inside the atrium she looked up, blinking against the sun coming in through the skylight to peer into the offices that looked out over the atrium. She found an empty table in the cafeteria, where Meena had begged to be taken out of her stroller. Sarala lifted her small body up and out and set her down in one of the plastic chairs, where Meena sat up on her knees and reached across the table for the salt and pepper shakers.

"Where's Daddy?" she asked.

"He'll be down soon," Sarala answered, removing the salt and pepper shakers from Meena's hands and placing them out of her reach.

As she waited for Abhijat to join them, Sarala looked around the cafeteria, where clusters of physicists, engineers, and technicians in golf shirts and glasses sat together. Here and there she caught bits of their conversations.

"Well, they're still debugging the equipment," one of them said, his tablemates shaking their heads in sympathy. "In some sense, it's reassuring. They were wrong, but wrong by five orders of magnitude." At this the other men let out hearty, guffawing laughs.

Meena played with the table tent announcing International Folk Dancing Club—newcomers always welcome! and every so often, a triangle of geese cut across the windowed wall of the atrium.

Sarala had dressed Meena in a pink sundress with bows on the shoulders and tiny pink sandals, her hair cut in a short bob, bangs struck out across her forehead just above her large brown eyes. A few of the aproned and baseball-capped cafeteria ladies came over to the table to admire her, bringing Meena a small cup of ice cream and a dish of raisins from the salad bar. They smiled at Sarala. "So nice to have a child in the building," one of them said.

Sarala could hear a scientist at a nearby table explaining to his lunch companion, "I told them, once they've got things sorted out they ought to be looking for an interaction that looks like—" and here she caught sight of Abhijat coming toward them from across the atrium, a broad smile on his face.

"Well, it won't be long before we're obsolete," the man at the other table continued. "Before there's a bigger, faster collider to be built. Let's just hope we're able to build it here. I wouldn't like to think what will happen once we're no longer operating at the highest energy levels."

"Now where did you get those treats, young miss?" Abhijat asked as he sat down beside Meena, tickling her under her chin. Meena smiled up at him and pointed happily at the cafeteria ladies who waved at her from behind the serving counters.

Sarala went through the cafeteria line, filling a tray for all three of them, while Abhijat sat with Meena, who tapped away at the calculator he had brought down from his office for her to play with. He cut up her chicken nuggets so they would cool and helped Meena sip milk through a straw in the small carton. Every few moments one of his colleagues came over to coo at Meena, "Such a good girl for her daddy." At one of the nearby tables, a grandfatherly scientist made faces at her, then hid his face behind his hands.

After lunch Meena waved to her father as the elevator doors closed, lifting him up to the top of Anderson Tower where, Sarala thought, he might, were he to look out of his office window, be able to watch their slow progress home. She wondered how often he took his eyes from the equations on his wall to look out over the prairie toward the city.

Back outside, she retraced her steps, pushing the stroller before her, walking along the paths in reverse, Meena chattering away, asking, "Mommy, what does *almost* mean?" "What does *before* mean?" then slipping slowly into sleep.

@

At home, Sarala lifted Meena's slack, sleep-heavy body from the stroller and carried her up the stairs, loosening her sandals and letting them drop in the hallway. She laid Meena down in her small twin bed, pulling her favorite blanket up over her sundress and stopping for a moment to admire her child, her plump lips open slightly in sleep, her round cheeks, the soft spray of eyelashes that fluttered against her skin.

Downstairs in the family room, Sarala set up the ironing board and plugged in the iron, pulling Abhijat's dress shirts one by one from the laundry basket. The house was silent, the neighborhood silent. She had never imagined such quiet. Had never thought it possible. She had always imagined a life like the one she'd grown up with, aunts and uncles and grandparents all living together under one lively, boisterous roof.

She turned the television on and knelt before it, clicking up and down the channels—a game show, a painting class on the public television station, a midday newscast—but finding nothing that interested her, she turned it off.

The house was still with Meena asleep, the iron letting out a gurgle of steam as Sarala turned Abhijat's shirts this way and that, working the iron into the tiny spots around the collar and over the rounded shoulders. She looked at the clock, calculating how long until Abhijat would be home for dinner, wondered whether after the meal, after Meena's bath and putting her to bed, he would return to the Lab or work in his study off the foyer.

She wondered how long Meena might sleep. She had come to the end of the pile of dress shirts, each hung neatly on hangers along the ironing board: Tuesday—Wednesday—Thursday—Friday. *Maybe she's about to wake up*, she thought.

Sarala carried Abhijat's shirts up to the master bedroom, tucking them in among the suits on his side of the closet. She closed the closet door behind her, a little louder than she would have had she not been hoping Meena would wake soon, then walked down the hall, the beige carpeting muffling her footsteps.

Unlike the other mothers she chatted with at the park, Sarala did not look forward to nap time, such a long period of strange silence in the house. She opened Meena's door and looked in.

She was probably just about to wake up anyway, Sarala thought as she sat down on the edge of the bed and reached out to brush the hair from Meena's face.

CHAPTER 5

New Symmetries

It was a point of pride with Rose, the way she and Randolph had arranged their lives outside the expected norms and traditions. Rose's upbringing had been so thoroughly and entirely conventional that she had been determined to find a different path for herself as an adult. Their family arrangement was uncommon, certainly, but it worked for them. *And yes, even for Lily,* she felt she had, always, to explain. *Lily and her father are devoted to one another and share a lively and meaningful correspondence.*

From Randolph, Rose and Lily received frequent dispatches concerning his recent adventures. In Malaysia, he'd tended water buffalo, leading them through muddy wetlands, having learned from the natives that the animal was not to be herded but rather that it would simply follow where he led.

In India, he'd stowed away on a steamship and sailed down the Brahmaputra. From his seat on the bow, he watched the ship's steady progress, palms arcing overhead. He had traveled the length of the river, from the Himalayas through Bangladesh to the Ganges delta, where he had seen tigers, crocodiles, mangroves, and slender boats skimming over water that in spring rose to flood levels as the snow melted in the mountains.

In the Kerala backwaters he'd lived in a thatched hut, and near Udaipur, he'd been delighted by the monkeys who came right up to the train as it stopped at the platform—little beggars, paws out, requesting the attentions of the passengers.

In one of his postcards to Lily, he listed his supplies for his latest trip: *We took twenty-four mules loaded with bedrolls, two yaks, tinned milk, ten bamboo tents, and four llamas (who did not get on well with the mules at all).*

There were parts of his trip, though, that he did not share with Rose and Lily.

These were the increasingly frequent instances in which he now encountered places that were no longer isolated, no longer separated and protected from modernity. Of these experiences, Randolph kept only a mental list:

The Coca-Cola sign in front of the camel breeder's modest home.

The Tiwi elders dressed half in traditional costume, half in what looked to Randolph like secondhand university t-shirts.

And worst of all, the tent he'd been invited into, in which he'd found the tribal leader and his wizened council watching a football match on a small television powered by a noisy generator.

As he added to this growing mental list of the ways in which modernity now seemed to encroach upon these places, he had begun to wonder if he was searching for a kind of untouched culture that no longer actually existed.

@

Randolph sat cross-legged with Lily on the soft carpet in the master bedroom, his trunk laid open in front of the closet. He had returned from his most recent trip just that morning and now smiled up at Rose, who watched from the hallway as Lily dug happily through the open trunk on the floor between them, pulling out treasure after treasure, certain that with each one would come a new story from her father. This was their ritual each time Randolph returned home. Rose joined them only to pluck Randolph's more malodorous articles of clothing from the trunk and transfer them to a laundry basket destined for her immediate and thorough attentions.

Each time he returned from an expedition, Rose labeled his travel journal with the dates and destinations of his trip, adding it to the long row of journals that lined the mahogany bookshelves in his study. There, among his record of daily activities could be found sketches of native art, notes on travel routes and supplies, lists of objects acquired and of animals observed, handwritten receipts, well-worn maps gone soft at the folds and threatening to tear, official-looking permits bearing indecipherable stamps, foreign banknotes, customs forms issued by stern and harried clerks, now folded into small squares—all of these tucked, like bookmarks, into his journals. The mementos she catalogued and arranged in the display cases in his study, tucking a tribal mask in next to a clay sculpture or a tiny hand-woven basket, closing the case carefully and stepping back to admire each new addition.

In a small tin box on the bookshelf, Rose saved all of their letters. Sorting through his trunk after Lily had unearthed all of the treasures with which he'd returned, what delighted Rose most was to come upon the letters she had sent him, bound and bundled together, and which he had carried with him throughout his travels. These she added to the collection each time he returned, so that the tin box contained within it both the original correspondence and the response, a record of their extraordinary marriage, of what Rose thought of, always, as their great love story.

@

When it was again time for Randolph to pack, it was Randolph and Lily's ritual to do that together also, Lily sometimes slipping in a drawing, a note, or some small treasure. These, Randolph discovered well into his trip, smiling to think of Lily doing this on the sly as he tucked his belongings into the trunk.

Lily prided herself on maintaining a stiff upper lip when it was time for her father to depart. She had never cried, not once. She felt it would have been disloyal. Her mother had taught her to be proud of their unconventional life—that there were many different ways to be a family, and that though it was different from what most people chose, this was the way of being a family that worked best for them. This was what she reminded herself firmly, emphatically, on the days when her father left.

In kindergarten, Lily came home from school one day distressed to have learned from a classmate that parents who didn't live together no longer loved each other. Rose had gently corrected her. Certainly sometimes parents stopped loving one another, she explained, but that would never be the case with Lily's mother and father, who loved each other so strongly that even Lily had to admit to never having seen her parents argue.

"Our family is different, yes," Rose said, taking her daughter's small hands in hers, "but that is something we should be proud of. It makes us unique."

@

Rose had read all of the great political biographies—Churchill, Kennedy, Truman, Roosevelt. As a girl growing up in a small farm town in the shadow of the great city of the Midwest, she had cried with her classmates over Kennedy's death, but unlike her girlfriends, she was crying not because their handsome young president was dead, leaving behind a widow and small children who, even in mourning, looked like they had just stepped out of a catalog, but because she had had such great hopes for his political career.

As a teenager, she had not imagined herself in any role other than that of a diligent helpmate to a spouse with his own promising political future. "Politics is men's work, like plowing, or fixing a tractor," her father, a stout farmer, said when Rose revealed her interest in the subject. Her mother, more sympathetic, pointed out the many ways in which Rose might fulfill her interests from behind the scenes, cutting out for her daughter photos from magazines and newspapers of a perfectly groomed Jackie Kennedy meeting Indian Prime Minister Jawaharlal Nehru or being presented to the president and first lady of Mexico.

But when Rose surprised everyone, including herself, by eloping with Randolph at eighteen, she had come to realize that he would be an unlikely political candidate for a number of reasons, not the least of which was the infrequency with which he stayed put in a given location. And so, after Lily's birth, Rose signed up for a correspondence course in political science at the state university, and, excelling in that class, had continued on until she had graduated with honors, with a deep sense of personal pride and accomplishment, and with a new plan for her life.

When Lily began school, Rose began her political career in earnest, first campaigning for and winning a seat on the local school board. At her first election, Randolph had been full of pride. Rose, uncertain about her chances, had worried that she might not win. But who better to represent the citizenry, Randolph encouraged her, than a daughter of Nicolet, now returned?

It was, perhaps, the frequency and unapologetic nosiness of the questions Rose received about the whereabouts of her husband (or, more often, of "Lily's father," as they tended to refer to him, unable to imagine that a man so infrequently present might still be a spouse, a partner, a helpmate) that had steeled Rose for a career in local politics. She'd been elected Alderman of Nicolet's twelfth ward and had thrown herself into the work with zeal and dedication. Already she had overseen the installation of speed bumps in the Lost Colony neighborhood, spearheaded an ordinance fining citizens who failed to clear snow from their sidewalks, and initiated the implementation of a hotline for residents to report suspected rabid wildlife (mainly squirrels).

In this new role, Rose discovered her passion, and though she still thought fondly of her exploring days with Randolph, lately, her dreams were of an entirely different sort of adventure—climbing the political ladder, perhaps one day becoming mayor.

@

One of the things Rose liked best about this new Nicolet were the cultural activities at the Lab. She and Lily were frequent patrons, taking advantage of the opportunity to enjoy visiting musicians, theatre troupes, and lecturers. Lily had displayed an early and intense curiosity about all things scientific, and her favorite events at the Lab were the lectures by visiting scholars on popular issues of science.

On their first visit, Rose drove past the gate and along the winding drive toward the towering building that had sprung up during her time away. The Research Tower it was called, and she marveled at the way it loomed over this land she remembered as orderly rows of corn and soybeans. They parked in the Research Tower lot and made their way, Lily's hand in hers, toward the outdoor amphitheater that had been constructed where the Heggestadt farmhouse once stood.

As they took their seats, Lily diligently studying the program open on her lap, Rose counted more empty seats than full. A shame, she thought, not to take advantage of the chance to see a first-rate production right here in Nicolet. Still, she couldn't imagine the Heggestadts, or her own parents for that matter, in attendance. Most of the audience, she thought, looking around, were new citizens of Nicolet.

After the performance, Rose decided to take the opportunity to explore the vast grounds of the Lab campus. As they drove along the roads that cut through the prairie grasses, she pointed out to Lily the farmhouses now relocated, the barns, the new buildings that had been constructed around them. Rose had never been to one of the Lab's open houses for displaced families, but she had heard about them from those who had: how strange it was to find their former homes, farmhouses that had once stood so far from one another on such wide expanses of land, now arranged in a neat cul-de-sac, side by side like the houses in a subdivision. And how strange, too, to find their childhood bedrooms turned into offices or temporary housing for visiting scientists.

When she'd returned to Nicolet, it had, in many ways, felt to Rose like she'd moved to an entirely new town. Now, as she drove past the cemetery full of familiar last names, past landmarks she remembered, and through the Lab's expansive campus, she felt like she was showing Lily the ghost of a part of Nicolet that had once existed.

CHAPTER 6

Elementary Particles

The urge to travel and explore probably originated in my childhood. Certainly it was an unusual childhood.
—WILFRED THESIGER, *THE LAST NOMAD*

MEENA AND LILY MET IN THE THIRD GRADE. THEY'D SPENT THE year racing to see who could finish their weekly math test first. Every Wednesday morning at 9:35 it was a draw as Lily arrived at the right side of the teacher's desk and Meena at the left. And every Wednesday at 9:36 they exchanged polite smiles and began the long, disappointing walks back to their own desks. But they'd bonded over the sly looks they exchanged as they waited for the rest of the class to shuffle forward at the bell with their half-completed tests.

Meena had noticed that Lily always brought the best things for show and tell—a shrunken head from Bali, a dried and stuffed piranha from the Amazon, which she passed around the classroom proudly, the fish's desiccated body mounted on a small wooden pedestal.

One day, finding no other available seats on the bus ride home, they'd been forced to sit together and had begrudgingly begun a conversation. Soon they were spending every Saturday afternoon together in the Nicolet Public Library, a large brick building that overlooked the town's scenic river walkway.

Lily preferred the quiet study room, spending her weekends working ahead in their textbook, *Steps toward Science*, shushing adults who whispered or folded their newspapers too loudly. Meena liked to browse the shelves, returning with armloads of obscure books from the reference section that caught her eye: *Noteworthy Weather Events: 1680-1981, Extraordinary Popular Delusions and the Madness of Crowds*, coffee table art books, mystery novels, and field guides, which she pored over beside Lily.

©

In the mornings, NPR on the radio on the kitchen counter, Lily and her mother ate breakfast in silence, ears alert for any mention of the countries where Randolph had set off on his latest expedition. Sitting across the table from each other, they passed the crossword back and forth as they ate. Rose had taught Lily tricks like filling in the *-S*s on plural clues, the *-ED*s on the past-tense clues, and how she might discover further clues within the clues themselves.

For Meena, mornings were a parade of novelty breakfast foods that had caught Sarala's eye in the supermarket—Pop Tarts, frozen waffles, frozen pancakes, frozen pancakes wrapped around a frozen sausage, sausage biscuits, biscuits and gravy in a microwaveable bowl, packets of oatmeal with colorful bits of dehydrated fruit that came to life under a stream of hot water from the teakettle.

After dinner, their small family of three spent the evenings in the kitchen, Sarala cleaning up, Abhijat beside Meena at the table helping her as she worked through her homework.

Meena's schoolwork, Sarala had noticed, was one of the few things that could tear Abhijat away from his study in the evenings. As she loaded the dishwasher, she watched with pride the patient way he explained the things Meena struggled with, the way he listened carefully to each of her questions, even as, she knew, he was already beginning to craft his response. These were the moments in which Sarala loved Abhijat best, in which she best knew that he loved both her and Meena.

@

Rose encouraged Lily's intellect, enrolling her in summer enrichment courses in art, music, science, and math. By ten, Lily had a layperson's grasp of Heidegger, an unflagging interest in Freudian psychoanalysis, and had begun compiling a list of her own criticisms of Frederick Jackson Turner's frontier thesis.

On weekends, Lily divided her time between the public library and the YMCA, where she could be found among the aging patrons, swishing along on the rowing machine.

On her bedroom mirror, Lily kept a photograph of her father, blue turban wound round his head, skin darkened and worn by the sun, beard closely cropped, indicating the beginning rather than the end of an expedition (which was itself distinguished by the presence of a long, tangled, and unkempt beard her mother insisted he trim immediately down to a refined Van Dyke). The photo had been taken in the Sahara, where he had joined a salt caravan and, in native dress, led his camel by a rope through the desert. Lily loved to hear again and again the story of the light-handed pickpocket Randolph had met there, who had offered to help Randolph negotiate a suitable bride price for the lady of his choice. "Oh, I've already got a lovely bride, thank you," he had replied, pulling out the photo of Rose and Lily he kept on him always, brandishing it with pride.

Randolph came home during the holidays—Christmas, Lily's birthday, and Rose's—but these were short trips, temporary. The house was a house of women—Lily and her mother, their nights spent together, Rose reading to Lily from the letters Randolph sent from his expeditions—North Africa, the Greek Isles, New Guinea.

Rose kept one room on the first floor of the house, just off the foyer, as a study for Randolph, a dark-paneled room with a sidebar on which sat a bottle of whiskey and a polished silver seltzer dispenser. Here, she kept his leather-bound expedition journals arranged chronologically on the bookshelves along the wall.

Above the bookshelves hung framed photographs of Randolph and Rose on safari, of their trusted porter on a trip to Nepal, and an impressive collection of rare maps. An imposing mahogany desk, which Rose kept polished to a high gloss, sat in the center of the room, and facing the desk, two leather wing chairs. The whole setup suggested an office that, in addition to being regularly occupied (which it was not), also hosted regular visitors (which it did not), who might occupy the wing chairs, admire the photos, and flip through the expedition journals. In fact, with the exception of Lily, who liked to curl up in one of the deep leather armchairs, a framed photo of a pygmy nuthatch hanging over her head as she applied herself conscientiously to her schoolwork, the room was almost always empty.

@

Sarala and Abhijat had always attended Meena's parent-teacher nights together, Abhijat asking most of the questions about Meena's performance and making notes on the small pad of paper he kept in the breast pocket of his jacket. This year, however, he'd been scheduled to present at a conference, so Sarala had promised to take detailed notes and report back on all pertinent information when Abhijat returned.

She dropped Meena off in the school's library, where Meena made a beeline for the low shelf of books near the librarian's desk, and Sarala made her way down the wide hall toward Meena's classroom: Mrs. Hamilton, Grade 3, Room 125. The halls were filled with harried parents. "You meet with Jenny's teacher. I'll meet with Randy's," one woman, a baby on her hip, shouted down the hall to her husband, and Sarala thought of how here, again, was evidence that Abhijat had been right: that with one child, they need not spread their attentions, their resources, so thin.

Inside, Sarala took in the bright primary colors of the posters decorating nearly every inch of wall space. She thought of the schoolhouse at Heritage Village, with its spare walls and stern signs. She took her seat at the small desk labeled with Meena's name on a piece of construction paper in careful cursive. A teacher's handwriting, Sarala thought, smiling at the other parents sitting uncomfortably in the too-small chairs.

Mrs. Hamilton began by asking each of the parents to introduce themselves, and Sarala listened intently as they did so, trying to imagine something about their children, in whose company Meena spent her days.

Once the introductions were finished, the woman next to her leaned toward Sarala, extending her hand. "We should have met long ago. I'm Rose Winchester, Lily's mother."

"Oh, yes," Sarala said, taking her hand. "I'm very pleased to meet you. Meena talks about Lily, well, nearly all the time."

"It's the same at our house," Rose said, smiling.

There was something so perfect about Rose, in her twinset and pumps, glasses on a chain around her neck, Sarala thought, looking at her, though she wasn't so much attractive as orderly looking, Sarala decided.

At the front of the classroom, Mrs. Hamilton began her part of the evening's presentation—a description of the students' daily schedules, an introduction to the textbooks for the year—and as she began, both Sarala and Rose pulled notebooks and pens from their purses. They were the only two parents taking notes, Sarala observed.

"For my husband," Rose explained, gesturing at the notepad spread open on her daughter's desk.

At conferences, Rose always took notes to share with Randolph in her next letter, and, in the weeks following the conference, she hand-delivered a letter from Randolph to Lily's teacher, by way of illustrating that while theirs was an unconventional family arrangement, Randolph was by no means an absentee parent.

"For my husband, too," Sarala said, holding up her pen. The women exchanged warm smiles, sharing this small thing between them. Sarala wondered if perhaps Lily's father had a job as demanding as Abhijat's.

☺

Despite their many differences, both the Mital and the Winchester homes shared one thing in common—a long bookshelf filled with a maroon set of World Book Encyclopedias. It had been Lily's idea that the girls should, together, embark upon a scheme of self-improvement whereby they would both read, each night before bed, a pre-selected entry in the World Book.

They moved through the set alphabetically, taking turns selecting the day's reading, and at 7:30 each night, the phone in one house or the other could be heard ringing as the girls telephoned each other to announce the evening's selection, at lunch the next day, their common reading providing them with a subject for conversation: ENLIGHTENMENT PHILOSOPHERS over peanut butter and jelly, MASTERS OF GERMAN LITERATURE over Fruit Roll-Ups, THE HALLMARKS OF FEUDAL SOCIETY over string cheese.

KINDS OF BRIDGES

At night, by light of campfire or oil lamp, Randolph wrote letters to Rose and Lily, which they took turns reading aloud at dinner on the happy days when the letters arrived bearing strange foreign stamps, his thick cream-colored writing paper marked with the signs of his travel—dirt, sweat, rainwater-smudged ink, exotic smells rising up from the paper as they unfolded it. In his letters, Randolph took them through the day's adventures, and it was like being there with him. Almost.

When Lily missed her father, she retreated to his study, where his collection of *National Geographic*s dating back to the 1930s weighed down a series of floor-to-ceiling bookshelves, their bright yellow spines a kind of wallpaper. Here, Lily curled up in the leather armchair, flipping through back issues of *Popular Explorer*, imagining her father hiking, setting up camp for the night, or traveling among a passel of goat herders, conjuring him into the pictures in his articles.

In Portugal, Randolph had learned from the local women how to balance a basket the size of a small table, filled with chickens, on his head for carrying to market. Home for Christmas, he'd tried to teach Lily, and she'd practiced diligently, walking gingerly to the bus stop at the corner, her backpack balanced precariously on her head.

"What are you doing?" Meena asked as Lily made her way down the narrow aisle of the bus slowly, eyes looking up, willing the backpack to stay put.

"Get a move on!" the bus driver shouted at her.

A History of Magic during the Middle Ages

The first time Lily was invited over to Meena's house, she'd been beside herself with excitement at the idea that she would be having dinner with an actual, real, flesh-and-blood physicist. She came home with Meena on the bus, Meena calling out, "Mom, we're home!" as they opened the door, dropping her coat and backpack in the foyer next to a pile of slippers.

Lily removed her shoes, lined them up along the wall next to the slippers, and folded her coat in half, placing it carefully on top of her shoes.

Sarala had made them an after-school snack of lime Jell-O with rainbow-colored marshmallows floating, suspended, in its strange not-quite-liquid, not-quite-solid state. This she served proudly, though the girls were less enthusiastic, poking at it disinterestedly with their spoons.

They worked together on their homework, sitting side by side at the desk in Meena's room until Sarala called them down to dinner.

There, Abhijat stood at the head of the table and waited for the girls to take their seats before being seated himself.

"We are delighted to meet the celebrated Miss Winchester," Abhijat said, holding his glass aloft in a toast. "Meena has told us a great deal about you."

Lily blushed and felt as though she were dining with President Reagan himself.

Throughout the meal, she peppered Abhijat with questions about his work, his research, his daily routine at the Lab, and the difference between an experimental and a theoretical physicist. Abhijat was delighted by her animated curiosity. (This was one of the few traits she shared with her mother, favoring Randolph in appearance and temperament.) She was a perfect companion for Meena, Abhijat thought.

For Meena, it was—as this moment is for nearly all children who find themselves seeing a parent through the eyes of another—startling. Watching her father grow spirited and enthusiastic as he talked about his work, she felt as though she, too, had met someone new that night.

"And your father?" Sarala asked, turning the conversation to Lily. "What does he do, if I may ask?"

"Of course," Lily nodded. "He's an explorer."

Sarala looked at her for a moment, and decided there must be some meaning lost in the translation. She resolved to look it up in the *Webster's Unabridged* in Abhijat's study after dinner.

CODES AND CIPHERS

Although Lily's status in the social hierarchy of elementary school suffered for her awkwardness (which Meena often tried to mitigate with her more nuanced grasp of elementary-age social cues), her impatience with the intellects of her classmates (which Meena privately shared but was savvy enough not to display), and her often eccentric taste in personal attire (showing up, for example, one morning, in a kitenge topped with a Hello Kitty T-shirt her mother had insisted on adding to the ensemble for reasons of both warmth—for it was winter in Illinois—and modesty), when it came to show and tell, even the students who thought Lily was a weirdo had to admit that she aced it.

"My dad brought me this teddy bear back from a business trip. I forget where," Abby Johnson mumbled, holding the stuffed animal aloft listlessly by the ear and sounding bored, even by herself. "He got my mom one, too."

Lily, however, had requested that Mrs. Hamilton make available to her a slide projector and had informed her teacher that she expected to require thirty minutes for her presentation, not including Q&A. Had Mrs. Hamilton not been so exhausted at this point in the school year, having had her fill of wiping noses and breaking up scuffles on the playground, and having been kept up the night before by her husband's snoring, she might not have allowed it, but as it was, she chose to see it as a blessing, as thirty minutes of class time she did not have to fill.

Lily shared with them slides of her father's most recent expeditions. From New Guinea he had brought Lily a ceremonial drum made with lizard skin and human blood, which she had passed around the room and which the children held in their hands reverentially, equally horrified and curious, just as she'd known they would be.

Animals of the Grasslands

It was field trip season—spring—by which it was understood that the teachers were exhausted and the children were restless, and thus any excuse to get everyone out of the classroom was leapt upon. Mrs. Hamilton, upon learning that Meena's father worked at the Lab, asked him to give the class a personal tour of the facility, and Abhijat had been more than pleased to oblige, consulting in advance with Meena and Lily about what their classmates would find most intriguing.

On the appointed day, the children, jostling and chattering, spilled in an unruly crowd from the bright yellow school bus, which idled noisily in front of the Lab's education center, a low building surrounded by prairie grasses and a reproduction Conestoga wagon. Here they were met by Abhijat and a docent, who had been dispatched by the education center to translate theoretical physicist to layperson, as needed.

The docent introduced Abhijat to Mrs. Hamilton. "Dr. Mital." Mrs. Hamilton took his hand in hers to shake it, beckoning the children who had begun to stray back to the fold. "We are so grateful to you for taking time out of your busy schedule to show us around the Lab."

"Not at all," Abhijat said. "It is my great pleasure to have you all here as our distinguished guests."

"Perhaps you know our chaperone, Mrs. Winchester? Lily's mother."

Abhijat took Rose's hand in his. "Very honored to meet you, Madame Alderperson."

"Please. Rose," she corrected. During all of her interactions with the Mitals, dropping off and picking up Lily and Meena from their many activities together, Rose had only ever met Sarala. She'd been curious about Meena's father.

"I understand our daughters have taken quite a liking to each other," Abhijat said.

"Yes, I've been so pleased to see that." Rose smiled.

Together they looked at the girls, who stood a bit away from the rest of the children, notebooks and pencils already in their eager hands.

"Children, may I have your attention, please?" Mrs. Hamilton's voice rang out over the chatter, her hand held up in the air as she spoke. "I'd like to introduce Meena's father, Dr. Mital. Dr. Mital will be our expert guide today and will tell us all about his work here at the Lab."

The children gathered in a squirmy half circle around Abhijat. "Yes, yes," he said. "Very pleased to meet you all," Abhijat began, nodding at the children. He was astonished by the way Mrs. Hamilton had so quickly brought order and quiet to the crowd of children, who now looked up at him in anticipation. "To begin, I wonder how many of you are familiar with what it is we do here at the Lab?"

Lily's hand shot up into the air.

"Yes, Miss Winchester, but perhaps one of your other colleagues?"

Abhijat waited for a long moment, but no other hands rose.

"Well, then, Miss Winchester, perhaps you will provide an explanation?"

"At the Lab," Lily began, "you're studying elementary particles that are the building blocks of the universe," sounding as though she were reading from a textbook, "as well as the forces that hold those particles together or push them apart. The particle accelerator and its detectors are like a giant microscope that helps you see these particles. Well, not really see them—they're much too small to be seen," she corrected herself, already beginning, Abhijat saw, to grasp the difficulty of explaining this work simply.

"Thank you, Miss Winchester. Very informative," Abhijat said, a smile lingering on his face, proud of how carefully she must have listened to his own description of his work. "Now, will you all please come this way?"

He led them in a long, wriggling line toward the Research Tower, the noise of the children, who had again resumed their chattering, rivaling that of the geese that eyed them suspiciously as they made their way past the reflecting pond, up the stairs, and into the atrium.

Rose looked up toward the ceiling of the atrium, its interior walls lined with glass, reaching up to the heavens. While on the surface the building couldn't have been more different, it reminded her, somehow, of the great cathedrals of France.

"The accelerator," Abhijat continued, turning to speak to the children as they paused in the atrium, "of which I will give you an aerial view in just a moment, is, some believe, the most important instrument for physics that exists in the world today. *Why?*, you may be wondering. Because of speed. Because in order to answer today's most pressing, most exciting questions in physics, one must have the fastest accelerator operating at the highest energy level. And here, at the Lab, we are fortunate to have just such an instrument."

The elevators carried them to the top of the Research Tower. On the highest floor, large plate-glass windows looked out over the prairie; from here, visitors could observe the surrounding land as it had been before the beginning of its transformation into farmland, into suburbia. The children lined up before the windows, noses pressed against the glass. Rose looked out over the great expanse of the Lab's campus, thinking of how she had never before seen Nicolet from this height, so much of it visible all at once, arranged just beyond the borders of the Lab's grounds.

"There, in the shape of a ring," Abhijat said, "you will see the outline of the accelerator, which exists many feet below ground, four miles in circumference." He traced the shape of the circle on the glass with his finger. "Looking out even farther, you will see how vast the campus of the Lab is. We are nearly seven thousand acres."

Rose looked out over the land she remembered as neighboring farms, prairie grasses now reclaiming the soil. The Nicolet Lily would grow up thinking of as home was so different from the Nicolet Rose had known—so different, she thought, as to be almost unrecognizable.

"And now, may I please turn your attention to this exhibit—" Abhijat gestured at a large segment of metal tubing stretching the length of the hallway, "—which shows a replica of the magnets used to power the accelerator. Here at the Lab," he explained, "we are searching for tiny parts of the world we believe may exist. To do this, we use an accelerator, in which we send two particles around and around in a circle, going faster and faster until—smash!" He clapped his hands together and held them there for a moment. "We have crashed them!"

"Why?" Meena asked, her voice coming from beside him where she stood next to Lily, watching as Abhijat spoke. Hearing her father describing his work, her curiosity had overpowered her sense that these were things she ought already to know. But her father so rarely talked with her or her mother about his work. She knew the Lab as a facility with a lovely butterfly garden, a cross-country ski path, a dog park, lectures, arts events, and symphonies—not as her father knew it.

"Ah, yes. A useful question from our colleague, Miss Mital," Abhijat said, looking surprised. "It is, to put it simply, to see what happens."

"And what does happen?" Meena asked.

Abhijat looked at his daughter, intrigued by her curiosity. He felt for a moment as though he were speaking only to her. "You see," he explained, "when they collide, they break apart into even smaller particles. Particles so small we can't even see them. All we can see are the paths they make as they go spinning and flying out into the world. And those paths help us to know what kind of a particle it is we are looking at."

A chattering in the corner, which Mrs. Hamilton quickly shushed, broke the illusion and brought Abhijat back to the group of students.

"Now, you may be wondering, why should we want to do such a thing," he continued. "Why build such a facility just to look at such tiny, tiny things? Who among us is wondering this?"

A few timid hands went up into the air.

He smiled. "Well, my distinguished guests, it is for a very good reason. These tiny, tiny particles help us to learn what the world was like at the very beginning of time." He paused here for effect, his eyes wide.

"Like Adam and Eve?" one of the children, a pale, blonde-haired girl, asked.

"Oh, no, long before then," Abhijat said, smiling.

"And what was it like?" Lily asked.

Abhijat looked out at them, eyebrows raised, his face animated. "Very curious indeed." He clapped his hands together. "Now, if you will please follow me."

Lily and Meena trotted along at the head of the group, close to Abhijat. As they passed the offices of the physicists, Rose noticed the chalkboard walls filled with equations, a beautiful script that reminded her for a moment of the hieroglyphs she and Randolph had seen in the temple of Karnak.

"You see," Abhijat continued, "every particle gives an energy signal. As Miss Winchester suggested, you might think of the particle accelerator as a kind of microscope. When the protons collide, they create mass in the form of other particles, and here, sometimes, are new particles we have before only ever imagined. In order to see these, we must use a quite ingenious machine called a detector, which is watching all day, every day for the signals from these particles. It gives us, in a nutshell, a tsunami of data. Because, you see, the accelerator is creating over a million collisions per second. So someone must look at these collisions and see what they're telling us."

"And what are they telling you?" Lily asked.

Abhijat smiled. "Well, you must be patient with us, Miss Winchester, as we work to discover that. Now, if you will please follow me, here we will look at part of the detector." Abhijat led the children over to a bank of computers, where a number of young men sat glued to their screens. "Birali is the colleague who is making sure the machine is running correctly," Abhijat said, indicating a younger man, who looked up from his computer screen and smiled at the children. "And he will today show us what the paths of some particles look like after a collision."

On his screen, the young technician pulled up an image of a collision event, the paths of the particles outlined against a black background, arcing and spiraling off by way of announcing their existence.

Rose thought of how the paths of the particles, inked out against the dark background looked like chrysanthemums, like the explosions she and Randolph had watched blooming against a dark sky during the fireworks festivals of Japan.

"What we will do next," Abhijat continued, "if you please, is to visit the experiment hall. Please, I think this you will find most exciting. So with your permission, we will head in this direction." He led the snaking line of students back through the atrium to a nearby building, the docent trotting along at the back of the group to help herd the strays. "On the way," Abhijat continued, "we will pass a very interesting part of our facility, the neutron therapy department. Here, with experimental medical treatments connected to our work, we are treating patients with very serious conditions." He gestured at the building as they passed and crowded together at the door of their destination. "Now in the experiment hall, I must ask you please not to touch anything. We must all keep our curious fingers to ourselves."

Inside, silver canisters of liquid nitrogen stood along the walls surrounded by strange machinery, and Rose thought it seemed more like being inside a factory than anything else. How, she wondered, did one connect the delicate image of the particle paths she had just seen, so like a flower, to this noisy, hissing, chuffing room?

"My colleagues you see working here are experimental physicists," Abhijat continued, his voice raised over the hum of the machines. "They work with the equipment we will see today, conducting experiments and gathering data."

Abhijat did not share this opinion with the students, but he had always felt that there was something ugly about all that tinkering, all that machinery. He privately felt that a good idea ought to be able to be sorted out in his head, on paper, or on the crowded chalkboard in his office. He thought of it as an untidy business—building and operating these accelerators. But it was a necessary business, he knew. For without this machinery, what were his theories, the argument went, but elegant ideas, grand guesses at the shape of the world?

"I, on the other hand, am a theoretical physicist," he continued. "We concern ourselves mainly with the philosophy and mathematics behind the physical world as it exists around us. If you will permit me a little joke, to quote Sir Arthur Eddington, 'I hope it will not shock experimental physicists too much if I say that we do not accept their observations unless they are confirmed by theory.'"

Here Abhijat waited what seemed to him a rather long time for the group's laughter. Finding it not forthcoming, he plowed onward.

"Yes, well, now we shall return to the education center, where I will be happy to take your questions."

The group approached the education center and gathered on the part of the lawn that had been neatly mowed, around which sprang up the tall, native prairie grasses now blowing in the warm breeze.

"So, please, have you any questions for me or for our colleague Mary Ann from the Education Department?" Abhijat asked, indicating the docent who now stood beside him. She had been surprised at how well Abhijat had been able to tailor his explanations to the age group.

But by now the allure of the warm spring day had begun to take hold of the children. The circle of students had already begun to fray out at the edges, a group of boys running circles around a large, outdoor sculpture of a Möbius strip.

"Well, then, hearing no questions, I thank you very much, young ladies and gentlemen, for your interest and attention." Abhijat folded his hands one over the other before him and nodded as though to punctuate the end of the tour.

Led by Mrs. Hamilton, the students called out in a sing-songy group, "Thank you, Dr. Mital. Thank you, Miss Mary Ann."

Most of the students bolted to join the boys in their game. Abhijat, Meena, Lily, and Rose stood where they were, watching the road for the approach of the large yellow school bus that would transport the children back to their classroom.

"It was very kind of you to give up this time for the students," Rose said. "And very interesting. I've never had the chance to tour the facilities—only ever the grounds." She thought about how many people there were now working at the Lab and living in Nicolet who had never known the town as she had.

"Not at all," Abhijat said. "I am delighted to see that they, and you, are curious about such things."

"Yes, it's an important human quality—curiosity," Rose said.

"The most important," Abhijat agreed.

And from around the corner, they heard the loud diesel approach of the school bus.

CHAPTER 7

Exotic Particles, Expected and Unexpected

1984

NOW, WITH MEENA OFF AT SCHOOL AND ABHIJAT AT THE LAB, Sarala found herself with entire days alone, long quiet hours in which she watched the clock, waiting for the sound of the school bus on the corner, of Abhijat's car in the drive. The house was in order. Meals were on the table each evening at precisely six o'clock.

"Why don't you take up a hobby?" Abhijat suggested. He considered it the highest form of luxury to be able to provide his wife with a life in which she need not occupy herself with work.

But what Sarala had decided she needed was her first good American friend. And, as though timed perfectly with her resolution, a new couple had moved in across the street.

From the window of Abhijat's study, Sarala watched with interest as a large Mayflower truck pulled up in front of the house across the street, followed closely by another car, from which emerged a woman in shorts, bouncy red hair held back with a pink silk scarf, sunglasses catching the daylight as she pointed here then there, directing the movers and the tall tanned man in a golf shirt who must, Sarala decided, be her husband. By the time the school bus delivered Meena home from school, the truck was gone. Sarala peered over her shoulder at the house as she walked Meena home from the bus stop.

That night, Sarala opened her red-gingham-print *Better Homes and Gardens Cookbook* and made a batch of cookies—chocolate chip—with which to welcome her new neighbors. In the morning, she combed her hair, studying her reflection in the mirror and trying out a bright, welcoming smile.

The house across the street was a green saltbox with yellow shutters and already looked to Sarala as though someone had been living there for years—an American flag flying from the porch, a stone goose standing sentry, wearing an apron, a matching kerchief tied over its head. Sarala knocked on the front door, the plate of cookies balanced in her open palm.

The door was opened by the woman with the bouncy red hair, which was today held back by a bright yellow headband.

Sarala held the plate of cookies out before her. "Welcome to the neighborhood," she said, producing the friendly smile she had practiced in the mirror. "I am Sarala. My husband, Abhijat, and I are your neighbors across the street."

"Well isn't this sweet of you." The woman held her hand up to her heart. "Come in please," she said, waving Sarala into the foyer. "I'm Carol, and this is my husband Bill—well, where has he gone off to? He must be out in the backyard setting up his grill. He's just crazy about that grill." Carol smiled knowingly at Sarala, took the plate, and beckoned for her to follow her into the kitchen, which Sarala did.

"You'll have to forgive the frightful mess. We're still getting settled in," Carol said over her shoulder, leading the way through the foyer and into the kitchen.

But Sarala, taking in the rooms around her, was perplexed, for though she was sure she'd seen the moving truck pull away from the house late in the afternoon just the day before, there was now nothing to suggest that Carol and Bill had not been living there for years—pictures on the walls, throw pillows plumped and arranged in the corners of the sofa, and not a single cardboard box to be seen.

Carol poured them each a cup of coffee and set the plate of cookies in the center of the kitchen table. Sarala took a seat, noting the bright flowered tablecloth and plush floral-print rug under the table.

Carol leaned toward Sarala. "Well, you'll just have to tell me all about yourself, and where you're from, and your husband, and everything."

Sarala, smiling, told Carol about her move to the States and all about Meena.

"And what does your husband do?"

"He's a theoretical physicist."

"He must work over at that laboratory. We heard a little about it when we were house hunting, but I have to tell you, I don't really understand what it is they do over there."

Sarala was used to this. Always, as though following some sort of script, the neighbors, upon learning where Abhijat worked, seemed to say one of two things: "I've always wondered what they do over there," or: "It must be fascinating, but it's all beyond me."

"To be absolutely frank," Sarala confided, "I'm not sure that I do, either," and Carol laughed, a full and warm laugh that seemed to suggest this was the most delightful thing anyone had said to her in ages.

Carol and Bill were transplants from Alabama, "on account of Bill's job," Carol explained. He was climbing the corporate ladder, so they were becoming old pros at these relocations and had just made a killing on the last house they'd sold, she confessed. "And I keep busy with my Mary Kay, of course."

"She is your daughter?" Sarala asked.

Carol laughed. "Oh my goodness, no. Don't tell me you've never heard of Mary Kay!"

Carol began to bustle around the small desk just below where the telephone hung affixed to the wall. She handed Sarala a book. On the cover was a blonde woman whose enormous and elaborately arranged hair filled the frame of the picture and then some. "This is Mary Kay Ash, my personal heroine."

By the end of the morning, Sarala left with a stack of glossy pink brochures and a small bag of makeup samples. Walking back home from the bright green saltbox, Sarala was struck by how dark and imposing her and Abhijat's house looked by comparison. If it could be said that a house looked stern, she thought, then theirs surely did.

"Why don't you come over for coffee tomorrow morning, after the boys leave for work?" Carol called out from the front porch as Sarala made her way back across the street.

@

That night after dinner, when Abhijat had returned to his study and Meena had curled up on the couch with one of the *Little House on the Prairie* books she was reading voraciously, Sarala made her way upstairs and opened the small pink bag of samples, spreading them out over the counter of the master bath, leafing through the brochures featuring models with elaborate frosted hairstyles moussed and hairsprayed into place, blush in bright swaths across their cheeks. She leaned in toward the mirror, holding the image of one of the women up beside her own face. Sarala looked at the colors in the samples— pearly pastels, pinks and blues. She could see them on the face of the woman beside her in the mirror, but she couldn't imagine them on her. Sarala put the samples and brochures back into the pink plastic bag. She opened the drawer under the counter and shoved the bag into the back, closing it behind her.

CHAPTER 8

Partners in Collaborative Research

1984

RANDOLPH VISITED NICOLET EVERY FEW MONTHS, BETWEEN expeditions. Often, Rose and Lily didn't even know to expect him. On those days, Lily returned home from school to find a familiar backpack in the front hall.

During these visits home, she and her father spent long hours together, Randolph regaling her with stories from his latest adventure, Lily filling him in on her latest school projects. In these conversations, they took on the classic postures of analysis—Randolph stretched out on his back on the living room sofa, eyes on the ceiling as though recounting film clips being played against that blank screen, and Lily beside him in the high-backed wing chair, listening in rapt attention as he described the pack of zebras he had watched one blazingly hot afternoon gathering under the shade of a few sparse trees, vying for the best position.

He told her how, in Tunisia, his motorcar had broken down in the middle of the desert and he had spent the night in the back seat until he was rescued by a gang of Berber boys who came upon him stranded in the sand. How the boys, rug weavers, had taken him back to their village, where he learned to his surprise that he was, as it turned out, not a half bad rug weaver himself.

He told her about the months he'd spent in Tanzania learning to speak the isolate language of Hadzane, now down to about a thousand speakers—hunting kudu with the Hadza people, sleeping with them in brush-covered dwellings. Of how he had learned to carefully measure lion tracks through the bush to identify a mother traveling with cubs, a dangerous encounter best avoided.

And he told her how for a time, for one of his articles, he had lived among the Tiwi tribesmen of Melville Island, who, during funeral ceremonies, donned false beards and face paint so that the spirit of the dead person could not recognize and harm them.

Rose was hesitant to intrude on these sessions. She sat at her small desk in the kitchen, and someone happening upon the scene might have guessed that she was, as it appeared, reviewing the minutes of the last city council meeting. In fact, she was listening as Randolph's stories unfolded, his voice warm and familiar, and she was as captivated as Lily. Rose could remember how she, too, had come to life on their trips, her senses heightened. Getting close enough to smell an animal. The sound of the wilderness around them, like a lullaby, as they slept.

Their life here was good, though, she reminded herself in these moments. She had enjoyed her adventures with Randolph, but she was glad to be back. It felt right to be home, even though home was now so different.

@

For both Lily and Meena, the highlight of the fourth grade was the unit introducing them to the methods and techniques of research, which Mrs. Webster had unimaginatively titled "Writing a Report." The unit began with an introduction to note-taking. They practiced creating outlines and studied the importance of visual aids. From there, the students were to break into pairs to research and prepare a short written report and presentation. Mrs. Webster had handed out a long list of preselected topics from which they might choose:

Creatures of the Sea
Good Nutrition
Illinois
Kinds of Birds
The Heart
The History of the Bicycle
The Shrimp
The Invention of Baseball
The American Flag
Flowers
How Trees Grow

But Lily and Meena had begged to be allowed to choose a topic of their own, and Mrs. Webster had, after much pestering and critique of her assembled topic choices on their parts, reluctantly agreed. Lily and Meena selected the life and times of Lady Florence Baker, explorer of central Africa and co-discoverer, with her husband, of Lake Albert.

For a week, the class spent the Language Arts portion of the school day visiting the small library around which the school's classrooms had been organized. Mrs. Smedstadt, the librarian, introduced them to the large wooden card catalogs near the checkout desk and walked them through the complexities of the Dewey Decimal System. Lily and Meena loved leafing through the soft-edged manila cards of the card catalog. Together they assembled a list of books to gather:

916 Af The Great Explorers of Africa
917.704 Sp The Discovery of the Source of the Nile
910.82 Da Hints to Lady Travellers
917.76 Mi Baker of the Nile
916.76 Ha Lovers on the Nile
962.4 Ba Morning Star: Florence Baker's diary of the
    expedition to put down the slave trade on the Nile,
    1870-1873

It was, perhaps, not surprising that Lily and Meena were the only fourth graders to request materials from another library. They had been distressed to find that their topic received scant coverage in their World Books, among the several-page spreads devoted to American presidents, state flowers, and breeds of dog.

Together Lily and Meena read through their stack of books and filled a neat pile of index cards, color-coded pink for biographical details, blue for historical context, green for information on their subject—Lady Florence Baker herself—white for information on her husband, and yellow for notes on other explorers who had been their contemporaries.

So, while the other students' index cards read like this:

Shrimp are a type of crustacean.
Shrimp are caught in nets.
There are many species of shrimp.
Shrimp eat plants.

Lily and Meena's looked like this:

Born Barbara Maria Szász in 1845 in Transylvania.
Kidnapped and sold into slavery at the age of four.
Raised as a harem girl in the home of a local merchant.
1859: put up for sale at a slave auction at the age of fourteen.
    Two men bid for her. One—a servant of the pasha of Vi-
    din. The other—Samuel Baker.
The pasha's servant places the highest bid, but Baker bribes
    Florence's attendant to allow him to take her. He and his
    friend, the Maharaja Duleep Singh (an Indian prince),
    escape with Florence.
1861: Samuel and Florence set out to discover the source of the
    Nile.
1865: Florence and Samuel Baker are married.
1866: Samuel knighted by Queen Victoria of England. The

Queen refuses to receive Florence because of the scandal of Florence and Samuel traveling together unchaperoned before their marriage.

1916: Florence Baker dies.

Certainly Florence's marriage to Samuel had been an unconventional one, and it had pleased Lily to discover this, feeling a sudden kinship with the couple. Lily loved the task of copying out the relevant passages of text onto her crisp note cards, enclosing them carefully in quotation marks and noting the source at the bottom of each card. At night, at her desk, she ordered and reordered them, imagining the best approach to organizing their report and presentation. Meena argued that the only sensible approach to organization was chronological, but Lily had wondered whether they might not start first with a key event of Florence's adult life—being snubbed by Queen Victoria, perhaps—and then circle back through the biographical details chronologically, using the opening scene as a kind of bookend, as some of the more sophisticated biographies she had read tended to do. "Lady Florence Baker was born Barbara Maria Szász in 1845 in Transylvania." Lily shook her head. She couldn't bear that type of inelegant introduction.

The assignment had been to produce a three-page report and a five-minute presentation, including one optional visual aid. For their oral presentation, Meena had created a posterboard timeline noting the key events in Florence's life, illustrated with photocopied pictures of Florence and Samuel and a map she had created, on which she had outlined the "Route of Florence and Samuel Baker's First Expedition, 1861-1865."

Meena and Lily's report, "Lady Florence Baker: The Journey from Slavery to Exploration," weighed in at twenty pages, not including endnotes, bibliography, and the following index, which Meena had carefully prepared:

Abduction
    childhood and, 1-3, 5

This Lily and Meena presented to the blank stares and confusion of their classmates and teacher.

CHAPTER 9

Everything of Consequence for the Fate of the Universe

It was particle physics...that reigned supreme during that first dazzling microsecond [after the Big Bang], when virtually everything of consequence for the fate of the universe took place.

—To the Heart of Matter: The Superconducting Super Collider, 1987

The men of the neighborhood left for work each morning dressed in sweaters and polo shirts, but Abhijat emerged each morning in a suit, his ensemble varying only in his choice of tie, a habit since his university years. It was a practice often mistaken for sartorial particularity, but in reality, the habit of the suit, its reliable, unwavering sameness, was comforting to Abhijat. He wore it almost like a uniform, and it was when he donned this uniform and prepared to leave for the Lab that he felt most at ease, knowing that he was headed toward the place where he felt most at home in the world.

Evenings, when he returned to Eagle's Crest, he joined the great parade of husbands returning home, greeting one another with a raised hand or a nod as they made their way into the neighborhood and toward their homes through the maze of the subdivision's circles, drives, and cul-de-sacs.

Each night, Abhijat parked the car in the garage and walked down the driveway to the mailbox to collect the day's mail. Frequently, he found himself performing this ritual at the precise moment Carol's husband, Bill, was doing so as well, and here they exchanged the kind of awkward greeting that passes between men who have little in common and know it, their conversations inevitably stilted and perplexing on both ends.

Abhijat felt most comfortable conversing with his colleagues, and he looked forward each morning to his arrival at the Lab. Unlike his neighbors and, he imagined, most Americans, Abhijat did not look forward to the weekends, for they were a time of forced exile (at Sarala's suggestion) from the Lab. If he must work on the weekends, she had asked, couldn't he at least do so from his study at home? Abhijat had agreed to this compromise, but it was time he did not relish because, as he worked, he was acutely aware that just outside his window, the other husbands of the neighborhood were at work in their yards and garages, on home improvement projects, playing catch in the yard with their children. And it was then that he felt so keenly different. So other.

The window of his study looked out over Bill and Carol's garage, where Bill kept his antique sports car (with the exception of summer weekends, when he wheeled it out into the driveway to wax and polish it as gently as if he were bathing an infant). Each time Abhijat looked up from his desk, he saw Bill at work on the car or endlessly puttering in the yard. What, Abhijat wondered, did he find to do out there?

Abhijat had taken to working during the weekends behind a closed door, blinds twisted tightly shut against the reminder of this parallel world to which he did not belong.

@

Sarala had come to realize that, with the exception of Meena, Carol was the first friend she'd had in years. She had, of course, been friendly with Lily's mother for as long as the girls had been friends, exchanging pleasantries as they dropped the girls off and picked them up at one house or the other. But Carol was the first friend who felt like she belonged to Sarala, a friend by choice rather than circumstance.

She spent her mornings now at Carol's house sipping coffee while Carol filled orders and updated her clients' product histories. "It helps me keep track of what they like and don't like," she explained.

Sarala sat beside her, leafing through a set of the flip charts Carol used to prepare for her Mary Kay parties—images of beautiful, sophisticated American women and the Mary Kay products that had helped them achieve that look. They were mostly white women, here and there a token black or Asian woman included. There were, as Sarala had come to expect, no women who looked like her. On the back of the photos were tips for the consultants: "Help your hostess feel special by gesturing to her as you say her name."

"When does Abhijat come back from his conference?" Carol asked, looking up from the pink binder in which she was recording the minutia of her clients' cosmetic preferences.

Abhijat had left earlier in the week for the International Workshop on Charm Physics, where he was delivering a paper on Hidden Charm. During his absence, Sarala had taken the opportunity to clean his study, a part of the house she rarely ventured into, being so infrequently invited. As she made her way into the room, she could sense the disturbance she made in the air, in the dust that coated the bookshelves and the spaces on his desk not covered in paper. Armed with one of Meena's old cloth diapers and a bottle of Pledge, she had set about cleaning what she could without disarranging anything. Here and there she found triangles of desktop peeking out from among the lined white paper on which he had scribbled equations, and these she approached gingerly, with a fingertip, loath to move something out of place that might someday explain this enormous and astonishing world in which they lived.

As she worked, she found herself recalling with perfect clarity, much to her own surprise, something she'd read in one of her schoolbooks years ago: "A well-ordered home helps to make well-ordered men."

What would Abhijat be like, she wondered, without his position at the Lab, without all of this. She looked out over his desktop. On top of the piles of paper that covered the desk sat a yellow legal pad covered with Abhijat's neat, bold handwriting:

HOW MANY QUARK SPECIES ARE THERE?
HOW DO THE QUARKS BEHAVE WITH HADRONIC MATTER?
WHAT IS THE NATURE OF THE WEAK NEUTRAL CURRENT?

As she cleaned, she was surprised and a little sad to realize that his absence that week had hardly registered for her, nor, it seemed, for Meena. It was as though they had both come to think of Abhijat as a person who existed only in the mind rather than in their shared physical space.

Even the things he studied weren't really present in the physical sense, she thought. Their very existence was hypothetical. He and the other theorists were predicting that these tiny parts of the world existed. But ultimately, who knew?

Sarala had begun to think that, in this sense, Abhijat's work was not so very unlike that of the fortune tellers she had seen on the streets of Bombay, who might take your hand and, tracing the lines of your palm, hypothesize a future for you.

She had seen images of the paths created by the collisions of particles, paths which, by their arcing and turning, would tell the story of what they were. Muons, neutrinos, hadrons, gluons. It wasn't unlike magic, she thought, remembering something she'd heard one of the other physicists' wives saying a few months earlier at the Lab's Christmas party: "Well, you know what I always say when people ask what a theorist does. I tell them it's a kind of transubstantiation—they turn coffee into papers."

@

When he returned home from the conference, Abhijat found himself distracted by the idle physics-world gossip that suggested there might be plans in the works for an even larger particle accelerator—one that would render the Lab's current accelerator as antiquated and obsolete as the Lab's old rusting and abandoned fixed-target accelerator.

Though he had never before taken much interest in the details of the accelerators, Abhijat had begun, lately, to think about this a great deal. The work he'd been doing had been well received, but if he were to make the kind of lasting legacy in the physics world he'd always expected to, then the theories he'd been working on would need to be confirmed by the experimenters. And the area of his work was fast outpacing the capabilities of the Lab's current accelerator.

Preoccupied, Abhijat found himself standing at his office window, looking out along the old fixed-target beam line, wondering what might be in store for the Lab in the future. He thought of the buildings of the old accelerator, now empty in disuse, which ran along the beam line out toward the boundary of the Lab's campus and the beginning of the town. He rested his head against the window, feeling the cool pane of glass against his skin.

Even if these rumors were not true, Abhijat realized, there would surely come a time when the Lab's technological capabilities were surpassed by those of another facility. And then what?

He returned to his seat at his desk, fingers drumming nervously against the desktop as he willed his eyes and attention back to the work at hand.

@

Near the back of the Lab's seminar room, Abhijat took a seat next to Dr. Cardiff, his colleague and contemporary, in one of the room's creaking orange chairs, which broadcast one's every stretch and repositioning. It was easy to identify the young man who would be the afternoon's presenter. He sat at the front of the room, beside one of Abhijat's colleagues in the first row, one leg crossed over another, foot bouncing up and down nervously, eyes on the door, watching to see who arrived to hear his talk.

Abhijat and Dr. Cardiff both made note of this, exchanging a smile. Abhijat could still remember being that young a man—junior scientist eager to share his work. He remembered how nervous he, too, had been.

But now, he had reached what could reasonably, statistically, be predicted as the midpoint of his life. Here he sat, with the job he had always dreamed of, at the world's premier research facility. And yet, much as he had wanted it; much as he had expected it; much as he had studied, read, and prepared for it; he had come to a point where he had begun to fear he might never be a great physicist.

He had always dreamed of one day ranking among his idols— Pauli, Dirac, Gell-Mann. Certainly he was a good physicist—strong international reputation, well respected at the Lab and throughout his field, impressive publications. But his work, while good—solidly and consistently good—had not been transformative. His theories had floated out into the world in the form of articles and papers he delivered at conferences. There were junior scientists who cited his work, colleagues who admired him, academics who taught his theories. But he had come to fear that, in the grand scheme of history, his would not be a name that was remembered. Since he'd begun his studies, his career, his greatest fear had been that he would be a failure. A B+ physicist.

@

The young speaker was introduced by Abhijat's colleague. A promising young man, Abhijat thought, listening—strong undergraduate pedigree, excellent Ph.D. program, already a number of well-regarded publications.

The young physicist moved across the half-circle stage as he spoke, framed by the floor-to-ceiling chalkboards. (Abhijat had yet to witness a speaker kneeling on the floor to utilize the bottom third of the available chalkboard space, but he felt sure that someday he would, that space becoming valuable real estate as the rest of the wall filled with equations.) As the young physicist became more and more nervous, his voice reached higher and higher into his register and began, here and there, to crack, betraying his youth, his sense of awe, of panicked reverence at addressing this group of scientists assembled before him.

"Afterward, there is of course propagation in a background," the physicist said, looking out into the crowd as though to test his own certainty on the matter. "And now this complicated equation that we will forget about," he said, smiling, trying his hand at a bit of levity. He had pulled down the screen that hung in front of the chalkboard and was now making notes on an overhead projector, his equation magnified on the screen behind him.

Abhijat began, without realizing it, to shake his head almost imperceptibly. To think that this young scientist was nervous partly because of him, because of the room full of scientists just like him.

"This shows great promise," the speaker continued, animated. "They are highly desirable and very strange," the young physicist said, smiling again, the overhead projecting onto his face as he moved in front of the screen.

What warmed Abhijat's heart was the way this young scientist seemed to harbor such enthusiasm, bordering on genuine affection, for the particles, for the equations that predicted their existence.

"Oh, and this is my favorite one," the young physicist said, his face lighting up.

Abhijat could remember being possessed by that kind of enthusiasm, that kind of energy, but it occurred to him that it had been quite a long time since he had felt it.

Since he had arrived at the Lab, the theoretical particle physics community had begun moving into an area of such high energy that the Lab's current accelerator was unable to verify or disprove many of the most cutting-edge theories. And so, Abhijat, like many of his colleagues, found themselves stuck in the frustrating position of waiting for a machine of high enough energy to confirm these theories so that they might know whether they were on the right track or not.

What was at stake: the great prizes, the ones that ensured a place in the history of physics. For a theory that wasn't proven by the experimental physicists was nothing more than an interesting idea.

Abhijat thought again of the rumor of the larger, faster accelerator. It could mean confirmation, validation of his work. Until then, almost all of the important physics prizes, eligibility for which required that the theory be confirmed by experiments as well as by standing the test of time, were out of reach for Abhijat and many of his colleagues.

He knew that some of his older colleagues had begun to wonder if they would live long enough to see their theories confirmed and their work recognized. And that many—including, Abhijat suspected, his friend and colleague Dr. Cardiff—had long ago let go of their hopes of this sort of recognition, of a Nobel or a Wolf. Abhijat, however, had not.

Dr. Cardiff seemed to Abhijat to be at peace with this. For Dr. Cardiff, it was the work, not the recognition, that seemed to bring him happiness, and at times, Abhijat found himself envious of such peace, though equally confused about how one might so easily set down the burden of one's ambitions.

In this, Dr. Cardiff sometimes reminded Abhijat of his mother, who had always insisted that one could best find success by first finding peace and contentment.

At the conclusion of his presentation, the young speaker, as expected, took questions from the audience. They came rapid-fire. Some, Abhijat could tell right away, were attempts to trip up the young physicist. These were usually delivered by the speaker's peers, who might use the opportunity to try to impress one of their senior colleagues. (Dr. Cardiff liked to joke that one could always spot such questions, for they inevitably began: "Let me preface my question by saying…") Others were less a question and more a demonstration of the questioner's familiarity with the work he referenced. When a good question came his way (these usually came from the older scientists, now eager to encourage their young colleagues), a smile floated across the face of the young scientist, and Abhijat watched how he paused in answering, as though trying to rein in a racing mind.

@

Days at home in the empty house, Sarala had begun practicing a flat, Midwestern accent, having studied her neighbors' smooth *I*s, hard *D*s, and clipped *T*s. She watched herself in the mirror as she spoke, willing her mouth around the round, nasal *A*s: Chic-ah-go.

Since her arrival in the country, Sarala had replaced her wardrobe of saris with jogging suits and seasonal and holiday-themed sweaters she ordered from QVC.

The wooden box of her mother's recipes had been pushed farther and farther back into the cupboard, behind her collection of Tupperware, and had been replaced with new cookbooks recommended by Carol and the neighbor ladies Sarala now power-walked with each morning, doing laps around the mall before the stores opened—*Betty Crocker, the Good Housekeeping All-American Cookbook, Microwave Cooking Made Easy.*

"I thought you might enjoy reading this," Carol had said that morning over coffee, presenting Sarala with her prized (and autographed, she pointed out, indicating the flourishing signature across the title page) copy of Mary Kay Ash's biography.

Sarala had begun reading as soon as she got home. It pleased her to note the character traits they both shared: tenacity, commitment, enthusiasm, fortitude.

Alone in the house, Abhijat off at work, Meena off at Lily's, Sarala kept right on reading through the long, quiet afternoon until it was time to begin preparing dinner, and then she propped the book up in a cookbook holder, reading as she stirred the pot simmering on the stove, a new recipe she was trying out called Yankee Noodle Dandy.

Outside, the sun had gone down. Meena would return soon from Lily's house, Abhijat from the Lab. From the kitchen window, Sarala could see Carol across the street as she emerged from her house, two smart carrying cases in each hand. These she loaded into the trunk of her pink Cadillac and, checking her lipstick in the rearview mirror, backed out of the garage and down the driveway. Sarala wondered where Carol was heading, red brake lights glowing for a moment as she stopped, just barely, for the stop sign in front of the elementary school, then rolled through the intersection and off into the night.

@

Sarala, who so keenly noticed so many things about the world, had, it must be said, a bit of a blind spot when it came to perceiving Abhijat's less-than-enthusiastic responses to the cuisine she present-ed him with each evening at dinner. She thought of the meals she prepared as a way to help Abhijat assimilate, to feel more at home in their adopted country. But Abhijat missed the food of his childhood.

Some nights, after growing hungry, picking at the American dinners Sarala placed before him, Abhijat took down the wooden box of Sarala's mother's recipes from the shelf over the oven, pulling it out from behind the collection of Tupperware.

On these nights, he carried it furtively into his study and read through the recipes, fragile pieces of paper in her mother's pencil-light handwriting.

For when you feel the pain of distance.

And her recipe for puran poli.

For when the problems of the world knock at the door,
begging entry to your home.

Her recipe for kheer.

As he read through the recipes, his mouth watering, eyes tearing at the mention of ground red pepper, cloves, cardamom, ginger paste, and raw mango, he remembered peeking into the kitchen of his childhood home, where the women sat, bent low over pots, peeling vegetables and grinding spices.

He had begun to cook for himself late at night, after he had finished wrestling with his latest paper. He grated ginger root into a bowl, Sarala upstairs watching television, Meena asleep or reading under her comforter by flashlight. At night, as they slept, the smell of his cooking creeping into their dreams, where Sarala found herself returning again and again to the kitchen of her girlhood.

CHAPTER 10

Sex Ed for the Gifted and Talented

Frantz Fanon discusses a critical stage in the development of children socialized in Western culture, regardless of their race, in which racist stereotypes of the savage and the primitive are assimilated through the consumption of popular culture: comics, movies, cartoons, etc. These stereotypical images are often part of myths of colonial dominion (for example, cowboy defeats Indian, conquistador triumphs over Aztec Empire, colonial soldier conquers African chief, and so on). This dynamic also contains a sexual dimension, usually expressed as anxiety.

—COCO FUSCO, *THE OTHER HISTORY
OF INTERCULTURAL PERFORMANCE*

1987

BY THE END OF ELEMENTARY SCHOOL, IT HAD BECOME CLEAR THAT where Meena and Lily belonged was not with the rest of the children, mingling with the general population, but as part of the new, experimental, Gifted and Talented program, and thus, when they began junior high, they were pulled from what began to be referred to as "the regular classes" and placed in what the school board had elected to call the Free Learning Zone.

The Free Learning Zone was populated with the brightest students from the four elementary schools that fed into Nicolet Junior High. The classroom was long and narrow, filled with round tables rather than desks, quiet corners furnished with pillows, and cozy chairs in which students might curl up and read when struck by a particularly driving curiosity. Here, the students' studies were self-directed. Long, low bookshelves lined the walls beneath a wide bank of windows. Colorful posters and artwork hung from the ceiling, suspended by fishing wire, giving the impression of the pictures floating in the air. There were easels where students might paint, computers grouped around a large round table, a problem-solving center, a debate corner, and, near the door, a desk for Ms Lessing, always piled high with precariously stacked books and papers, pens and pencils rolling off onto the brightly colored carpet. Ms Lessing had wild, curly red hair held back each day with a series of colorful scarves that sometimes matched the rest of her outfit, but more usually did not.

Among the privileges of the Free Learning Zone was that students could leave the classroom and visit the school library whenever they liked, and Meena and Lily took advantage of this opportunity frequently, becoming intimately familiar with the library's collection of books, newspapers, periodicals, and reference materials.

Meena loved the way she might wander down an aisle, running her fingers over the spines of the books and choose one at random, any number of worlds opening up before her. She didn't, however, like to think of all the other small worlds left on the shelves. It induced in her a sense of panic, the thought that it might not actually be possible to read all of the books in the world.

She loved, too, the library's numerous sets of encyclopedias—Britannica, Columbia, New Standard. In them, she looked up Bombay, tried to imagine her parents' previous lives, tried to imagine herself there. Her mother had taken her back to India twice. Both times she had been too young to remember anything of the trip, of the country, aside from the grandmothers who doted on her, stuffing her with a parade of sweets. And both times, her father had been unable (or unwilling, Meena was never quite sure) to tear himself away from his work to join them.

She looked up the Lab, which was described just as her father described it, as "housing the world's premier particle accelerator facility, currently the most important tool for the study of subatomic physics." It seemed important that the place where her own father worked appeared in the encyclopedia. She felt a sort of pride by association.

There, in the school's library, the Free Learning Zone students sometimes encountered students from the regular classes whose teachers had arranged a visit to the library for some project or other, and on these days Meena and Lily sometimes caught glimpses of their old elementary-school classmates. They regarded each other curiously across the library as though eyeing a wild animal.

What were the other kids learning, Lily wondered? She had no sense of what she might talk about with them, were they to meet on the playground for recess or, as Ms Lessing called it, expressive play. Had they done the unit on Cubism yet? Would they know what a fractal was? How far separated had they become, she wondered. Tom Hebert made it sound like the regular kids now spent most of their time learning to fix automobile engines and give haircuts. Erick Jarvis, whose glasses turned from regular glasses into sunglasses and back again whenever he went into or out of the building, and who had a brother who was still in the regular classes, reported that, according to his source, it was all just exactly the same as before.

Among the regular kids, though, there had, it seemed, cropped up a collection of apocryphal legends about what had become of the gifted and talented kids who had been disappeared from their classes. One said he had heard that the gifted kids were all aliens who'd been identified by the government and had been shut up in the Free Learning Zone to undergo a series of top-secret experiments.

Tom Hebert said his next-door neighbor believed the gifted kids had been identified as "Commie spies" and had been sent to the Free Learning Zone for deprogramming. But the other Free Learning Zone students gave this theory little attention, having felt for some time that Tom was not really one of them. They had heard that he'd had to beg his way into the Free Learning Zone, a series of increasingly shrill phone calls from his parents until the principal had finally relented, shaking his head and thinking, *Fine, kid. It's your funeral.*

Regarding the regular classes, many of the Free Learning Zone students had begun to develop a barely concealed contempt. Although the term *regular* might be more commonly understood to suggest "that which is normal, standard, or expected," among the Free Learning Zone students there could be no greater insult than to be thought of as regular. Why be regular, normal, standard, when one could be exceptional, gifted, advanced?

@

In February, just as the citizens of Nicolet were beginning to tire of the grey slush of winter, the students of the Free Learning Zone began a unit titled "Our Changing Bodies."

Meena and Lily could tell this was going to be something different from the way Ms Lessing colored when she began the first lesson, her voice going a little breathy, as though hoping not to be overheard by anyone who might be passing just then in the hallway. Gone was the self-directed learning. Ms Lessing insisted that all of the Free Learning Zone students take seats facing her. Suddenly, Ms Lessing was using the chalkboard, overheads, slides even, and strangest of all, reading from the book. She grasped it as she spoke as though it were a life preserver, the only thing keeping her afloat.

Lily paid careful attention. *Ovaries*, she lettered in her notebook in her slow, deliberate handwriting. *Testes.* She avoided looking at any of the boys in the class as she wrote.

Meena had propped up her health textbook on her desk so that it appeared as though she was following along as Ms Lessing lectured. But inside the textbook, she had secreted away her latest obsession, which she had discovered at the Friends of the Nicolet Public Library's used book sale the previous weekend and had been carrying around since then—a strange, yellowed old book called *The Secret Museum of Mankind*. Turning the pages, her eyes on the grainy images and their captions, it was this book she read as Ms Lessing lectured.

There were photos of scantily clad men, earlobes stretched around clay disks; bare-breasted women in skirts of grass, naked babies resting on their hips; a boy hunter wielding a spear. In the background, she could hear Ms Lessing reading aloud from the textbook.

"You may begin to notice changes in your body."

But Meena's eyes were on the grainy photographs of *The Secret Museum*. She was nearing the end of the section titled "The Secret Album of Oceana," in which the author noted, *The shores are dotted with these careless children of nature, lightly clad.*

From the front of the room, Ms Lessing had adopted what she hoped was a reassuring tone.

"These changes are part of what is called puberty."

P-U-B-E-R-T-Y she spelled out carefully on the chalkboard in all capital letters.

Here, in a classroom that was a sea of white suburban faces, Meena pored over the images in *The Secret Museum*, all identified as "natives" or as "representative specimens of their race," all of them dark-skinned, the images in the book and the lecture, going on in the background like a kind of soundtrack, becoming intimately connected as she half listened and half took in the photos and their captions. *Kalinga girls are fond of this style in which the bodice ends early and the skirt begins late.*

"Soon, you may find that you have developed body odor."

Here, an image of young women, their faces marked with elaborate patterns of cuts and tattoos, a caption reading, *Tribal marks deform their not-unpleasing faces.*

"Your breasts will begin to develop, and at first, they may be tender."

There were almost no instances in which the individuals in the photos were identified by their names, Meena noticed. Rather, they were stand-ins, "a Kalabit" or "a Dayak," each group represented by a single photo and informative caption.

"These changes are caused by hormones," Ms Lessing continued.

To Meena's right, Lily was carefully taking notes, but Meena was transfixed by the picture before her, a young woman ornamented in an elaborate feathered headdress: *This striking personage, upon whom you will find all the young men's eyes, is among her tribeswomen, considered to be a rare beauty.*

"For boys, the shoulders will grow broader."

These girls do most of the work in the fields, while men pursue or evade vendettas.

"Your voices may become deeper."

Here, an image of bare-bottomed men with bows and arrows.

"Both boys and girls will develop hair under their arms and in their pubic areas."

Naked, dark-skinned women stood together staring out of the photograph and, it seemed to Meena, right at her, their bodies painted, breasts hanging flat against their chests.

Tom Hebert, in the seat behind her, tapped her on the shoulder. "What are you looking at?" he whispered.

"Shut up," she hissed, whipping around to glare at him, her long braid catching him across the face as she turned back around.

"Girls will develop a regular menstrual period."

The next page showed a group of women, their skirts pulled up, legs spread wide around the washbasins at which they worked.

"You will begin to feel strong emotions, and you may find yourself becoming frustrated, angry, or sad more easily."

A woman standing in front of a hut, her nakedness hidden by cleverly arranged beadwork.

For Meena, it was as though two mysteries of the adult world were being revealed simultaneously to her—one by the book and one by the shocking news Ms Lessing was breaking to them all.

"Shall we talk about our questions, our concerns?"

Ms Lessing removed her eyes from the book and regarded the classroom full of students, their faces turned up toward her. Normally, the Free Learning Zone students were avid, if overenthusiastic, participants in class discussion, but now the classroom was weighted with a thick, awkward silence. Ms Lessing blinked out at the gifted and talented students for a moment as though trying to summon patience or courage or a little of both.

"Well then, let's continue." She plodded steadily forward through the overheads. "Now we will discuss sexually transmitted diseases," she explained, placing on the overhead a particularly alarming image. "This is a chancre." The students looked away, letting out an audible groan, almost in unison.

At the conclusion of the lecture, the class sat quietly in a kind of stunned silence. The lecture on their developing bodies had shocked both Lily and Meena, neither of whom had yet registered the possibility that this might happen to them.

For Lily, the careful notes she penned had been an academic exercise in keeping her anxiety at bay. Meena, closing her textbook and tucking *The Secret Museum* into her backpack, felt she had only just barely survived an arduous and terrifying initiation into near-adulthood.

CHAPTER 11

Atom Smasher

In the end, physics is an empirical science. It needs clever experiments; and such experiments need nifty devices. Without them, many beautiful theories would be merely that—beautiful. It is only thanks to tinkerers ... that some of them also turn out to be true.

—Obituary: Simon van der Meer,
The Economist, March 19, 2011

Physicists don't like the expression "atom smasher." It makes them think of what (for example) a watch smasher would do. Out of the collisions of watches and clocks, you would expect to find the components of watches and clocks: hands, springs, cogwheels, and frames. You would not expect to find from such collisions additional clocks, and certainly not clock towers. Incredibly, this is just what sometimes happens when two energetic subatomic particles are smashed together. New and more exotic particles emerge from the collisions.

—*The Charm of Strange Quarks: Mysteries and Revolutions of Particle Physics*

For some time, nearly all of the particle physics conferences Abhijat attended had been dominated by discussion of the need to conduct experiments at higher energy levels, and there had been rumblings, unconfirmed, of course, that it might be the National Accelerator Research Lab that would be chosen as the site for such an instrument.

The accelerator currently housed on the campus of the Lab was four miles in circumference, but it had become clear that in order to chase after the new questions that were emerging, to test many of the most recent and most fascinating theories, a new accelerator would be required, something much, much larger than anything that currently existed.

It was a hunt that had stretched out over the entirety of Abhijat's career—each time the physics community thought they'd found the smallest, most elementary particle, something still smaller, still more mystifying emerged.

For some physicists, it seemed like a frustrating chase that might never end, each time the prize moving just beyond their reach. But Abhijat believed that this was an illustration of the supreme beauty of the universe. If there was a god, he had once told Sarala, then he must surely be a mathematician.

@

Anderson Hall was the Research Tower's large lecture hall, reserved for the Lab's cultural activities—plays, lecture series, performances by orchestras—and the occasional all-staff announcements made by the Lab's director. One Monday, on a bright spring morning, the Lab staff were summoned to Anderson Hall, where Dr. Palmer, the Lab director, announced that the Department of Energy was, in fact, considering building a new, much larger accelerator, and that the Lab was, in fact, the facility under consideration to house it. If built, it would be the largest particle accelerator in the world.

For a moment, Abhijat's breath caught in his throat. This was it, he realized. This was his chance at establishing his legacy. His chance at accomplishing what he had always hoped for, always worked toward—his chance to grasp, finally, what he had begun to fear might remain frustratingly just out of reach.

The excitement in the Lab cafeteria following the announcement was palpable. At each table, physicists chatted animatedly, wondering what might be revealed by collisions at such high energy. Would it expose gaps in the Standard Model of particle physics? Would they be able to find the Higgs boson, a particle hypothesized but never yet observed, whose existence was essential if the Standard Model was to work? Would it allow for the discovery of a Grand Unified Theory? Was it possible that additional families of quarks and leptons existed?

Abhijat sat quietly among his colleagues at lunch, but beneath his calm exterior was more excitement than anyone would have suspected. This new machine meant that he might no longer languish in the murky middle of good physicists who had failed to be great. With this increased size came increased power, and with that, the possibility of finally testing the theories he'd been working on for years. His mind raced, a series of possibilities—theories tested, confirmed, and then, perhaps a prize. But—he caught himself—he should not allow himself to get carried away.

He had counted the hours, the minutes until he would return home for dinner and share the news with Sarala and Meena. In his office, he could hardly focus, playing his announcement out ahead of time.

@

"But with such a large circumference, where will they build it?" Sarala, seated beside him at the dinner table, had asked, after he shared the news. Watching him talk, she had thought of how she hadn't seen him this animated in years.

"Part of it on the Lab's campus—the accelerator, the particle detector, the experiment halls—and part of it stretching out," he answered.

"Stretching out—to where?" Sarala asked, catching Meena's eye, who, Sarala could tell, was wondering the same thing.

"Through Nicolet," he answered. "Or rather, under it."

"Yes, but under where, exactly?" Sarala asked.

Abhijat would later come to think of this moment—Sarala's question, the concern in her voice—as the first moment he glimpsed the way this might sound to the rest of the community. "Well." He found himself proceeding cautiously. "That is still under consideration." *But it's unimportant*, he'd wanted to tell her, hoping to redirect her attention instead to where his own lay: to the possibilities this opened for his work, his reputation.

In the cafeteria that afternoon, following the announcement, he and his fellow colleagues had been so focused on the changes this would mean for the field, so excited by what this would mean for each of their careers, that it hadn't occurred to them how such a proposal would be perceived in the community.

"I'm not sure this is going to go over well in town," Sarala said gently, hating to put out the light of excitement in Abhijat's eyes, but certain that ahead lay troubled times.

@

Sarala had been right. By the following morning, news of the proposed collider appeared on the front page of the *Chicago Tribune* and the *Nicolet Herald-Gleaner*, along with a proposed path for the collider ring superimposed over a map of Nicolet, showing the collider's tunnels running under the town's subdivisions, schools, and what the newspaper identified as "prime farmland." ATOM SMASHER, the headline read in all caps.

Reporters have learned that the National Accelerator Research Lab is in discussions with the Department of Energy to build a large collider ring, called the "Superconducting Super Collider," in an underground tunnel that will encircle the town of Nicolet, running under homes, schools, and farmland.

Sarala presented the paper to Abhijat as he took his seat at the table for breakfast.

"Abhijat, this map," she said softly, after he had taken a moment to skim the front page. "It would go right under our neighborhood, under Meena's school, under Heritage Village."

"But this is only a proposed path," he assured her. "It's far from certain."

"But," Sarala continued, "I don't understand why the Lab can't build this on the property they already have."

"It's much, much bigger than the accelerator we have now," Abhijat explained. "Much bigger than the property we have. The current advances in tunneling, though, mean the Lab wouldn't have to acquire the land." These points had been noted by the Lab director the day before in his announcement. Here, Abhijat's voice took on a hopeful tone. "No one would have to give up their farms or homes as when the Lab campus was built. Now we can just tunnel under these things, and people can retain their homes."

Sarala looked at him dubiously.

"Oh, but you must understand," he continued. "This is not a machine to be feared. It is something we should be in awe of, honored to have built here. Think of the answers it will reveal to us. Think of what it might mean for our family."

Sarala was thinking of that. "But under our town? Under our homes?" she asked.

"Yes, but there is no danger. What possible danger could there be?"

But Sarala did not have an answer for this.

@

By the time Abhijat arrived at the Lab that morning, the staff had been summoned back to Anderson Hall where, just the day before, they had received what had seemed to them to be happy news. Again, the Lab director at the podium. Again the restless chattering among the staff in the audience. Again the director's hand held up to quell this, and then his voice.

"Many of you have likely seen the covers of today's papers. This is not how we planned the information to be disseminated to the public, but here it is and we must make the best of it."

@

The day the cover story about the collider appeared in the paper, Rose, at the tiny desk in the corner of the kitchen from which she ran her political career, had begun to imagine greater things. With an issue like this, sure to galvanize the voters, she thought, she might—if she played her cards just right—have a chance next year at the mayor's office.

CHAPTER 12

Conditions at the Creation
of the Universe

Truth is ever to be found in simplicity, and not in the multiplicity and confusion of things. He is the God of order and not of confusion.

—Sir Isaac Newton, quoted in *To the Heart of Matter: The Superconducting Super Collider*, 1987

In the weeks since the announcement about the new accelerator, Sarala noted that the front page of the *Herald-Gleaner* featured a steady march of articles on the history of the Lab, its safety record, and its scientific accomplishments. There were articles on land acquisition and the power of eminent domain, on the various methods that might be employed for tunneling beneath the homes and farmland of Nicolet. On the necessity for the Lab to secure the support of elected officials at the local, state, and national level if the project were to move forward. On subatomic particles like quarks and gluons. On the paradox of needing so large an instrument to study something so small. Abhijat had been surprised, then alarmed, at the amount of coverage the collider plan was getting in the news, not all of it good.

The decision about whether or not the super collider would be constructed was to be made, the citizens of Nicolet learned, not by them, but by the Department of Energy, which would conduct and then circulate environmental impact studies, feasibility studies, and would endeavor to gauge the response of the community to the idea by hosting a public hearing on the matter.

Representatives from the Lab and the Department of Energy were quoted, insisting that the path that had been outlined on the front page—in which the tunnel traveled west from the Lab's campus, running under homes in Eagle's Crest, under Heritage Village, and out into the surrounding farmland before arcing back around and making its way back to the Lab, passing under still more farmland, more homes, the elementary school, the junior high, and the high school—was only one of several possibilities still under consideration.

These same officials cited the Super Proton Synchrotron at CERN on the French-Swiss border, which had been constructed under French farmland, as a model, and as proof that there was no reason to fear living on top of such a facility.

Not long after the articles began to appear, Sarala noticed that the Editorials and Letters to the Editor sections of the *Herald-Gleaner* had begun, slowly, to be taken over entirely by the issue of the collider. Gone were scraps over increases in property taxes, rogue candidates for school board, and complaints over the noise produced by the cannons set off each summer during Heritage Village's annual Revolutionary War Days event.

The editor of the *Herald-Gleaner* would later come to remember the day of the super collider cover story as the last day the editorial pages featured content unrelated to the collider. From that day forward, letters about the collider began to arrive, at first in a slowish trickle, but that had been deceptive and unrepresentative of what was to come.

Throughout Nicolet, suspicion grew among the citizens as to just what the Lab was up to out there, whether they'd been planning this further takeover of the town's land all along. In place of the usual sorts of letters to the editor were diatribes questioning whether all of the public activities at the Lab—the cultural events, the butterfly gardens, the hiking trails—had only been naked attempts at improving the Lab's public image, luring in the wary public, who now eyed the Research Tower from their bedroom windows and imagined the superconductor snaking beneath their rec rooms, God-only-knows-what whizzing around below them as they slept. And then, once they collided, once they "succeeded," what then? The end of the world? Dark matter? A black hole that would swallow Nicolet whole, leaving a gaping crater of nothingness in the prairie?

@

Since the announcement of the collider issue, Lily's letters to Randolph had begun to focus almost exclusively on the subject, providing him with updates and articles clipped from the *Herald-Gleaner*. The local unions, she explained, argued that building the collider would bring thousands of construction jobs to the area, and were thus in favor of it. Local realtors worried that the location of the collider tunnel under homes would decrease property values in the area, so they had come out against it. Most teachers, Lily wrote, supported the project, as did many of the citizens who worked for computer or high-tech companies. These people, she explained in her letters, surely understood the research possibilities the collider would bring. But farmers, Lily noted, were split on the issue. There were those who were grateful for the Lab campus, for the way its land, returned to prairie grass, was the only land for miles that had not been swallowed up by suburban sprawl. But other farmers, remembering the land that had, years ago, been taken to build the Lab campus, were wary of the assurances that they'd still be able to own and farm the land under which the tunnels would be constructed. And on it went, the town divided.

To Lily, it seemed obvious that the collider was not only a good idea, but in fact an essential one. She found herself perplexed by the response of community members who did not support it, and had begun to feel as though she were living among foreigners whose strange customs she'd only ever half comprehended. Sitting in the wing chair in her father's study, she wondered if that was how her father felt during his explorations. But, she realized, looking around the room at his photos and collections, he seemed to find these differences exciting rather than worrisome.

©

Randolph read Lily's letters with a mixture of amusement at this strange, curious daughter he and Rose had produced and concern that she seemed so entirely uninterested in the things one might expect from a girl of her age.

He wrote to Rose: *How do you suppose we might interest Lily in some of the more conventional preoccupations of young women her age?*

But Rose, having never been particularly conventional herself, had been able to offer no fruitful suggestions. She remembered her own parents' letters about the construction of the Lab years ago, the newspaper clippings her mother had sent in the letters she'd posted to wherever Rose and Randolph were due to arrive next. For Rose, out in the world, in the midst of her adventures with Randolph, the whole thing had seemed like a story that was happening to someone else.

CHAPTER 13

Expeditions through Unmapped Territory

As the quantum physicist Finkelstein said: "As well as a Yes and a No, the universe also contains a Perhaps."
—PAOLO NOVARESIO, *THE EXPLORERS*

ALL WINTER LONG, COMING HOME FROM CAROL'S OR CATCHING A glimpse of her own home through Carol's big bay window as they shared coffee in the morning, Sarala had begun to think that her house did, in fact, look stern and imposing. She felt embarrassed that it had taken her so long to notice how spare and utilitarian the yard was—driveway, grass, sidewalk, porch. By the end of the long grey winter, her eyes craved color, and she began to make plans for changes come spring: bright flowerbeds to line their front walkway, a flowering tree for their front yard. She sketched it out on a piece of paper, borrowing ideas from the glossy magazines she kept in a pile on the living room coffee table.

@

By early spring, copies of the feasibility studies the Lab had conducted began to circulate. These noted that it would be necessary to negotiate easements with property owners under whose homes and businesses the collider's tunnels would run.

Then came the draft of the Environmental Impact Statement, which the Department of Energy had commissioned and which the citizens of Nicolet and the surrounding communities were invited to respond to. The statements arrived in eighteen-by-twelve-inch cardboard boxes, one to each home in Nicolet and the surrounding areas. Inside were reams of paper bound together, their blue covers reading Volume 1 of 21, Volume 2 of 21, and so on.

On the day the draft of the Environmental Impact Statement arrived at the Winchester home, Lily dragged the box through the foyer into Randolph's study, slit it open with his ox-bone letter opener, and began reading, page 1, volume 1, red pen in hand for suggested corrections.

> The collider ring will pass under farmland and residential communities.
>
> Geologic suitability is outstanding. Perceived potential loss of home values is a key element of the strong landowner opposition.

©

Slowly, in the yards of some of the more vocal opponents, signs reading No SSC, Not Under My House, and Not Under My School began to bloom.

Sarala noticed these first, and wondered how long it would be before Abhijat, in the course of his commute through the neighborhood to the Lab, would notice them. It had not taken long.

Though the signs had sprouted up all around the neighborhood, Abhijat had managed to remain composed, if privately frustrated. But the first sign to go up on their own street was a different matter. It had felt, to Abhijat, very much like a personal attack.

The sign appeared one day in front of Ted and Sheila Miller's house, just a few doors from the Mitals. Sarala noticed it first. She'd felt a sudden surge of embarrassment and shame. The Millers knew where Abhijat worked, but still the sign stood starkly in their yard, like a message to her and her family.

Abhijat noticed it that night on his way home. He slowed and pulled the car over to the side of the street. To Abhijat, the signs seemed tantamount to putting up a large placard in one's yard announcing: "I am poorly educated and illogically fearful." He couldn't imagine who in their right minds would be willing to publicly advertise such a thing.

Surely his own neighbors knew where he worked, that his career and the careers of hundreds of his coworkers were at stake. Don't you care, he'd wanted to shout, that you may cost people their occupations, their calling?

@

At the hardware store, Mr. Fricker, who'd taken a shine to this young mother who seemed, always, to come in without a husband, walked with Sarala through the store, helping her select the things she might need for the redesign of her yard: plastic trays in which to start the seeds, a small spade for when it was time to transplant the sprouting plants into the ground, potting soil, and slim envelopes of seeds. In the rotating seed display were flowers that reminded Sarala of her girlhood—orange, yellow, and pink marigolds—but she'd settled instead on an assortment of varieties in alternating arrangements of red, white, and blue.

@

As a bachelor who had lived alone all his life, Dr. Cardiff was a favorite dinner guest of the wives of the other Lab physicists, Sarala included, and when Abhijat's frustration over the steady stream of anti-super collider sentiment in Nicolet began to reach a crescendo, Sarala thought a dinner with Dr. Cardiff might cheer him up. Meena had asked whether Lily might join them, so the five of them gathered around the Mital dinner table one evening.

"And how is your father, Lily?" Sarala asked. "Where do his adventures take him these days?"

Sarala had introduced their two dinner guests, Lily and Dr. Cardiff, and now turned to explain to Dr. Cardiff that Lily's father was a—. She found herself unable to produce an accurate description.

Abhijat stepped in. "An explorer," he said, nodding at his colleague.

"I see." Dr. Cardiff smiled. "How very fascinating."

"He's in a mountainous region of Tibet right now," Lily said, answering Sarala's question. She could picture her father standing atop some peak, hand shading his eyes from the sun as he looked out over the rugged terrain ahead, plotting his next day's journey.

"You must miss him terribly when he's gone," Sarala said. Her voice was gentle and tentative, and in that tone Lily recognized that what Mrs. Mital was really asking, what so many people always seemed to be wondering, much to Lily's irritation, was whether she resented her father's absence and travel. Lily evaded Sarala's asked question, and instead responded to the implied one, a tactic that tended to unnerve Lily's conversational partners, leaving them wondering if she was some sort of mind reader and, for many, ensuring that this was the last time they engaged her in conversation.

Sarala, though, was not so easily unsettled.

"My father knows me better than my mother does," Lily said. "Sometimes letters are a better way to know someone than all of the silly, inconsequential interactions of daily life."

Abhijat regarded Lily carefully. He thought for a moment, of the letters he and Sarala had exchanged in the months just after their marriage.

"And how is your outreach mission faring, Dr. Cardiff?" Sarala asked, turning her attention to her other guest.

"Well, I'd like to be able to say that I'm making headway, relieving some of our neighbors' anxieties," Dr. Cardiff replied. "But I don't seem to be making the kind of progress I hoped." Dr. Cardiff was a squarish, grandfatherly man with gentle eyes framed by large black glasses. Because of his skill at interacting with the public, Dr. Cardiff had been dispatched by the Lab director to speak about the super collider throughout the community. Of all Abhijat's colleagues, Sarala couldn't imagine anyone better suited to the job of representing the Lab to the public. She had always loved his soft, gentle manner, his courtly way of taking her hand in his by way of greeting.

Dr. Cardiff was a theorist Abhijat held in the highest regard, and was better than most of their colleagues at explaining the collider in terms that might be understood by a layperson. But perhaps more important, he was skilled at listening to the residents' concerns and at empathizing with them. Since taking on the role of spokesperson he'd attended meetings of the city council, of the school board, and of the various homeowners' associations. In doing so, he had quickly realized that the most important part of his outreach was simply to be human, to put a familiar face on "those scientists out at the Lab."

In many of the sessions, though, he could tell that no matter how sincerely he tried to connect with the residents, to respect and respond to their concerns, there were many who thought of him as nothing more than a government stooge, someone dangerous to listen to. At one meeting, a woman had stood up and yelled, "You'll just show me something that will take away my fears, but it will be a trick, a Potemkin village!" And he had had to admit to himself to understanding why one might feel that way. This was science beyond what a non-specialist could understand, and at a certain point one would have to take a leap of faith, to trust the motives of those who did understand it.

Sarala, sensitive to the notion that, as a bachelor, Dr. Cardiff was so infrequently provided with a home-cooked meal, and to the amount of stress he had likely been under during the last few months, had wanted to prepare something that would, for him, be comfort food, and though he would have probably delighted in the chance to sample some of her mother's recipes, Sarala had chosen something she hoped he would find both familiar and reassuring.

"What is it?" Abhijat asked as she brought the dishes to the table.

"Kraft Dinner—macaroni and cheese—and Rice-A-Roni." Sarala held up the boxes proudly.

She passed the serving dishes around the table as Dr. Cardiff continued. "It's an unenviable position they're in, many of our neighbors. To know the science here well enough to feel certain that this is safe would require an impossible investment of time and effort. There is nothing for them to do but to trust that we have their best interests at heart. Think of those of us here tonight," he added, serving himself from the bowls as they made their way around the table. "Because you have the luxury of knowing Dr. Mital as a caring, ethical person, you can say, 'Even though I don't know the science well enough to assess the risks, I feel safe in the knowledge that Dr. Mital would never support this project were there a danger to living or working on top of it.' However, not all of our fellow citizens have that luxury. And the way we have described this project has not always done much to earn their confidence."

Dr. Cardiff had come to understand that for many residents, the Lab's attempt at simplifying the explanation by saying "We're recreating conditions not seen since shortly after the Big Bang" did more harm than good, leaving residents wondering, "Then what? After you recreate the Big Bang, then what of this world?"

What they should be saying, Dr. Cardiff had come to realize, and he had revised his remarks accordingly, was: "We're creating similar conditions in a controlled environment, but we're not recreating it."

Lily leaned forward in her seat. "Dr. Cardiff, do you really and truly believe that there would be nothing dangerous about living on top of the super collider?"

Dr. Cardiff smiled at Lily. "I do, Miss Winchester, I do. If I had a single lingering doubt about this, I would most certainly tell you, and the rest of Nicolet's citizens. But if that does not reassure you, I encourage you to review the draft of the Environmental Impact

Statement. Though," he held up his finger in warning, "it will require a significant time commitment."

"Oh, I already have," Lily said.

Abhijat and Dr. Cardiff exchanged surprised smiles, Abhijat's full of pride in Lily, who had begun to feel like an adopted member of the family, and Dr. Cardiff's at the pleasure of discovering a kindred spirit, a generation removed.

@

Unlike Lily, Meena had not attempted to read the Environmental Impact Statement. The open box sat in the middle of Abhijat's study, where he had pulled out and leafed through a few of the volumes.

Instead, Meena had focused her attention on the Letters to the Editor in the *Nicolet Herald-Gleaner*. These she read carefully, as though they might help her to gauge the mood her father was likely to be in on a given day: distant and preoccupied (these were the nights she sometimes had to knock at his study door to remind him to join them for dinner), or happy and hopeful (these were the days in which someone, preferably not from the Lab, had written in support of the project), for Abhijat, too, kept a careful eye on the papers.

I am Mrs. Dixie Edmonson, and I am the president of the Nicolet High School PTA. I am for our tax dollars being used in our classrooms, not under our classrooms. This is an experimental facility fraught with uncertainty. It does not belong in any populated area.

Abhijat's response to these letters was a growing sense of dread. It would be taken from him—his chance at a legacy, he worried. If they were allowed to prevail, if Sarala's concerns about the community were right, it would be snatched away, again just out of reach.

@

As the residents of Nicolet sat down to make their way through the daunting box of Draft Environmental Impact Statement documents, many were outraged to find themselves referred to as "human receptors" in a section detailing the potential for exposure to radiation.

At the entrance to the Lab, Abhijat and the other scientists now faced a throng of protesters each morning when they arrived and each evening when they left, stationed just outside the entrance, chanting, "We are people, not 'human receptors!'"

@

Rose, who was preparing to announce her candidacy for next year's mayoral race, had also been carefully monitoring the community response. As soon as the word "radiation" entered the conversation, Rose noticed that the arguments in the newspaper took on a fevered pitch, opponents insisting that no one really knew the risks of cancer for those who would live above the beam line. The letter writers pointed out that many experts argued that there was *no* safe dose of radiation. And to that, supporters (among them a number of physicists from the Lab) countered that the public was exposed to radiation all the time—in soil, rocks, food, and in the very air they breathed.

@

Each morning as she ate her breakfast, Sarala studied the paper and kept a silent tally of the letters for and against the collider.

We did not ask to have our homes located on top of this science experiment, this atom smasher. I won't allow you to build this death ring below my home.

I am not one to stand in the way of progress, but if you want me to support this you will have to guarantee three things: that my property values will not decrease, that my water supply will not be impacted, either by drying up or by being contaminated, and that there is no health risk to living on top of this experiment.

Sarala felt like a bit of a traitor when she found herself thinking that some of the concerns seemed, to her, entirely reasonable.

@

The seeds in the flats on the back porch had begun to sprout. Sarala had followed the directions on the slim envelopes, each bearing a map of the United States with colorful swaths indicating optimal times for planting. She'd watched the flats carefully, keeping the soil moist, moving them to different spots on the porch, following the patches of sunlight throughout the day.

She had felt such wonder when she'd spotted the first few sprouts unfolding themselves from the potting soil—that with water, soil, and sunlight, they'd come to life just as promised. She'd expected it, of course, but found it no less astonishing because of that. Soon it would be time to transplant them, to dig up the sod and prepare the beds along the front walkway. Soon they'd take root there, she thought, and bloom as the spring turned to summer, making their house look, in this small way, just a bit warmer, more welcoming.

@

In response to the sheer size, not to mention the dry, academic tone of the Draft Environmental Impact Statement, the Lab began to produce slick, glossy, magazine-style reports, offering "an overview of the issue."

Persons living in the vicinity of the SSC need not be concerned about the public safety aspects of the project. While some radioactivity would be generated, the radiation levels will be carefully monitored by sensitive instrumentation. Throughout the facility, stringent safety standards will be maintained.

Extensive, continuous monitoring, both inside and outside the tunnel, will assure the protection of SSC personnel and the local population alike.

But for many in the community, these assurances—packaged as they were in slick brochures delivered to each home in Nicolet—were suspected of being nothing more than advertising, than propaganda, and thus fell on deaf ears.

@

Sarala sat with Carol and Bill on their screened-in porch, enjoying the warm air of the approaching spring. Meena was spending the night at Lily's, and with Abhijat ensconced in his study, Sarala's own house was quiet by comparison. As the sun began to set, late in the day this time of year, the sounds of dogs barking and the neighborhood children being called in from their evening games floated out into the night.

Carol and Bill sat in a wicker love seat, Bill's arm around Carol.

"I just think they need to be clearer about what it is they're doing out there," Bill said. They were again discussing the matter of the collider. "For one thing, why do they need their own fire department? I used to think that seemed reassuring," he continued, "but now, I'll admit, it's got me wondering."

"What does Abhijat think of all the discussion in the papers?" Carol asked.

Sarala thought of how distant Abhijat had been lately, how absent he seemed. "I think he is very concerned that it may not happen," Sarala confided. She'd begun to feel caught—stuck between the town's growing suspicion of the Lab and her loyalty to Abhijat.

On the streets, in line at the bank, and at coffee shops, nearly all of the conversations were about the collider, about the Lab. People had begun, too, to wonder about the buffalo. Were they, as signage around the Lab indicated, there to hearken back to the land's simple prairie past? Or were they being monitored by the Lab staff, early indicators that something might be going wrong?

Sarala felt, sometimes, like she ought to apologize to Abhijat for the town's response. And she felt, other times, like she ought to apologize to the town for the Lab's.

Later that night, back at home, Sarala sat propped up in her and Abhijat's bed watching the latest episode of *Dallas*. As she watched, she flipped through yet another one of the glossy reports that had arrived in their mailbox the week before, and in every mailbox in Nicolet, courtesy of the Lab.

Sarala had herself begun to wonder about the collider. She imagined the accelerator below her home, the protons whirling and spinning, smashing into each other in a mad collision. Sometimes she imagined she could feel it, their house trembling above it.

Downstairs, she could smell Abhijat cooking again. Ginger, turmeric, oil dancing in a hot pan.

@

The next morning, Sarala set about digging up the sod along the front walkway and turning over the soil. It was difficult work, but it felt good. She dug down into the ground, clearing away the grass and revealing the rich, dark soil, scooping out small holes into which she could place the fragile, just-sprouting plants.

Into the dark, cool dirt she pressed her fingers, making space for each of the tiny constellations of roots. As she loosened the sprouting plants from the flats and settled them into their places in the ground, she covered their delicate roots with earth and marveled that she and the sun and the water had been all that was needed to coax them into life. She thought of the tunnels that might be built under these homes, imagined the particles circling somewhere down below. She thought of the small army of flowering plants that would bloom here as her own response to the signs that had begun to crop up along their street, emboldened by the arrival of the first. She wondered if Abhijat would notice the changes to the front yard. She realized, half smiling, half sad, how unlikely it was.

Each night at dinner he was there in body, but his thoughts were elsewhere. Even Meena seemed to notice, no longer working on her schoolwork there in the kitchen after dinner, peppering her father with questions, but instead withdrawing to her room to work on her schoolwork alone. The house had grown so silent it had begun to press in on Sarala, and some nights she turned on the television just for the sound of another voice.

"Why don't you talk with Abhijat about this, about how distant he seems?" Carol had suggested.

Once, this might have seemed possible, but not lately, Sarala thought. "Some conversations aren't worth having," she said. Carol looked at her sadly.

Sarala remembered how, in the early days of their marriage, she had kept a mental list of the ways she and Abhijat had begun to love one another. It had been a long time since she'd added to that list, she realized, feeling like she had failed at this.

@

New articles appeared in the *Herald-Gleaner* on the issues of groundwater contamination and on the potential for radioactivity to be released into the atmosphere. Letters to the editor urged officials to consider what they had begun calling the No-Action Alternative, which advocated not constructing the super collider. These, Lily carefully clipped from the newspaper and included in her letters to her father, annotating them with her own observations, most of which were expressions of exasperated frustration at how boneheaded, obstinate, and unwilling to listen to reason, to science, the citizens of Nicolet seemed to be on the matter.

@

Sarala was proud that the flowers along the front walk had come in nicely, petals unfolding with the warm days. She imagined the roots stretching deep into the dark black soil. In the mornings, when the ground was still wet from the dew, Sarala liked to kneel at the edges of the lawn, pulling budding weeds and stubborn blades of grass from among the flowers, her fingers working deep into the soil, loosening them from the earth.

Stepping back to admire her work, she thought of how carefully, in the early years of their marriage, she'd attended to the project of adapting and adjusting to their new home—and of how little attention Abhijat seemed to have devoted to this.

@

The scientists and other staff at the Lab had begun to worry that if the super collider wasn't built there, it would be built somewhere else, meaning that the Lab's technology would be surpassed, all but guaranteeing its demise.

Abhijat explained this to Lily, Meena, and Sarala one night over dinner, noting with a deep sense of sadness that the best physicists, who had for years been drawn to the Lab by virtue of its position at the forefront of high-energy particle physics, would, if the Lab were to lose its bid for the collider, almost certainly begin to make their way to other facilities. He could envision a time—he said this haltingly, as though not wanting to admit it, as though by saying it aloud he might invest this possibility with a sort of dangerous power—when the Lab might be shut down entirely.

@

This went on through the summer, through the long, cold winter, and through the spring, by which point the very fact that now, a year after news of it had leaked, the project was still only "under consideration" itself became part of the frustration.

In most cases, the citizens of Nicolet were assured, the planned tunnels could be built under existing structures, the land returned, after construction, to its original use. But in a handful of cases, where they might need to construct an access shaft or a maintenance facility, the land would have to be bought and the owners relocated, and soon, the letters to the editor that Sarala read each morning began to focus on the frustration of being left in this limbo.

We don't know from one day to the next if we'll lose our home. My wife and I saved for years to buy this house and now we're being told we may have to start all over again. Until a decision is made, our lives are on hold. We don't dare make any plans because we don't know what the future will have for us here.

And though the prospect of relocation, of being forced to sell their land and homes was troubling to those who faced it, equally troubled were those who were assured that they could remain where they were, the tunnel snaking its way in a long loop below their neighborhoods.

My husband and I used our hard-earned savings to build our house. It has been a home for our family and an investment in our future. But now we are left wondering, if we want to sell our home sometime in the future, will we have to disclose that this atom smasher runs underneath it? And if so, well, then frankly, I can't imagine who in their right mind would buy such a home. Leaving us holding the bag. This project is nothing more than welfare for the overeducated.

Sarala thought back to their own period of house hunting when she had arrived in Nicolet. Would she have felt comfortable buying such a home, she wondered.

In his own letter to the editor, Dr. Palmer, the Lab director, noted that his own home, one of the old white clapboard farmhouses that had been removed from their original homesteads and trucked to the village on the grounds of the Lab, sat right on top of the current accelerator's neutrino beam. "Do you think I would live here if there were something to be afraid of?" he asked.

But from the citizens of Nicolet, there was no response.

@

Once Rose announced her candidacy for the mayor's office, she'd been pressed to take a stand on the collider almost immediately. This will be the issue that wins or loses the election, her campaign advisors cautioned her. Whatever position Mayor Callahan, the incumbent, takes, they warned, you'll have to take the other. And it would be best to get out ahead of him on this, they pointed out. It would put you in a position of power.

Rose understood this, and agreed. She had set about trying to educate herself on the issue and its potential impact on Nicolet. But as she delved into the many volumes of the Environmental Impact Statement, she realized that it was not an issue around which one could easily wrap one's mind.

Watching the electorate carefully, Rose had noted that, on the matter of property values, even those who believed there wasn't any real danger in the collider had to admit to knowing enough of human nature, enough of their fellow citizens, to understand that it wouldn't matter in the end—that this fear, however unfounded, would, in fact, damage their property values. "If two homes of equal value were for sale," the argument went, "and one was located on top of this experiment, I think it's easy to recognize that most prospective home buyers would choose the one not located on top of such a facility."

As she made her way through the materials, weighing each side carefully, her advisors pressed her to come to a decision. They prepared press releases for both possible decisions so they'd be ready to move as soon as she made her choice. But in the end, Mayor Callahan beat her to it.

Lily woke one morning to find her mother asleep at her father's desk, highlighter in hand, the Environmental Impact Statement spread open before her, head resting in the crook of her arm. When Lily collected the paper and brought it to the kitchen table, the headline marching across the top of the *Nicolet Herald-Gleaner* caught her eye: MAYOR COMES OUT IN FAVOR OF THE SUPER COLLIDER.

Well, thought Rose, he'd beaten her to it. And he'd surprised her. She'd felt certain Mayor Callahan would come out against it.

"Yes, go ahead and send ours," Rose told her advisors. She felt at once both apologetic and defeated as she put down the phone. She'd understood the importance of making the first move. She'd been leaning toward supporting the project, but that wouldn't matter now. Her advisors felt certain that, given the direction public sentiment was heading, she'd ended up on the right side. She would chalk it up to a lesson learned—that sometimes an important decision must be made quickly rather than thoroughly.

@

Lily, being now a teenager, and attempting to make sense of the world by dividing it into neat and orderly categories—right and wrong, valid and invalid, useful and not useful—had been horrified when she'd learned about the public position Rose had taken on the issue of the collider.

"What were you thinking?" Lily asked the next morning, the paper spread open on the table, its headline announcing: LEADING CHALLENGER IN MAYORAL RACE COMES OUT AGAINST SUPER COLLIDER.

Rose, joining Lily at the breakfast table, explained that it was a political decision—that although she was sympathetic to the logic that the collider would allow scientists to answer many of the fundamental scientific questions about the origin of the universe, she had made a decision as a political figure to adopt a public opinion more in line with those of her constituents than reflective of her own understanding of the risks and rewards of the issue, something that was often required of politicians, she explained.

"But Mom, you know better than this," Lily protested.

"What I know," Rose said calmly, as though trying the line out on Lily, "is that our citizens need a leader who shares their concerns."

"But you don't really believe this is dangerous, do you?"

"I don't know," Rose said candidly. "But the voters need someone who understands their fear and will offer them some degree of protection."

"So you're pretending that you agree with something that's factually incorrect?"

"Lily." Here Rose took a deep, calming breath. "As you age, it is my firm belief that you will come to see that the world is not as black and white as you imagine it to be."

"But Dr. Mital says—"

"Dr. Mital works at the Lab. It is in his interest for the collider to be built."

"But he also lives here. You saw the map. It could go right under their house, as well as ours. Do you think he would support this if there were any danger?"

"Lily," Rose continued patiently, "I think you would be surprised to learn some of the seemingly incomprehensible things people may do when their careers are at stake."

Only after she'd said it, only after it escaped her mouth and she heard it out loud did Rose realize that Lily had won the argument. Sometimes she wondered if it wouldn't have been easier to raise a child who was not quite so bright, though when she shared this with Randolph in her next letter, he'd teased her: *But*

Rose, you'd be so disappointed if you didn't think she was smarter than the both of us.

@

Now, over breakfast, Lily and her mother no longer worked together on the crossword. Instead, Lily read the editorial page, her fingers worrying the amulet her father had sent her the month before from the markets of Marrakesh, while her mother fielded phone calls and worked on response letters to her constituents.

In her letters to Randolph, Rose had never permitted herself to bore him with the mundane details of their lives. Rather, she aimed in her letters to address more important, universal themes. However, once Lily had begun to so vocally criticize her mother's position on the collider issue, Rose found herself unable to resist noting in her next letter that Randolph really should enjoy not having to put up with being the target of contempt from such an opinionated child. *You are lucky to be the one she idolizes and not the one she takes for granted*, she wrote, scribbling her signature at the bottom of the page and shoving the letter into an envelope.

Lily, meanwhile, continued her own campaign, sending her father clippings of articles and annotating the more outrageous editorials that appeared in the paper.

Randolph, reading their letters by candlelight in the sparse cell of the mountaintop monastery where he had stopped to collect his mail and replenish his supplies, had begun to think of the issue of the collider not as a conflict brewing among the citizens of Nicolet, but more specifically, as a conflict brewing in his home between the two women he loved most in the world, and, more importantly, as one that he was not at all sure how to solve.

@

Many of the Lab's young physicists found it difficult to take seriously the concerns voiced by the protesters who gathered at the Lab entrance. Such fear seemed, to the young scientists, to be entirely baseless and thus impossible to comprehend. Many of them believed that the only real danger of a project like this wasn't radiation, but rather simple, old-fashioned construction accidents.

Lunch in the Lab cafeteria often included a table at which one of the young physicists read the day's letters to the editor aloud to his tablemates, all of them exasperated. Abhijat, however, did not feel so free to laugh at these letters. He had begun to worry that, ultimately, it didn't matter whether the town's fears were rational or not. Regardless of what the Lab did, it didn't look like the protestors—or their concerns—were going away any time soon, and surely the Department of Energy would take that into account when making their decision.

"How goes your campaign amongst the savages?" one of their younger experimentalist colleagues, Dr. Cohen, asked as he joined Abhijat and Dr. Cardiff at their table in the cafeteria.

"It does us no credit," Dr. Cardiff reminded him gently, "to engage in ad hominem attacks on those who see this issue in a different light than we do."

"I don't think it's an ad hominem attack," Dr. Cohen argued, "to point out the obvious—that their fear is based on nothing more than a lack of education." Several of his contemporaries nodded in agreement.

Dr. Cardiff maintained his ever-patient expression. "I think it is more accurate to say that their fear is based on a *difference* in education," for after speaking with many of the opponents, he knew it was far too simple to cast them as uneducated bumpkins. "It's not that they are incapable of understanding the science. It's simply that this is not what they've spent their lives doing, as we have. It does us no credit to think of them as stupid."

Another colleague chimed in, "If you ask me, the people who are really dangerous are the ones who understand a small amount of physics—enough to think they understand what's going on, but really, only enough to be paranoid."

"Perhaps," Dr. Cardiff allowed. "But then the responsibility to educate them on this issue rests with us."

"Really, Gerald?" Dr. Cohen's voice was quick to take on a thick veneer of sarcasm. "I'm supposed to put my work aside so I can teach these people the basic principles of particle physics, in hopes that they'll grasp even a *portion* of the issue and allow us to build this here. No. It's too much. That is not my job."

Abhijat couldn't help agreeing that it was a poor position in which to find themselves.

"What we must understand," Dr. Cardiff said, directing his comments at Dr. Cohen, but hoping his words would also reach his dear friend Dr. Mital, whom he knew to be both tortured by the uncertainty over the collider and full of frustration with his fellow citizens, "is that because they don't know the science, for our neighbors this is a matter of trusting that we have no nefarious motives, that we're not being blinded to some danger by our own career aspirations. And that sort of trust is a difficult thing to ask of people when the stakes are so high."

@

In the next issue of the *Herald-Gleaner*, there appeared yet another letter to the editor—this one by Dr. Abhijat Mital, theoretical physicist, National Accelerator Research Laboratory.

To all of my friends and neighbors who ask, *What good is this science? To what practical purpose?* I say this: We don't know what will be revealed to us by the experiments made possible by the Superconducting Super Collider.

We don't know, and that is exhilarating. It is the worst kind of stagnation of the imagination, of passion for life, and of curiosity to suppose that we already know everything worth knowing. What is progress, I ask, if not a belief, a faith in the idea that there is always more to know?

And, at the home of Ms Lily Winchester, a letter bearing an air-mail stamp and a postmark from Siberia arrived.

My dearest Lily,

While I have been impressed by and obliged to you for your very thorough reportage on the matter of the proposed super collider, I do hope that you will not overlook the opportunity to engage in all of the wonders attendant with discovering your own world as a young person growing into adulthood. This is a wondrous time of change in which you find yourself, and I trust that you will always keep your eyes open to the astonishing possibilities of your own life, your own world. I do hope, also, that you will try to go easy on your mother. She has her reasons for opposing this, and my hope for you is that as you grow, you will begin to understand the shades of grey that exist in a world that can often seem deceptively black and white. Now I must take my leave of you, for I am about to set off on a great trek across Siberia to join the Nenets people in their annual reindeer herd. I will be on the lookout for a special gift for you, to be delivered in person when I next return.

Your loving father,
Randolph

CHAPTER 14

In a Distant and Barbarous Land

April 9, 1988

Mr. Winchester,
I write to you on behalf of the Nicolet Ladies' Auxiliary in
hopes that you will consider accepting our invitation to serve as
the keynote speaker for our annual garden party and luncheon.
Your account of your expeditions will make a thrilling addition
to our program, and we would be honored by your acceptance.
Sincerely,
Mrs. Albert Steege
Nicolet Ladies Auxiliary,
Luncheon and Garden Party Committee Co-Chair

April 11, 1988

Mrs. Steege,
Thank you for your recent correspondence. My husband is
away on an expedition and out of contact until next month,
when I expect to speak with him briefly by phone from the Lu-
limbi Research Station. At that time, I will share with him your
invitation. Thank you for your interest in his work.
Sincerely,
Rose Winchester

May 24, 1988

Mrs. Steege,

Many thanks for your recent invitation to serve as the keynote speaker for the Nicolet Ladies' Auxiliary Club's annual garden party and luncheon. I apologize that my travels have prevented me from responding sooner. I would be delighted to accept your kind invitation. Your suggested date is most amenable, as it will correspond with my next visit home. You may contact my wife Rose to arrange further details for the event.

Yours in a spirit of everlasting adventure,
Randolph Winchester

It was with relief that the editor of the *Nicolet Herald-Gleaner* included the following article in the next issue, happy to note that it had nothing at all to do with the collider.

NOTED EXPLORER RANDOLPH WINCHESTER TO ADDRESS NICOLET LADIES' AUXILIARY

Noted explorer and local resident, Randolph Winchester, husband of Twelfth Ward Alderman and mayoral candidate Rose Winchester, will be the keynote speaker for the annual Nicolet Ladies' Auxiliary garden party and luncheon. Mr. Winchester's many expeditions have taken him around the world, to Africa, India, Manchuria, and elsewhere. A member of London's Travellers Club and New York's Explorers Club, Mr. Winchester's lively accounts and photographs of his numerous expeditions have appeared in *Popular Explorer Magazine,* *The Explorer's Journal,* and the *Royal Geographical Society Magazine.*

Mr. Winchester will share stories and photographs from his many expeditions at the luncheon. Mrs. Albert Steege, co-chair of the event, notes, "We are thrilled to have Mr. Winchester as our keynote speaker for this year's annual garden party and luncheon. Mr. Winchester's accounts of his explorations through the wild parts of the world will be a stimulating addition to the afternoon."

For more information about the event, please contact the Nicolet Country Club, Ladies' Auxiliary Committee.

@

The shades on the great plate-glass windows of the Nicolet Country Club's dining room had been drawn, the room lit dimly by chandeliers that hung over each table. Around the room, ladies in pastel suits and floral dresses took their seats as indicated by small place cards.

A low chatter filled the room. Randolph, Rose, and Lily were seated at the table beside the podium, as were Meena and Sarala, whom Randolph had invited as his special guests. Randolph's invitation had also been extended to Abhijat, but he had been unable to join them, Sarala found herself having to explain, as he was working through the details of an important new paper likely to occupy him all weekend. She smiled apologetically and surveyed their banquet table, momentarily transfixed by the vast number of plates, glasses, and pieces of silverware that made up her place setting. In the center of the table were still more dishes holding cream, butter, salad dressing, salt, and pepper, all perfectly arranged, all perfectly confusing, a kind of chaos in which, she imagined, some dedicated observer might find order.

Mrs. Albert Steege took the podium, the room quieting as she leaned, smiling, toward the microphone. "Thank you all for joining us today for the annual Ladies' Auxiliary luncheon and garden party."

From her seat beside Randolph, Rose looked about, noting the conspicuous lack of any garden nearby. She supposed that by "garden party," Mrs. Albert Steege and her co-chairs intended that at the conclusion of Randolph's remarks, the ladies might adjourn to the flagstone patio overlooking the golf course, and from there admire the well-maintained fairway.

Mrs. Albert Steege continued, "We are delighted to have with us here today, as our keynote speaker, noted explorer Randolph

Winchester, who has only just returned from his most recent expedition to regale us with tales of his adventures in the wild. Please join me in welcoming our distinguished guest."

The room filled with the Ladies' Auxiliary's quiet, polite applause. Randolph stood, smiling, and clasped Mrs. Albert Steege's hand in a gentle, two-handed embrace, somewhere between a bow and a proper handshake.

"Ladies," Randolph began, taking his place at the podium. "I am honored by this opportunity to speak to you today. I hope you will be kind enough to indulge the stories and photos of an old adventurer long past his prime."

Rose imagined a few of the women already falling in love at the sound of his voice, deep and velvety, his careful British English peppered here and there with a curious cadence acquired, they might guess, somewhere exotic. Looking out over the country club dining room from her seat, she thought of how the whole affair looked a bit like a wedding if not for the podium and projector screen set up beside it.

Rose looked out at the members of the Nicolet Ladies' Auxiliary. These were the wives of farmers—or rather, former farmers, who, years earlier, when the Lab campus had been "acquired," had sold (or, in some cases, had been forced to sell) their farmland. People who had expected to live their lives as members of a small rural town, consuming casseroles in church basements at golden anniversary parties, not with the hulking mass of the National Accelerator Research Lab's twenty-story Research Tower looming over them, and—as she had so often heard her fellow townsfolk saying—*God-only-knows-what zooming around in those tunnels under the soil.*

Now, though, these ladies had arranged themselves around ten-top tables draped in white linen, peering over the centerpieces at Randolph, who stood at the front of the room in a tweed jacket, dress shirt open at the neck, his beard, which had grown wild during his recent travels, once again trim and distinguished.

"My first great adventure, years ago, led me on foot through the mountains of the Hindu Kush," Randolph began, "and I remember distinctly how at home I felt, a sense that I might look forever at the wild world around me. I knew that before me lay a life of exploration and of wonder."

Sarala, watching from her seat at the table, smiled at the rapt attention with which Lily watched her father. She tried to imagine herself and Meena in the audience as Abhijat delivered one of his papers, or sitting, attentive, in his office at the Lab as he explained the symbols and equations that decorated his chalkboard wall.

"I must begin by telling you that I do not think of myself first and foremost as a photographer," Randolph continued. "The images I present today are merely a grasping—always futile, in the end—at capturing the experience. And of the peoples you will see represented here…" He paused a moment for dramatic effect. "It is useful to remember that they are as curious about us as we are about them."

It was Randolph's habit to begin his lectures with a favorite image, that of a man squatting before a campfire ringed with stakes upon which human heads had been impaled, empty eye sockets peering out through the smoke of the campfire and into the lecture venue. This image he projected onto the screen for a long moment before he began again to speak, waiting for the gasps and murmurs he could now, after years of experience, time almost exactly as they reached their crescendo.

"To begin, I must tell you that my work is rife with peril." Randolph's voice was low and serious, causing the ladies in the audience, Rose noticed, to lean forward a bit in their seats, ice tinkling as they set glasses of water with lemon down on the tables, the better to regard him with their uninterrupted attention. "Not the peril one might imagine at first—that of cannibals—" here Randolph gestured at the image on the screen "—or man-eating animals, but rather, the perils of inauthenticity."

Sarala caught herself taking a reassured breath and she looked around to see how many in the audience were doing the same.

"It is my firm belief," Randolph continued, "that the only worthwhile way to explore the world is to live among its people—to eat as they eat, to sleep where they sleep, to travel as they travel."

He had come to understand that pictures of landscapes, buildings, and their surroundings held an audience's interest for only so long. What they wanted to see were the people among whom he had lived. He gestured once more at the image on the screen.

"It is imperative that one photograph the natives in their natural setting, with as little disturbance to their way of life as one can effect. One must at all costs avoid posing a photo. Rather, one must watch patiently as the natives go about their daily tasks, performing their rituals."

Here, Sarala thought back to her first months in Nicolet, how she had watched so carefully to learn and understand the ways of her new home.

"For some," Randolph continued, "the only way to photograph them is to sneak up upon them in their sleep. They fear the camera as a kind of witchcraft."

Meena, flanked by her mother on one side and Lily on the other, found herself thinking of the startled, frightened, and perplexed faces in the images from *The Secret Museum*. She could imagine the people in the photos wondering who this strange man was, and what he was pointing at them. She had read, once, about the superstition that the act of being photographed could steal one's soul, and for a moment, she felt she could understand this fear.

Randolph projected the next image onto the screen.

"Here," Randolph continued, "you will find women laboring in the fields, sleeping infants strapped to their backs. They are of a sturdy stock, not averse to hard work."

Meena watched the Nicolet Ladies' Auxiliary as Randolph spoke, pocketbooks hanging from the backs of their chairs, half-finished glasses of iced tea on the tables before them, every once in a while, one of the women quietly buttering a dinner roll and consuming it in a way she imagined to be unobtrusive, tiny bites like a bird.

"And here is shown a vigorous race." Randolph projected onto the screen an image of barefoot natives, spears at their sides. "Theirs is a wild life, given to savagery and brutality meted out to surrounding tribes who encroach upon their territory or resources. One might well imagine their war chants," Randolph continued, "drums thundering through the bush." He moved closer to the screen, pointing. "These patterns of white chalk on the skin are seen by the native as a protective charm, a talisman against harm in warfare, and once thus ornamented, warriors seem to fear nothing. They are a violent people, bent on the destruction of their enemies, whether by murderous plots, cowardly sneak attacks in the dead of night, or by driving them into the inhospitable desert to certain death."

Meena wondered how these same people might have described themselves to this curious audience, who peered up at their images on the screen from half a world away.

Randolph moved through the pictures, holding the audience in quiet, rapt attention as he spoke. He advanced the slide projector with a click. This was, Randolph explained, "a Nuer man," who now stood before them, projected onto the screen, naked but for a string around his waist. The Nicolet Ladies' Auxiliary seemed to draw a collective breath. Some looked away. Some held their linen napkins up to their mouths, looking, to Meena, like small children peeking out from behind a favorite and comforting blanket.

Randolph exchanged a barely detectable smile with Rose. It had always amused him how infrequently groups of ladies like these were shocked by the naked female body—in the course of his lectures, he'd shown plenty of the standard images of naked-to-the-waist women, breasts hanging flat against their ribcages, to no noticeable fanfare—and yet, conversely, how predictable were those same ladies' responses to an image of a naked male.

The windows around the room looked out over the rolling hills of the golf course so that, while lunching, ladies might spot their husbands on the ninth tee, taking one swing and then another, and might thus anticipate whether they were likely to finish the round in a foul temper. Today, though, the curtains were drawn (thankfully so, thought Mrs. Albert Steege, who shuddered to imagine what someone might think were they to see the shocking image projected onto the screen beside Mr. Winchester as he spoke).

Randolph projected a new image onto the screen—a line of young men and women caught by the camera in a fleeting moment of their dance, feet hovering above the dusty earth as though levitating. How like the images from *The Secret Museum*, Meena thought.

"Here we find a group of revelers in their comely festival attire of paint and feathers," Randolph continued.

One member of the audience raised her hand timidly.

"Yes?" Randolph invited, favoring her with a broad, charming smile.

"I'm sorry to interrupt," the woman said. "But that man in the background. Is he wearing...a White Sox T-shirt?"

Randolph turned toward the screen. "Yes. It would appear that he is," he said, sounding, for a moment, surprised by the revelation. "These items of our modern society," he explained, "do occasionally make their way into these parts of the world, much as I would prefer to allow these cultures to continue on in their virgin state."

Meena thought for a moment—but wasn't Mr. Winchester himself, his articles and photos in *Popular Explorer*, part of exposing these cultures to the modern world? She looked around, wondering if anyone else was thinking the same thing. Beside her, though, Lily had not taken her eyes off her father, and Meena chose to hold her tongue on this matter.

Randolph returned to his presentation, projecting a new image onto the screen: a group of women standing before a dwelling of dried-mud walls, its roof thatched with wide leaves. "The people of this tribe are rather shockingly dependent upon superstition—magic, witchcraft, secret societies—decorating themselves and their homes with protective charms and amulets."

Sarala thought of her own home on Patriot Place. She wondered what Randolph would make of the framed blessing that hung in their foyer, of her mother's box of recipes—*for when you wish to call a child into this world, for when one must remember to be joyful.*

On the screen two men appeared carrying canvas-wrapped bundles on their backs. "Here are two of my porters," Randolph continued. "I engaged these gentlemen on the advice of a fellow traveler and found them to be fine, loyal, honest young men willing to bear a heavy load for long, challenging days of walking."

A tall, thin man in a long, loose-fitting robe looked out into the room from the screen, his wild hair held down by a headband he wore like a crown around the top of his head.

"Now, this fellow is a camel breeder, and it was from him that we acquired our means of locomotion through the desert. Here, I adopted Arab dress, finding it far superior to the clothing with which I had arrived."

Behind the camel breeder, in the background of the image, Sarala could see the animals processing in single file over the sand dunes toward the horizon line, the sky rising up above them.

"We started out across the desert at midnight," Randolph went on, "darkness all around us, caravan bells ringing as we went, the moon watching our slow progress, and the stars brighter than I have seen in all my travels. Aside from the sound of the camels' hooves and the tinkle of our caravan bells, it was the most silent night I have spent on this great earth. Along an age-old and well-worn road, there I went into an ancient land, full of mystery."

On that trek across the Sahara, he had learned to wrap a proper turban. He had trekked slowly up mountains of shifting sand by moonlight, learned to train hooded falcons, with their bells and hoods of kangaroo leather.

The screen showed a street filled with shoppers leaning over blankets lined with pots and market wares, inspecting the offerings, and overhead, balconies from which hung brightly colored, hand-woven carpets.

"Here you will find picturesque streets and bright, vibrant markets where the local tea merchants brewed for me a strong, dark tea one drinks in clay cups fashioned by hand from the earth that runs beside the river."

For Rose, watching from her place at the table, the pictures conjured up memories of her own travels with Randolph—the ornate, latticed windows through which the women watched the world passing by, the bustling markets and bazaars, rugs and vegetables and butchered animals all lying side by side, streets shaded with panels of fabric hung between buildings, slivers of sunlight peeking through gaps, making a pattern on the ground. There, the shops opened up onto the street, proprietors sitting among their wares, luring pedestrians with a compliment or a promise of an excellent bargain for all manner of things near priceless according to them, their goods hung out into the street—cloth, clothing, dishes, and tea. She remembered how the small Arab boys in their long flowing robes had looked to her so much like miniature men.

"Here, I lived for months in a houseboat," Randolph continued, his voice bringing Rose back to the room, to the members of the Nicolet Ladies' Auxiliary and the drawn curtains, beyond them the long green fairway, and beyond that their home—her home with Lily. Randolph continued "Up the river we traveled in our little steamer. Along the shores, children waved to us from their huts and dwellings near the water. So completely had I fallen in love with this land, with its people and their customs, that I could scarcely imagine returning home again."

For a moment, Rose's breath caught in her throat. She took a sip of water.

"In desert country," Randolph continued, "the eye grows hungry for trees. In the heat, for cool. In the cold, for warmth. But in all these hungers, these desires, one finds adventure."

And with that, Randolph turned toward the audience, the lights coming up to indicate the end of his lecture.

"Thank you very much, Mr. Winchester," said Mrs. Albert Steege, rising to take his place at the podium. There was, again, the polite applause of the Nicolet Ladies' Auxiliary. The ladies in the audience began to collect their handbags, and, as Randolph had come to expect, a number of them approached with questions at the ready.

"How very brave of you to venture out among those savages." Mrs. Reginald Larson held her hand to her throat as she spoke, the skin along her forearm thin, seeming to only barely cover her bones and the network of blue veins beneath it. "Why, at any moment, I suppose, you must be in danger of being assaulted by headhunters or wild animals or goodness knows what."

"Oh, I assure you it's not as dangerous as all that," Randolph insisted.

How, wondered Mrs. Ronald Carlson out loud, did the natives respond to his arrival? Why, he must so often be their first emissary from civilization, the first white man they had encountered save, she imagined, for a few intrepid missionaries.

"And what about you, dear?" Mrs. Norman Amundson asked, turning to Rose. "Might you join your husband on his next expedition?"

"Oh, I'm afraid not," Rose protested. "My exploring days are long over."

"You must be very proud of your husband," Sarala said.

"Yes, of course," Rose said absently, and Sarala thought she caught a shadow of unhappiness passing over her face. But in an instant it was gone. "We are so glad you and Meena could join us today," Rose added.

"We are honored to be your guests," Sarala said.

Beside them, Meena listened as Randolph responded to the Ladies' Auxiliary's questions and thought back to what he'd said about the perils of inauthenticity. Couldn't it be the case—and she wondered if this occurred to Randolph—that these natives he photographed might be putting on a kind of show for Randolph and his photographers? That his subjects, having gotten a sense of what was expected of them, might oblige by performing just that, without his knowing or understanding, carefully staging and posing the photographs for Randolph just as he had hoped to avoid?

If only, Meena thought, the photos could be taken by someone invisible, whose own presence wouldn't change the moment. How did he know with certainty, she wondered, that what he captured was authentic and not some sort of performance of authenticity?

She wanted to ask, but she couldn't think of a way to do so that wouldn't seem impolite. And among the other questions from the Ladies' Auxiliary, hers seemed wildly out of place.

"Very informative." Mrs. Eugene Vogt took Randolph's hand in her strong, formidable grip. "Now, though, what about the children? We must think of the children."

"Their children are, in general, very happy, it seems to me," Randolph answered with a benevolent smile.

"Well, you must write a book." Mrs. Norman Amundson took his hand in hers, patting it as she spoke. "About your adventures."

"Yes," Randolph nodded at her. "Many kind friends, including my lovely wife, have made that suggestion. I do a short article now and then, but a book would mean being trapped in my study, writing about my adventures rather than going on them. Perhaps one day, when I am an older man and my exploring days are well and truly over," he conceded.

"And where might your next adventure take you?" Mrs. Ronald Carlson asked.

"Well," Randolph smiled. "I believe there is magic and mystery to be found everywhere, even right here in Nicolet." At this the women laughed, as though the very idea was outrageous.

Mrs. Albert Steege swooped in. "Ladies, I think we must let Mr. and Mrs. Winchester and their guests take their leave."

ℂ

On the ride home, Lily asked her father whether he didn't sometimes find himself exasperated by the questions he received after his lectures.

"Ah, but it is all born of curiosity," he explained, "and that is an important quality to indulge."

Rose hardly listened to them, floating back to the photos, to her memories of the years when they had explored together, a happy, carefree time. She thought of the sound of oxen wearing wooden bells meant to frighten off evil spirits, of the night train from Siliguri, the tea plantations of Darjeeling, the small house where they had spent monsoon season.

But now there was Lily, and it wouldn't have done to have raised her on a caravan—no home to call her own, no friends her own age, let alone reliable, consistent schooling. It was better this way, Rose thought, agreeing with herself yet again, or convincing herself, she was never sure.

Rose thought of how Randolph had looked the day of his return, unpacking his trunk with Lily, unearthing treasures for her, regaling her with stories. Always, at the beginning of his trips to Nicolet, he was happy, this period between the end of one expedition and the beginning of another. It was only later that the itch to pack returned. This she had learned to recognize in him, the way he began to move from room to room, fingering the mementos from his previous trips she had so carefully arranged in his study. Then she knew he was once more ready to make his escape from civilization.

And it was true, she reminded herself, that she loved their women's home—hers and Lily's—filled with dispatches from exotic locales. That she relished her and Randolph's separation for the sweet attentiveness it brought to their reunions. She missed him, yes, but it was the kind of pain one sometimes liked to feel if only as a reminder of its presence. The kind of pain that also gave one a bit of pleasure.

Perhaps it was part of her farmer's upbringing—her sense that the harder something was to do, the more valuable it was.

CHAPTER 15

School of Navigation

For Lily and Meena, the transition to high school had been difficult. No longer were they cloistered in the Free Learning Zone. There were AP classes, where they spent the majority of their school day with their classmates from the old Free Learning Zone days, but there were also moments when they found themselves in class—for there was no AP gym, health, or lunch, though many of them had come to wish there was—with kids they had hardly seen since elementary school.

Meena found herself enjoying these opportunities to interact with her other classmates, but Lily found it agonizing (a feeling, Meena noticed, that was shared on both ends of the conversation). The few times Lily and Meena were invited to social events—birthday parties, a football game here and there—it became increasingly obvious that, whereas Lily seemed to find these interactions excruciating, Meena had a gift for them, moving easily among her peers, meeting new people, able to slip into and out of conversations with ease. She enjoyed these events, though she wondered if she might enjoy them even more without Lily to attend to.

Lily on the other hand, could usually be found with her voice teetering on the edge of exasperation, involved in some conversation it was clear her partners wanted nothing more than to escape from, and here Meena would often step in, extricating all parties from the social tangle they'd found themselves helplessly caught in, Lily relieved to be back by Meena's side, her partners grateful to be free to join less unpleasant conversations. Meena had begun growing concerned, though, noting that even at social events that included only their AP classmates, Lily still managed to behave as though she felt out of place.

@

As Rose and her team prepared their campaign strategy, they took advantage of each of the city council meetings, over which Mayor Callahan presided, to size up the competition.

Well-liked but not a political heavyweight, was Rose's assessment. The mayor was a former crop insurance salesman who, like many in Nicolet, had had career change thrust upon him as the area farms transformed, seemingly overnight, into subdivisions. He had, Rose noticed, a habit of using the expression "like I said" indiscriminately, on matters on which he had not previously offered comment, leaving her wondering whether he perhaps carried on in his mind a more substantive commentary in which he believed himself to have weighed in on these issues both sensibly and eloquently.

His campaign slogan, each time he ran, had been the same: "Larry Callahan: Your Mayor and Friend." This was not, in Rose's opinion, likely to cut the mustard in the current political climate.

But Rose had her own area of concern, for in each of her public appearances, there was, from the electorate, the whispered question: *What about this husband of hers? What kind of a marriage is this?* As though Rose and Randolph's arrangement might be a harbinger of poor judgment on Rose's part. How were they to know, some wondered, that she wouldn't take it into her head to go traipsing off after this husband of hers on one of his expeditions, leaving them high and dry?

@

Lily spent her school days immersed in her classes, attempting to avoid thinking about her mother's campaign, dreading the moment she felt sure would come, in which one of her classmates would corner her, demanding an explanation of her mother's stance on the issue. It hadn't occurred to her that, even among her AP classmates, with the exception of Meena there were few other students as focused on the issue as she was, and that this scenario was unlikely to arise. For Lily, her mother's position on the issue left her feeling publicly freakish, as if she'd been born with a second head.

At the end of the school day, Lily and Meena made their way through the halls to their lockers. From overhead, above the racket of the crowded hallway, came the disembodied voice of the principal, making his end-of-the-day announcements. "As a reminder, next month Nicolet Public High School will host the public hearing on the matter of the proposed Superconducting Super Collider. We expect you to help make all of our visitors welcome."

Lily and Meena loaded their backpacks with books. "Congrats, Meena!" a blond girl with a high ponytail called out as she passed. "So excited to have you on the squad!" echoed another girl, whom Lily didn't recognize. Meena waved to them and continued loading books and folders into her backpack.

"Who's that?" Lily asked.

Meena pretended not to have heard her.

"What does she mean, 'on the squad'?" Lily asked, hefting her backpack over one shoulder. "What squad?"

Tom Hebert leaned in between Lily and Meena's lockers. "Oh, didn't you hear, Lily?" He shoved a copy of the school newspaper into her hands. "Meena's one of the new soccer cheerleaders."

Meena glared at Tom as she made her way through the jostling crowd.

Lily looked down at the newspaper, then up, elbowing her way through the teeming hallway to catch up to her friend. "Is this a joke?" she asked, rifling through the pages of the newspaper as they made their way to the bus.

"No," Meena said, sliding into their usual seat just behind the driver.

Lily sat down beside her. *Freshmen soccer cheer squad: Meena Mital, Carrie Praeger, Jill…* She looked up at Meena. "But you never said anything about this."

Indeed, Meena had not, knowing precisely how Lily might respond on the off chance that she made the squad. "I just wanted to try something new," Meena said.

Lily was confused. "But," she began, "you don't just take up a new hobby, just like that, out of the blue." Her brow furrowed as though working through some difficult equation.

Meena looked at Lily, exasperated. "Of course you do. We're teenagers. That's exactly what we're supposed to be doing."

@

When Lily arrived home after school, Rose could tell by the faraway look in her daughter's eyes, by the frown line on her forehead, that something was amiss.

"Is something wrong?" she asked.

"I'm fine," Lily insisted. She sank into a chair in the living room and hid herself behind one of her schoolbooks. Rose watched her, curious, but did not press. She was herself preoccupied by a new wrinkle in her political ambitions.

It had become clear to Rose that if she were to stand any chance of unseating Mayor Callahan it would require an overhaul of her family's unconventional living arrangement. And so she had resolved to ask Randolph something she had promised herself she never would.

Earlier that day, she'd sat at Randolph's desk to write a letter, looking out over his curios as she began. *It is not, of course, necessary to cancel what you've already planned,* she wrote. *But I wonder if, perhaps, by the summer you could arrange to be—* Here she paused, wanting to say *home,* but realizing, as though for the first time, that the house in Nicolet had never felt like Randolph's home, even to her.

This draft, like each of her previous attempts, she had crumpled into a ball and swept into the wire wastebasket beside the desk.

@

After an awkward dinner, during which Lily had been nearly silent, Rose managing only to extract from her that her day had been "fine" and that she'd done "fine" on her history exam, Rose told Lily that she would be out for the evening for a campaign meeting. "I'll be home at nine, all right?" to which Lily, having returned to the living room and again hiding behind her book, replied only, "Fine." What was worse, Rose wondered—a vocal, disapproving Lily or this quiet, sullen version?

@

Lily liked having the house to herself. She listened to the sound of the garage door closing, of her mother's car backing down the driveway. The sump pump in the basement hummed, the dishwasher, loaded with dinner dishes, sloshed away, and it felt peaceful to be there alone.

She wandered into her father's study, ran her fingers along the shelves of mementos from his trips: pottery, antiques, figurines, vases—a collection by which he hoped to acquire a full and complete knowledge of the world. At the window, a telescope stood at the ready. Open on the big leather chair in the corner was a book filled with drawings of mythical creatures. Next to it sat an old steamer trunk, on top of which rested the shell of a tortoise. She felt close to him there, among his collections. She sat down at his desk, pulled a sheet of writing paper from the drawer, and began a letter.

I feel like I don't understand anyone anymore, or like they don't understand me.

As she wrote, she noticed in the waste bin beside the desk a collection of crumpled pieces of paper much like the one on which her pen now rested. Here and there, peeking from among the wrinkled folds, she caught glimpses of her mother's handwriting. *Home, difficult*, she could make out.

She reached into the bin, smoothing the first page out over her own letter, and began to read.

@

When Rose returned home that evening, she closed the door of the garage behind her, hung her coat on the hook along the laundry room wall, and slipped her feet out of her pumps.

Lily was waiting for her in the kitchen holding one of the discarded letters, now smoothed flat on the table before her.

"Oh, Lily, you startled me," Rose said, coming into the kitchen. She looked at what her daughter had spread out on the table before her. She could make out the arcs and swirls of her own handwriting in among the spots where the paper had been crumpled, then smoothed flat.

"You always told me to be proud of our family," Lily said, her face stern.

Rose took a deep breath.

"You're caving," Lily continued. "You're caving to social pressures that you should be smart enough to ignore."

Rose pressed her hands to the counter, remembering Lily's face as a child, turned up to hers, worry marking the corners of her eyes—something she'd picked up on the playground. *Is it true*, she'd asked? She'd sniffled when Rose had finally coaxed it out of her—*that a mother and father living apart no longer loved each other?* "Oh my goodness, no," Rose had said, taking Lily on her lap. How patiently she had explained to Lily that their family was different, but that they loved one another just as much as any of the families who lived together all the time.

"Lily," Rose began. "Like many things in this world, this is not as simple as you're making it out to be."

"I'm so sick of people always saying that," Lily said. "It's like the thing adults tell kids when they don't want to admit that they're selling out."

There was a long moment of silence between them, the quiet sounds of the house continuing on in the background.

"I haven't sent it," Rose said finally. "I didn't send any of those letters." She wondered now if she ever would. If she could ever find the right words to ask this of Randolph.

@

The following morning, Lily trekked grimly to the bus. Unlike every other day, she walked past the empty seat beside Meena and instead selected the empty seat beside Anderson Small, a junior band member (clarinet) who was very much perplexed (and, truth be told, a little alarmed at what this abrupt change in seatmates would mean for his admittedly already quite tenuous position in the social strata of Nicolet Public High School). Meena kept her eyes forward, studying the back of the bus driver's head as they made their way to school.

On Tuesdays and Thursdays, the school employed a program whereby the students progressed through the daily schedule in reverse, so as the day began the girls found themselves in pre-calc. Before the class began, though, Mr. Boden called Lily and Meena to his desk and informed them that they were both expected in the guidance counselor's office.

"Busted," Tom Hebert whispered under his breath.

Lily glared at him, but she and Meena were both wondering what had prompted so unprecedented a summons. They made their way without speaking through the empty halls to the Guidance Office, where they were instructed to take a seat until called by the secretary. "What do you think this is about?" Lily asked Meena, whispering quietly, finally breaking the silence between them.

"No idea," Meena answered, reluctant to slip so easily back to normal. She tucked her legs under the chair and watched the secretary, who peered at the girls from over the rim of a pair of reading glasses that had slid precariously close to the tip of her nose.

@

Sarala sat across from Carol at the kitchen table, her hands around the mug of coffee she'd learned to enjoy, though she preferred it with a small amount of milk and a large amount of sugar. She'd been telling Carol how absent Abhijat seemed lately, how entirely occupied he was by the matter of the collider and how it might impact his career.

"It seems like you've been saying this a lot lately," Carol said.

Yes, Sarala thought—it was probably true. Ever since the matter of the collider had descended upon the town, upon their home, it felt less and less like Abhijat was there and present in their daily lives. It wasn't, in fact, all that different from Randolph's absence from Rose and Lily, she'd realized. She'd so often wondered about its effect on Lily and Rose, but was their own life so very different? She thought of how often she had to dispatch Meena to pull Abhijat out of his thoughts, out from behind his closed study door, to join them for meals.

Sarala found herself thinking, then, of her mother-in-law's warning about Abhijat's constant striving, about her hope that Sarala would help him find a greater degree of balance in his life. Perhaps, Sarala thought, she had been naïve. Perhaps, by making their home life so unobtrusive, she had, in fact, made it possible for Abhijat to withdraw. Perhaps, she had, without realizing it, made it even more difficult, even less likely for him to find this balance his mother had believed in so firmly.

A sense of her own failure settled over her. His mother had hoped that Sarala would help to bring balance to Abhijat's world, but instead, Sarala had only allowed him to withdraw from it more. She wondered if she'd made a terrible and irreparable error in judgment.

Carol refilled Sarala's coffee mug. "Sweetheart," she said, putting her hand on Sarala's arm. "As your friend, I have to tell you that you seem unhappy and you seem lonesome. Now, I'm not one to advocate breaking up a family, but I do think it's important that you understand your options here."

She handed Sarala a pamphlet neatly folded in thirds. So You're Considering Separation read the title across the top.

☺

The guidance counselor, Mr. Delacroix, called Lily and Meena, finally, into his office. He was a short man, bald, with a wiry black moustache, and Meena thought for a moment that he looked exactly how she had always imagined Hercule Poirot might look. The girls took the empty seats opposite his desk and waited for him to speak. Mr. Delacroix regarded them across the wide expanse of his desk. "Well, I suppose you're both wondering why I've called you in today."

The girls nodded.

"I'm pleased to tell you that you've been identified as two of our most academically talented students. As such, you've been encouraged to consider applying for a new program called the Academy of Science and Math. It's a residential high school for gifted math and science students from all over the state. Students are accepted in their sophomore years."

He slid brochures across the desk to each of the girls, who opened them as he spoke.

"We've prepared a letter for your parents," Mr. Delacroix continued, sliding identical envelopes across the desk, one to each of them, "explaining the opportunity and laying out the application process. I hope you'll both consider this very seriously. Take a few days to look over the materials and to talk with your families. In the meantime, if you have any questions, I'll be happy to talk with you further."

The girls nodded again. Thus dismissed, Lily and Meena made

their way back through the strangely silent halls. Lily reached out and clutched at Meena's hand as they walked. "This is the best thing that has ever happened to us," Lily said, breathless with excitement.

Meena nodded, but privately she was not sure she agreed.

☺

The letters Lily and Meena carried home each met a different fate. Lily's was delivered proudly into her mother's hands, then photocopied and included in her next letter to her father.

Meena's was slipped, surreptitiously, into the garbage can beside the desk in her bedroom.

☺

That afternoon, after returning from Carol's house, Sarala began a letter of her own, addressed to Abhijat's mother.

You always told me that you hoped I would help Abhijat find happiness in the world. I worry now, though, that I've made a terrible mistake.

Sarala was afraid that she had been seduced by his work, by his ambition, much as Abhijat had been. That she had been wrong to believe it might make him happy.

I wanted so much to make a place for it, for him, she wrote. *But now, he seems frustrated. Unhappy, and lost to us.*

She described the quiet that had come over him, the worried brow that was now a nearly permanent fixture. *He's not happy,* she confessed, and she felt her failure again drape itself heavily over her shoulders.

She tucked the letter into the thin airmail envelope with its red, white, and blue borders and tucked it into her purse. She didn't want to mail it from home on the off chance that Abhijat might see it.

At the grocery store, she stood in front of the squat blue post office box, uncertain. For a moment, she considered not sending it.

Perhaps his mother would only see it as a confirmation that Sarala had not heeded her good advice, as proof that this wife she'd selected for her son had been a poor choice after all.

Then, before she could change her mind, Sarala dropped the letter into the slim mouth of the blue box and went inside to do the week's shopping.

©

In the halls of Nicolet Public High School, word about the Academy soon made its way through the AP students, who had begun to describe it as a boarding school for baby geniuses.

Lily assumed that she and Meena would both apply. She did not know that Meena's letter and application materials had never even been opened, nor did she know that, lately, Meena had begun wondering whether it was a good idea for her and the other advanced students to be so separated from the rest of the student population.

Over the last few weeks, Meena had been thinking about this and about how clear it seemed, in each of the articles and editorials on the collider she read, that the people on either side of the issue simply didn't know how to talk to one another.

CHAPTER 16

Charm Offensive

WHILE MOST OF THE TOWN'S READING MATERIAL INCLUDED THE *Herald-Gleaner*'s latest accounts of the battle over the collider and the voluminous final version of the Environmental Impact Statement that had been delivered to their doorsteps, Sarala continued her own informal education. After finishing the Mary Kay autobiography, she had become a regular borrower of the Nicolet Public Library's significant collection of self-improvement and motivational literature. She was especially taken with *Color Me Beautiful*, breaking what she understood to be a cardinal rule about marking a library book by underlining (very lightly and in pencil) the following (feeling justified on the grounds that it was good advice, and, one might argue that she was doing future readers the service of directing their attention toward it):

> *Practice standing this way in front of a mirror, looking at yourself from the front and from the side. Practice walking while pulling up through your midriff, head carried high, shoulders down. When you walk, swing your leg from the joint at the hip rather than the knee. This stride is smooth and elegant.*

Her attention was caught again, later, by the following:

Long hair is fine for young women, but after thirty-five it is aging. Then it is best to keep shoulder-length the limit.

She was not, however, eager that Abhijat should find and comment upon her choice of reading material, so she kept these books in a drawer in the china cabinet in the dining room, a part of the house into which Abhijat rarely ventured.

@

Meena and Lily had been the recipients of two socially uncoveted invitations to Erick Jarvis's birthday party, and although Lily indicated that she had no intention of going, Meena urged her to reconsider. "It would be nice, Lily."

"Oh, fine," Lily acquiesced, and the two had been dropped off at the Jarvis house by Abhijat, as rare an excursion for him as for the girls.

Erick's mother had insisted that he invite not only his brother to the party, but also his cousins, with whom Erick had an uneasy relationship, themselves being dedicated students of the high school's auto shop classes and finding nothing so damaging to their social reputations as having a cousin in the nerd classes.

Lily had not strayed far from Meena's side the whole evening.

"I hear you're going to that school for geniuses," Erick said, addressing Lily, who responded to this attention by turning slightly away.

"You mean the nerd academy," Tom Hebert said loudly, hoping to attract the admiration of Erick's brother and cousins with his quip.

"You don't just decide you're going to go," Lily explained, her eyes half closed, arms crossed in front of her, a posture Meena noticed that Lily adopted when she was nervous. "It's a competitive application process."

"So do you think you'll get in?" Erick asked, ignoring both Tom and his cousins, who were now shotgunning cans of Mountain Dew in the living room.

"I don't know," Lily responded, eyes still half closed, arms still crossed. "I hope so."

"Will you guys be roommates?" he pressed on.

"Probably," Lily answered. But at the same moment, Meena responded, "I don't know if I'll get in."

Lily looked at her, perplexed. "Of course you'll get in."

@

Most of the town's residents were now nervously anticipating the public hearing on the matter of the super collider, which had been scheduled for May and would be held in the auditorium of the Nicolet Public High School.

Lily's mind, however, had turned entirely to the matter of the Academy. She worked diligently on her application each evening and could, it seemed to Meena, be counted on to talk about nothing else.

For Lily, the Academy represented the promise of a world of peers who would understand her eagerness in the classroom, to whom her quirks might seem normal. The idea that such a place existed, a ready home for her, seemed to Lily like a dream come true.

At school, she found herself poring over the Academy brochure, imagining the room she would share with Meena, how she would come to think of her single year of regular high school as a lost year—a horrible glimpse at the tiresome football games and ridiculous cafeteria dances she would soon shake off in favor of more worthy endeavors.

@

Meena had counted on her father's preoccupation with the matter of the collider to allow the announcement of the opening of the Math and Science Academy to slip, unnoticed, past eyes that were otherwise ever vigilant for opportunities to enrich her academic environment.

The plan she had settled on was to say nothing, and with any luck, by the time the matter of the collider had been settled, should her father catch wind of the Academy opportunity, the deadline for application would have long since passed.

She had a sense, though they hadn't discussed it, that her mother would have taken her side. Would have argued that the Nicolet school system was perfectly fine, better than fine. That it was, after all, why they had chosen to live there. That Meena would have time enough on her own in college and beyond without forcing her out into the world at this age. And she had a sense also that her mother (whom she sometimes noticed watching longingly as the other fathers on the block conversed easily with one another, leaning against their lawnmowers or snow blowers) would understand Meena's wariness about moving so completely away from her classmates, her concern that she might become as unable as her father was to connect with them.

This was not, however, a decision Meena had shared with Lily, who, she imagined, would find it nearly impossible to comprehend.

Lately, Meena had begun to realize that the more time she spent with Lily, the more isolated she felt. There were an increasing number of moments in which she'd noticed, growing within her, a lurking and unpleasant suspicion: that it would be easier to do some things without Lily—social events she would have liked to enjoy without the specter of Lily at her side, needing to be attended to. This, though, had left Meena feeling both guilty and ashamed.

How different it was from when they were younger, Meena thought. She could still remember the first time she'd been invited to Lily's house to play. She'd understood it to be a great honor and a sign of the depth of their friendship when, one Saturday afternoon, Lily invited her into Randolph's study—a grand cabinet of curiosities filled with specimens in glass jars, the fossilized bones of strange creatures, sculptures, wood carvings, well-worn travel books (his favorites, Lily explained, and thus, well loved). It was as though Lily's house contained within it a miniature museum.

Meena thought how unlike Randolph Lily had turned out to be, and how a bit more of his curiosity about the world might serve her friend well.

As for breaking the news about the Academy to Lily, Meena did not yet have a plan. Instead, she kept silent while Lily pored over her application, too engrossed in her own application materials to notice that, rather than commiserating, Meena barely responded each time Lily brought up the subject of her application essay, her quest for the strongest letters of recommendation.

Meena never told Lily that she had applied. But she never told her that she hadn't, either. For Meena, this seemed an important distinction—a talisman against any future accusation that she had acted with dishonesty or deceit.

@

The week before the public hearing, the Lab had arranged a meeting to brief all employees on how they would be expected to conduct themselves should they choose to participate in the hearings. Dr. Palmer, the Lab director, stood once more at the podium in Anderson Hall, addressing the assembled employees. "I'm sure you all know by now," he began, "that the public hearing on the projected super collider will be held on Wednesday at the Nicolet Public High School. For those of you who have preregistered to speak—and I understand there are a number of you who have—I'd like to make a few important things clear. If you choose to speak, and we encourage you to do so, you may identify yourselves as Lab employees, but you must also make it clear that you are speaking for yourselves as private citizens, that you are not speaking on behalf of the Lab. Please remember that your conduct at these hearings will reflect on the Lab and may well influence the Department of Energy's decision regarding the collider. We would urge you to do your best to talk in terms that will be easily understood by laypersons."

Here there were chuckles from the audience.

Dr. Palmer held up his hand, smiling. "Yes, I am aware that this is difficult for many of us. In light of that, Gerald here," he gestured at Dr. Cardiff in the front row, "has been working over the past few weeks on something we're calling the checkout-line project. Essentially, it's a quick physicist-to-layperson translation of some of the central issues. What we're thinking about is how you might quickly and clearly describe what we're doing to one of your neighbors in the checkout line at the Jewel. Gerald will be handing out some of the talking points he's put together, and I'd encourage you all to make use of them.

"Now," he continued, resting his elbows on the podium, "I know there is a good deal of frustration in this room with the people who want to put a stop to this project, and I know there is also significant concern over what will happen to the Lab if this collider isn't built. But the thing we've got to remember at this hearing is that these are our friends and neighbors."

Here, Abhijat thought he detected the voice of Dr. Cardiff in Dr. Palmer's remarks.

"And no matter how unfounded we think their concerns are, the most important thing to remember is that they believe them to be true. All we can do is to try our best to educate them and to allay those fears."

@

In the atrium after the meeting, over coffee and Danish, Abhijat listened with concern to his colleagues, wondering how well those who had chosen to speak would be able to adhere to the director's advice.

"I don't know what we can say to these people," one of Abhijat's junior colleagues was saying to a circle of fellow physicists. "These are the same geniuses who think a mobile phone is going to give them cancer."

"Or living near power lines," added another.

"It's not looking good for us, is it, mate?" one of his colleagues said, patting Abhijat on the back, and setting a few tiny muffins on his plate.

"I have confidence," Abhijat said, nodding as if to demonstrate this. "I have confidence in our fellow citizens."

"I hope that's not misplaced," his colleague said, popping one of the muffins into his mouth and looking out over the prairie.

@

Though it had always been Abhijat's habit to collect the mail at the end of the day when he returned from the Lab, Sarala had begun to do this, hoping to intercept any return correspondence from Abhijat's mother before he might see it and wonder why his mother should be writing to Sarala alone as opposed to both of them, as she always had before.

When the letter arrived, Sarala snatched it out of the pile of mail she left for Abhijat on the kitchen counter and took it into the living room to read.

> *My dear Sarala,*
>
> *I was both touched and saddened to receive your letter. Touched that you should think of me as a confidant, and sad to see how unhappy this has made you both. You are correct that I had hoped that you might help Abhijat to see beyond his often very limited horizons. I had hoped for this, and you have—you and Meena both.*
>
> *You must always remember that you have allowed him to live a much fuller life than he would have otherwise. And though he may not yet see that, I believe he will someday come to recognize this, that he will someday come to understand how important it has been.*
>
> *He is a difficult man to love, I imagine. Yet without those parts of him, he would not be the man we love, all three of us.*

My great hope for my son is not that he becomes a renowned and famous physicist, but rather that he should look up from his work and come to see the beauty of the world he has—the world that is tangible and knowable and present.

CHAPTER 17

Charm and Beauty

W̲ITHOUT A WORD TO ANYONE, S̲ARALA HAD MADE THE APPOINTMENT, her long hair falling into a pile around the stylist's chair. With a blow dryer, the hairstylist restrained Sarala's dark curls, shaping them into soft wings that fanned out around her face, drawing attention to her high cheekbones, the whole arrangement set with a soft lacquer of hairspray. Sarala was unsure whether she could reproduce the effect, but, for the day, at least, it was enough to catch a glimpse of herself in the mirror each time she passed.

When Meena and Abhijat returned home that evening, Sarala revealed her transformation.

"You look," Abhijat said, after regarding her for a moment, "like Carol."

"I think it looks great, Mom," Meena said.

Abhijat excused himself to change out of his suit. As he made his way up the stairs, he permitted himself another peek at Sarala and admitted, only to himself, that it did, in fact, suit her.

Upstairs, he slipped out of his jacket and returned it to its hanger. He stood for a moment in the large walk-in closet, which had, when they first bought the house, seemed to him excessively large. Pushed to the back were the bright saris Sarala no longer wore, her side of the closet now filled with matching jogging suits, Velcro tennis shoes, and holiday-themed sweaters. He ran his fingers over the saris' thin, delicate fabric, then turned back to his side of the closet, removing his tie and returning it to its place among the others.

@

At the dinner table, Abhijat looked down at his plate, scooping up a bit of the grey-green matter on his spoon and letting it slide off with a resounding splat. "What is this?" he asked, sounding weary, tired of it already, before Sarala even answered.

"Green bean casserole." She held up the photo from the cookbook. "I learned from Carol."

"Carol," Abhijat said under his breath. He held up another spoonful, sniffing at it suspiciously.

From across the table, Meena raised her eyebrows, nodding at him like a mother cajoling a toddler into taking a bite.

He exhaled into the quiet of the room. "I don't like you spending so much time with her," Abhijat said. He had not failed to notice the Not Under My Home sign that had appeared in Carol and Bill's front yard.

Meena watched nervously from her place at the table.

"Surely there is someone more, more…" Abhijat searched for the word. "…edifying for you to spend time with."

Sarala didn't answer. For her, it had become answer enough to say nothing.

@

After she had cleared away the dinner dishes and returned the kitchen to order, Sarala made her way the few blocks to her neighbor's house. "You should come," Carol had said that morning with an encouraging smile.

As she walked, Sarala noticed the new sensation of cold around her neck and found her fingers drawn again and again to the ends of her newly short hair.

It seemed strange to Sarala, upon arriving, to find the driveway full of cars when she knew that none of the women there lived any farther from Judy's house than Sarala did.

"Look at you!" Carol exclaimed when Sarala came through the door. "You look fantastic!" Carol embraced Sarala, then stepped back to take in the transformation again. "I absolutely love it," she announced.

Judy's living room felt crowded, full of overstuffed sofas that looked, to Sarala, as though they might burst were she to sit down on one. In the center of the room, a floral area rug sat on top of the wall-to-wall carpet.

"Her husband got a huge promotion last year, and she's just re-done her living room," Carol confided to Sarala. "That's really the only reason she's hosting. She just wanted to show it off to everyone."

Around Judy's dining room table, Carol had arranged pink plastic trays into which she placed Styrofoam inserts, disposable wands for mascara, and sponge-tipped applicators for eye shadow. Beside each of these place settings sat a pink terrycloth headband, a sales ticket, and a pen. A pink runner marched down the center of the table.

The women had congregated in the living room, where they sat, tiny plates of appetizers balanced on top of their wine glasses, trading in neighborhood gossip.

Sarala watched as Carol, from her spot at the head of the dining room table, opened her pink case, its tiny compartments unfolding to reveal lipsticks, perfume samples, and eye shadow.

"Ladies," Carol began, her voice ringing out over the chatter. "Let's come find a seat when you're ready."

Mirrors attached to the trays reflected the women's faces back to them as they took their seats, each woman's place indicated by her name written out in a flourishy cursive on the sales ticket that sat beside each tray. Carol began to speak once the women had taken their seats.

"Everything begins with skin care. Whatever problem you have with your skin, we have something that can help. Oily skin, we have something for that. Combination skin, we have something. Even for those of you whose skin can't quite make up its mind," here she winked at one of the women, who laughed. "Now, let's begin."

The women put on their headbands, their carefully arranged hairdos pulled back from their faces, and began to remove their makeup. Sarala had no makeup to remove, but she did as they did, slipping the terrycloth headband over her dark hair, applying cold cream to her cheeks and forehead, wiping a cotton ball dipped in eye-makeup remover over her lids.

"Now, I am not here to sell you anything." Carol continued with a gentle stream of talking points that Sarala found strangely soothing to listen to, Carol's voice warm and inviting. "I'm here to teach you about good skin care. I don't want to be your sales consultant. I want to be your best girlfriend who, when you run out of mascara on a snowy morning and don't want to load the kids into the car to run to the drugstore or the mall, you can call me, and I will bring it to you. All I want tonight is for you to let me pamper you."

Once they had removed their makeup, the women around the table began to practice putting on their faces again, following Carol's careful instruction.

"And how is everyone's face feeling?" Carol made the rounds of the table with tubes of foundation, assessing skin tone—"Lenore, I'm thinking you're a beige number one"—and dispensing squirts of the appropriately matched foundation into the small indentation in their Styrofoam trays. "Marjorie, I'm thinking ivory for you."

At Sarala, Carol stopped, went back to her case, rummaged inside for a moment, and emerged with a darker tube of foundation than the ones she'd offered the rest of the table. Compared to the other well-used tubes, Sarala noticed, this one was nearly untouched. Carol squirted a bit into Sarala's tray. "I think this will be just the thing," she said.

Carol moved around the table dispensing guidance, making adjustments, as one might to someone learning a new yoga pose. "You'll want to hold the brush like so.

"Now here," she continued, "is a new lipstick that's just come out for the spring season. I think of this as a very wearable red. You see reds all the time that look great on the shelf, don't you? And then you bring them home and think, why on earth did I buy this? I can't go out in public like this! And this is another one of the benefits of Mary Kay. We let you try it all before you buy it, so while it may cost a bit more than the drugstore brand, you'll always go home with something you love and can wear the next day. Now Marjorie, you look skeptical."

Sarala's eyes followed Carol's to the woman beside her.

"I guess I'm just not much of a red lipstick lady," Marjorie said sheepishly. In contrast to the other women at the table, Sarala had noticed that Marjorie had comparatively little makeup to remove when the party began.

"Until tonight!" Carol said, dabbing a bit of the new color onto Marjorie's Styrofoam tray. "What do you say ladies, can Marjorie be a red lipstick lady?"

"Try it!" they encouraged. Even Sarala found herself nodding along in encouragement.

Marjorie applied a small bit with the tip of her finger, then studied herself in the mirror. "It's not as bad as I expected," she decided.

"Not as bad as you expected!" Carol laughed. "You look gorgeous! Your husband will be chasing you up the stairs tonight when you come home!"

Sarala hadn't before seen Carol as she presented, and it was mesmerizing. She was polished and well spoken, and she worked the room like a pro. For a moment or two she would engage in small talk, neighborhood gossip, and then, almost unnoticed, would swing back around to the latest shade of eye shadow or the fabulous deal on toner and night cream going on only for a limited time.

Sarala had seen Carol, on show nights, emerging from her house in a dress coat and high heels, her pink totes in hand. Tonight she watched Carol from up close, her skin so smooth it might have been polished, navigating the table in her high-heeled, pointy-toed shoes.

Sarala tried not to count how many of the women there had signs in their yards opposing the collider, but with the public hearing only a few days away, the whole thing felt a bit like the elephant in the room, an idiom Sarala had come to appreciate.

@

Upstairs in her room, Meena relished the quiet, working methodically, peacefully through her pre-calc homework, calmed and encouraged by the careful process through which, if she followed each step precisely, she would arrive at a reassuringly correct answer. Lately it seemed her ears were filled always with Lily's chatter about the Academy and her constant questions about Meena's own application, which were becoming tiresome and increasingly difficult to deflect.

"You should have your father help you with it," Lily suggested.

But Meena said she didn't want to bother her father while he was so preoccupied with the super collider.

"I'm sure my mom would be happy to help look over your essays, like she did for me," Lily offered.

"No, that's okay, I'll be fine on my own," Meena assured her, but the truth was that Meena's letter about the Academy was by now buried deep in the Nicolet landfill.

Lily's other recent favorite topic of conversation was the issue of the super collider, and for Meena, their conversations on this matter were even less enjoyable.

Meena had privately begun to sympathize with the opponents. She didn't understand the science behind the collider any more than they did. But she had the luxury of a father to trust, to know that if it were a dangerous thing, he would not allow it to be built under his home, under her school. Many of the opponents, however, did not have the benefit of someone else's knowledge to lean on. Here, she echoed Dr. Cardiff's thoughts on the issue, for he seemed to Meena to be a reasonable and compassionate person.

"I think I can understand why they're so afraid," Meena confessed finally.

Lily looked her as though she'd been struck. "Honestly, Meena, you sound like my mother."

@

Abhijat had intended to spend the evening in his study, working, as was his habit, but he found himself unable to concentrate, a steady parade of intrusive thoughts interrupting each time he looked down at his notes. First, his thoughts were of the collider—the hearing, the letters to the editor, the growing number of signs in his neighbors' yards. Then he found himself thinking about what he'd said to Sarala at dinner, how he'd taken his frustration over the issue of the collider out on her, unfairly. Carol was not the problem, he chastised himself. She'd been a good friend to Sarala, for years now.

Unable to focus, he wandered into the family room and turned on the television, an indulgence he rarely allowed himself. A bad habit, a poor use of time, he'd always argued.

He ought, probably, to apologize, he thought.

@

"Well, all I know is that I don't want this thing running under my house," Sarala heard one of the women at the far end of the table saying. "I don't care what it is."

Carol caught Sarala's eye and gave her an encouraging smile.

"God only knows what they're really doing over there in that Lab," Judy said as she lined the bottom lid of her eye, her mouth open a bit, tongue snaking around as she concentrated.

"You know, Judy," Carol interrupted, handing her a new color. "You might try something in a smoky blue. To bring out your eyes."

"I heard it's something to do with nuclear waste," a woman across the table from Sarala said.

Carol pressed on. "Now take a look at this blush, ladies. Would you believe it actually works on every skin tone? Honestly. Give it a try. I'll pass it around."

Sarala tried it. She looked around the table at the other women. It did, in fact, suit them, but on her own face, it looked pearly and strange. She wiped it off with a cotton ball.

"We'll be another Three Mile Island if we let them have their way," Judy continued, undiverted.

"Well, according to that map in the paper, it's not supposed to run under our house," Marjorie joined in, "but honestly, I've thought about selling either way. Before, I didn't take much notice of what they did there, but the more I learn, the less I like it."

"Someone has got to put a stop to this," said Lenore.

"You know, if you want to speak at that public hearing next week, you've got to sign up by Wednesday," Judy noted. "Otherwise you can write a letter. But I think it'll be important to be there. For them to see us there in person."

"Oh, come now, ladies," Carol said smiling. "Don't let's spend the whole evening talking politics. It's not good for the complexion."

Sarala was surprised to find that her lip was trembling, and she blinked back the tears that had leapt to her lashes more quickly than she would have expected, tears that hovered there as though held back only for the time being, certain to return the moment she let her guard down. She thought of how Abhijat and his job were at once the reason they were here in Nicolet, as well as the reason she might never feel entirely at home here.

Carol caught Sarala's eye and gave her a small smile of encouragement. "Now then," Carol continued, and Sarala was grateful for the way the women's heads swiveled back in her direction. "Really big for spring this year is the smoky eye." Carol leaned into the light of the chandelier that hung over the dining room table so the women might admire her own eye makeup. "I didn't quite do a smoky eye tonight, but I did the dark blue, which is a nice kind of baby step toward the true smoky eye.

"Are there any questions?" Carol paused and looked around the table. "Now, as you finish up, I'm going to go around and write down everything that's on your face. Whatever you'd like to start with is fine with me."

Sarala blinked at how seamlessly Carol had moved into the sales portion of the event. The other women began taking their headbands off, rearranging their hair in the mirror, admiring the lipstick or rouge they had tried, and fishing in the purses that hung on the backs of their chairs for their checkbooks.

The women began to gather their purses and pink plastic bags filled with their new purchases. Carol turned to Sarala as she repacked her tote bags. "Why don't you let me give you a ride home?"

"Thank you. I think I will prefer walking, though," Sarala said. She thanked Judy and collected her purse as the rest of the women said their goodbyes.

Outside, the air was cool. Again she felt the cold creeping in around her newly bare neck. Sarala walked through the neighborhood, most of the houses lit from within by the dancing blue light of a television in the family room.

Until the discussion of the collider had intruded, it had been nice to be out of the house for the evening. Sarala imagined the quiet that would hover over her home when she returned—Abhijat closed up in his study until late into the night, Meena busy upstairs with her schoolwork, which she never seemed to need help with anymore. Sarala wondered sometimes how Meena felt about the collider, if she thought about it at all.

She was glad that Abhijat had never asked her thoughts on the collider. She wouldn't have liked to tell him.

Her own home stood on the corner, dark but for a light in Abhijat's study and one in Meena's room. Sarala looked up as she neared it.

The feeling of belonging nowhere pressed down upon her. The sky was dark but for a bit of light pollution coming from the center of town. She belonged neither with those women, nor, lately, it seemed, with Abhijat, from whom she felt keenly aware that she was drifting further and further.

Instead of going inside, Sarala kept walking. She thought of Abhijat's mother, of her own mother, a continent away, past a deep blue sea. She wondered if they, too, had grown far from their husbands, even while wanting nothing more than to go on loving them.

She wanted to be a woman who counted her blessings. Who thought each day of how lucky she was to live in a beautiful home, in a pleasant town, with a child and a husband she loved. Here, the tears she had held back in Judy's dining room returned, and since she was now alone and in the dark, she let them run quietly down her face. She didn't cry, exactly. It felt, instead, like they just leaked out of her.

Maybe everyone was secretly unhappy, she thought.

@

When Sarala returned home, she was surprised to find Abhijat in the family room watching television. He had startled, hearing her come through the door, jumped up, and turned off the television, as though he'd been caught doing something unseemly.

Standing in front of the now-dark television, he composed himself. "How was your evening?" he asked.

"Just fine," Sarala said, and he noticed, with a twinge of shame, the note of surprise in her voice as she answered. She was surprised by the question, he realized. Surprised to find him interested in her activities.

He should apologize, he thought again.

"And your evening?" she asked.

"Oh, fine," Abhijat answered. There was a thick, strange silence between them. "Meena's upstairs," he offered. "Schoolwork."

"I'll just check on her, then," Sarala said, and she turned and was gone, her footsteps on the stairs.

I should have apologized, Abhijat repeated to himself as he sat down again on the sofa. Distantly, he could hear Meena and Sarala talking.

He should go upstairs and apologize, he knew. But instead, he listened, discerning the sounds of Sarala changing out of her clothes, the scrape of a hanger against the rod in the closet, water running in the bathroom, then the sounds of her settling into bed, the television in their room tuned to one of the shows she followed—all of them, it seemed to him, about rich and impossibly good-looking American families.

◎

Abhijat spent the night awake long into the small hours, worrying. As the date of the hearing approached, he'd found it increasingly difficult to sleep, focused on the idea that the hearing would be where the matter of his legacy was decided. Where it would either be held out to him or snatched away.

Sarala and Meena had long since gone to bed, and the house hummed with silence. He found himself searching the living room bookshelves in hopes of finding a text that might—what? he chided himself. Offer some guess about how things might turn out, about what decision would be made? Provide some prophecy about how this mess with the collider would all turn out?

He ran his fingers along the spines of the books, stopping at the copy of de Toqueville's *Democracy in America* he had purchased for Sarala so many years ago. He pulled at it, tugging it gently from the other books and letting it fall open, heavy in his palm.

He flipped backward to the book's table of contents, his eyes wandering over the chapters he remembered from his own reading. He turned, expectantly, to Book 1, Chapter 10: "Why the Americans Are More Addicted to Practical than to Theoretical Science."

But he found no solace in it, no explanation of the situation in which the town and the Lab now found themselves, no suggestions about how one might resolve this impasse. Leafing through the book's pages, though, what he did find was the inscription he had made inside the book when he had given it to Sarala so many years before. There, on the dark blue paper of the flyleaf, was his inscription. He ran his finger over his own handwriting.

For my beautiful and beloved wife—

It felt as though he had discovered the private, secret correspondence of two strangers.

@

Abhijat sat at his desk, his lamp glowing out into the otherwise dark house. He realized how very little he knew about Sarala's interests anymore, how infrequently he asked her about her world. It had been a habit so easy to slip into—busy with work, busy with Meena—that he'd hardly noticed how long it had been since they'd had a proper conversation, one that did not involve Meena's schedule, her schoolwork, or, he realized, the situation at the Lab.

Upstairs, Sarala had fallen asleep. Abhijat turned off the television and watched as she shifted under the comforter in sleep.

@

In the morning, Abhijat watched Sarala for signs that her irritation at his comment had blown over. But she was quiet, and even as she prepared breakfast and packed Meena's lunch, she avoided looking at him.

Meena noticed this too, the strange silence of the kitchen. She watched a small frown of concern bloom on father's forehead, his face bent low over his breakfast.

Sarala went out to the driveway to collect the newspaper. She hadn't yet talked with Abhijat about her plan. She thought it would be best to wait until after the matter of the collider was decided. Even then, though, she wasn't sure it was something he was ready to hear.

©

After arriving at the Lab and giving Dr. Cardiff what he hoped was enough time to settle in for the day, Abhijat knocked gently on the open door of his friend's office. Though Dr. Cardiff always kept his door open and welcomed his colleagues to drop in, Abhijat maintained the careful protocol of knocking first.

"Come in, come in," Dr. Cardiff called, still looking down at the papers on his desk as Abhijat entered. "Have a seat, old friend." Dr. Cardiff indicated one of the two chairs that sat opposite his desk.

Dr. Cardiff's office looked out into the atrium of the Research Tower, and Abhijat looked down at the small people making their way across the lobby. Across the atrium, he could see into the other offices, his colleagues in profile at their desks or standing to chalk out an equation on the slate walls. Dr. Cardiff followed his gaze.

"It's an inspiring view," he said, and waited for Abhijat to speak.

"Gerald," Abhijat began. He took a seat in the chair Dr. Cardiff had indicated. Abhijat's hands began to beat a nervous staccato in his lap. "In your opinion, if I may ask, what do you believe will happen to the Lab, to us, if the collider does not go forward?"

Dr. Cardiff took a breath, rolling away from his desk and settling more comfortably into his chair. "Well," he said, "they may consider building it somewhere else in the U.S."

Abhijat nodded. He had already considered this possibility.

"But I think it's far more likely," here Dr. Cardiff took a deep breath, "that it, or something like it, would be built in another country. It may mean the end of this country's dominance at truly high energy levels."

Abhijat thought for a moment about this. If the Lab were no longer the preeminent facility, then, in terms of his career advancement, it would set him back to stay. He wondered whether Sarala and Meena would agree to a move. Early on, he thought, Sarala could perhaps have been more easily convinced, but now? "And where would you go, Dr. Cardiff, in that event?" he asked.

Dr. Cardiff smiled at his friend, imagining something of the thoughts Abhijat must be turning over in his mind. "Oh, I imagine I'll stay right here. At my age, being at the top facility no longer seems as imperative as it once did."

The phrase "at my age" struck Abhijat. He and Dr. Cardiff were contemporaries. Abhijat had not yet begun to feel old, to feel like the sort of man who might use this expression "at my age," the sort of scientist who might imagine the endpoint of his career as not very far away. But, he realized, this was, in fact, precisely what he was.

"I see." Abhijat thought for a moment. "Thank you," he said, rising and making his way quickly toward the doorway, "for sharing your thoughts."

"Of course," Dr. Cardiff said. Then, gently, "Try not to worry too much about this, Abhijat. Really, at this point, it's quite out of our hands."

"Yes," Abhijat agreed softly. "Yes, I think you are right."

Dr. Cardiff did not tell Abhijat that he had begun to think it was unlikely they would prevail. That it seemed to him doubtful that the collider would be built in Nicolet or, indeed, anywhere in the U.S.

CHAPTER 18

Prairie Burn

*The gladdest moment in human life is the departure upon
a distant journey into unknown lands.*
—Richard Burton

By Tuesday morning, most of the town was buzzing about
the public hearing, which would begin at 8 a.m. the following day.
And with the event looming, the tension had begun to rise among
the town's residents. Many of them, unaccustomed to public speaking, were now poring over their notes, spending long nights at
their kitchen tables deciding what would best fit into their allotted five-minute time slot, what would be most effective, what they
might say to sway the decision in one direction or another.

At the Lab, Abhijat spent most of the afternoon in a meeting in a
conference room that looked out over the atrium; with a lull in the conversation, he could hear the quiet hum of the Research Tower's central
air. It was only when he returned to his own office, caught the smell of it
creeping into the building, and looked out over the prairie that he saw it.

The orange flames had spread quickly through the dry prairie
grasses, sending up a cloud of smoke that rose slowly into the air.
From his office on the nineteenth floor, Abhijat watched the glow
from the grass now ablaze and looked out over the flame-red prairie.

From town, Sarala smelled the smoke. It reminded her of the camp-fires around which reenactors arranged their tents during Heritage Village's annual Revolutionary War Days.

She stepped out onto the porch. From far off, billowing gray clouds of smoke rose up from the grounds of the Lab.

As she turned to go back inside, she noticed a flyer that had been rolled up and tucked between the front door and the screen. She pulled it out and unrolled it.

"Don't forget to join us tomorrow at the public hearing. This is your last chance to protect your homes and families. Bring your friends. Wear your T-shirts and buttons. Arrive early—our opponents will!"

The phone at the emergency response dispatch unit had already begun to ring off the hook.

☺

The prairie burn was an annual event. Conducted by the Lab's grounds crew and supervised by the Lab fire department, it was something the Lab had done every year, a way to rejuvenate the land, to allow the growth of new vegetation, clearing the way for fresh shoots of native prairie grasses through the ash. But this year, amid all of the clamor over the super collider, it had collectively slipped the minds of nearly all of the citizens of Nicolet.

Abhijat walked to his car and began his short, winding drive home. In his rearview mirror, the smoke and heat rose up from the grasses as they turned to clouds of ash, reaching up into the evening sky and obscuring the Research Tower. At the entrance to the Lab were the usual protesters, but now they seemed angrier, louder, and Abhijat could hear them from inside his car as he passed by more slowly than usual.

"You think you can burn us out? We won't be intimidated by your scare tactics."

Abhijat drove home in silence, realizing as he did so that the prairie burn had been—this year—poorly timed.

CHAPTER 19

The Last Trek into the Wild

TRAVELING THROUGHOUT SOUTHERN ASIA THAT FALL, RANDOLPH had collected a thoughtful assortment of gifts for Lily and Rose, which he looked forward to presenting to them upon his next sojourn in the States. Through Lily's letters, he had been kept abreast of the gathering storm the super collider had become for the citizens of Nicolet, and for his wife and daughter as well.

Randolph's final stop on the journey would be the Andaman Islands, where he had arranged to live among the inhabitants of a small fishing village for several weeks in a hut on the beach.

In a small cardboard jewelry box, swaddled in cotton, Randolph had sent Lily the tiny corpse of a deathwatch beetle, and a note, describing to her how the small creatures bored into dead wood, and from there sent their mating calls, a repetitive tapping sound, out into the night.

@

Randolph had fallen asleep soundly, a well-earned rest after a busy day working alongside the fishermen, learning their techniques for constructing and repairing the nets they used to gather the fish that had sustained their people for generations. Before bed, he'd read Lily's most recent letter, chronicling the state of the town as the public hearing loomed, and Rose's most recent letter, chronicling the state of Lily's application to the new Science and Math Academy.

@

He woke to the sound of shouting. The sun had just begun to rise, and when he peered out the entrance of his shelter, he was astonished to see that the ocean had receded miles and miles from shore, revealing wrinkled wet sand as far as the eye could see, as though someone had pulled a plug and the great sea had simply drained away.

All around him, there was the sound of commotion, and when Randolph turned back to the village to make sense of it, he found the fishermen and their families frantically loading children and prized possessions onto rickety bikes, some of them already hurrying inland toward the swell of land where the mountains began.

CHAPTER 20

The Public Hearing

*In this advance, the frontier is the outer edge of the wave—
the meeting point between savagery and civilization.*
—FREDERICK JACKSON TURNER, *THE SIGNIFICANCE
OF THE FRONTIER IN AMERICAN HISTORY*

OUTSIDE THE HIGH SCHOOL, PROTESTERS AND SUPPORTERS HAD
gathered with signs and posters, shouting at one another and at the
Department of Energy representatives as they made their way inside.
As Sarala and Abhijat passed through the crowd, Sarala noted the
presence of police officers near the entrance, arms crossed over their
chests, watching for signs of unrest.

Most of the crowd carried signs and wore T-shirts reading No
SSC IN NICOLET or BUILD YOUR EXPERIMENT ELSEWHERE, but
there were a small number of supporters there as well, some of whom
Abhijat recognized from the Lab and greeted with a nod as he and
Sarala passed through the crowd. Among the opponents, Sarala recognized a number of their neighbors and some of the women from
the Mary Kay party. She kept her head down, avoiding eye contact,
but just as they were almost to the door, she caught sight of Carol,
who broke away from the group of protesters and took her hand.

"Sarala, I'm so sorry," she said. "I know you're in a difficult place
here, but I feel like I have to take a stand on this."

"I understand," Sarala said. She smiled warmly at her friend. Indeed, over the last few months she had begun to wonder whether,

were she not married to Abhijat, she would be standing with Carol and the rest of their neighbors.

Carol embraced her. "We're still friends," she said, her words somewhere between a statement and a question.

"Of course." Sarala gave Carol's hand a squeeze and hurried to catch up to Abhijat, who stood at the door, holding it open for her.

☺

Earlier that morning, as she dressed for the hearing, Abhijat had brought Sarala a letter. She sat down with it, on the edge of their bed, and he watched her as she read.

I think that I have been insensitive to your feelings, it began. She read on, Abhijat beside her on the bed, expectant, uncertain.

She looked for a moment at the letter in her hands when she finished. It was so like Abhijat—its language scientific, analytical. She remembered how appealing Abhijat's logical, organized mind had felt to her when they'd first married—how reassuring. But now?

She took his hand in hers, finally. "It's time for us to go," she said.

☺

Inside the lobby, the students of Nicolet Public High School, Lily and Meena among them, had gathered during the passing period to watch the protesters. Meena caught sight of her parents making their way through the crowd and joined them.

Lily watched the crowd for her mother, whom she found standing with a group of protestors, passing out campaign literature. They made eye contact for a brief moment before Lily looked away and made her way toward the auditorium, where she joined Meena, Abhijat, and Sarala, who sat next to Dr. Cardiff in a row of seats near the middle of the room.

The auditorium had neatly divided itself—supporters of the super collider on one side and protesters on the other, and, as though they were all guests at a wedding, each person who entered the auditorium looked up into the crowd on either side of the long entrance tunnel that split the seats into two sides and made a choice.

Up on the auditorium stage, which typically showcased awkward but earnest high school musicals, officials from the Department of Energy took their seats behind a long table looking out over the auditorium, their names on placards before them.

The organizers of the hearing had scheduled a three-hour period for public comment, but 1,500 people had shown up, nearly a hundred of whom had preregistered to comment, and the auditorium soon began to overflow, audience members sitting in the aisles and standing along the entrance tunnel, where they leaned against the gray concrete walls.

From his seat at the long table on stage, the moderator called the hearing to order, explaining the rules of conduct and pointing out the podium near the foot of the stage, from which each speaker would make his or her remarks.

Sarala noticed that its placement, whether by design or necessity, meant that the speakers would be looking up at the stage and at the officials behind their long table, like children looking up at an adult.

The moderator continued. "I have been retained by the Department of Energy for the purpose of facilitating today's hearing. In this role, I am neither an advocate for nor against this proposed project."

"Bullshit!" came a shout from the protestors' side of the audience.

"Well, then," the moderator continued. "I suppose now is as good a time as any to remind you that this hearing is being recorded. Your comments today will become part of the public record."

@

As the hearing began, Sarala watched the parade of speakers as they made their way to the podium, one after another.

There were speakers who, remembering the Lab's original means of acquiring its campus, now cautioned that this was nothing more than another land grab, another abuse of eminent domain. "You hear a lot of folks going on about what a good place the Lab is, all its important contributions," one of them noted. "But what about those folks who lost their land? They'll sing you a different tune. And now, thirty years later, here we are again. And what about in another twenty years? They might be coming for your house, for your land then."

There were speakers who argued that they were sick and tired of being told why they should give up the houses they saved for and raised their families in just so "a bunch of scientists could have a fancy new toy to play with."

"If they want this thing so badly," one man said, "let them build it under their own houses."

There were questions that revealed the depth of the fear many in the audience felt about the prospect of the collider: "Will the men in the area become sterile?" "In the event of a war, would this be the first place to be bombed?" one woman asked, and Sarala could sense Abhijat, beside her, beginning to stiffen in frustration.

@

Randolph had returned to the shelter to gather his things, but as he did so, he heard the villagers' swift walking turn to running, and Randolph—whose years of exploration had taught him nothing if not to trust the locals—took what he had in his arms and began to run, too, his eyes scouring the terrain ahead, searching for higher ground.

@

As the morning progressed, officials and scientists from state agencies presented reports on floodplain mitigation, well impacts, potential increases in construction traffic, and the viability of deep tunneling through area geological formations. In an attempt to make sense of and bring order to what felt to her like an unfocused, meandering presentation of information and emotion, Lily had divided her yellow legal pad into separate sections and she took careful notes, placing them under the appropriate heading.

Under <u>Local Real Estate Values</u> she first noted the reports indicating that there was no evidence whatsoever that the collider would have any negative impact on local real estate values, but crossed it out a moment later when the next speaker's reports claimed exactly the opposite. Her notes on <u>Contamination of the Water Supply</u> became equally muddled, each assurance, each report cancelled out by another. She crossed out what she had written and instead wrote "uncertain." Under <u>Environmental Concerns</u> she'd listed the remarks of the director of the State Environmental Protection Agency, who noted that the Lab's efforts to return the land to its original prairie had resulted in "significant improvements to the habitats of many native species of plants and animals."

As the hands on her watch neared ten o'clock, the moderator leaned toward the microphone before him. "We will now take a short recess and will commence again in fifteen minutes."

©

During the recess, the audience members relocated to the school's cafeteria, where they sat at the long lunch tables drinking coffee, having again self-segregated into groups of supporters and opponents. The recess had coincided with the high school's passing period, and students, the majority of whom had decided not to attend the hearings, moved around the edges of the cafeteria slowly, regarding the adults with curiosity.

After waiting out the long line for the women's restroom, Rose approached the table where Lily sat with the Mitals and Dr. Cardiff. "Good morning, Dr. Mital, Mrs. Mital," she said. She stood behind Lily and placed her hands lightly on her daughter's shoulders. Lily looked down at the table and did not acknowledge her mother.

"Madame Alderperson." Abhijat nodded stiffly.

Sarala smiled at Rose as warmly as she could, having noted the coolness in Abhijat's voice and that Lily had yet to make eye contact with her mother. "Mrs. Winchester, allow me to introduce my husband's colleague, Dr. Gerald Cardiff."

"Very pleased to meet you," Dr. Cardiff said, taking Rose's hand in his. His smile, Sarala noted, was also warm, and she felt relieved on Rose's behalf.

"Likewise," Rose said. "And thank you both," she said, turning back toward Sarala and Abhijat, "for looking after my daughter today. I imagine she feels like a bit of an orphan during this hearing." She ran her hand over Lily's back, but Lily continued her project of conducting a careful study of the mock wood grain of the table.

☺

Back in the auditorium, the audience again took their seats, the officials returning to their places at the long table on the stage.

Looking around the auditorium from her seat on the supporters' side, Meena felt like she could sense the fear and anger in the room. Fear of the super collider on the part of the protesters. Fear of the protesters on the part of the scientists, who had begun to worry over what would become of the Lab if the super collider wasn't built. And on both sides, anger that the other side wouldn't listen to reason. It was a room in which everyone was afraid of everyone else. Meena turned back to face the stage. She had never seen adults like this.

The moderator called the audience back to order. "We will now reconvene today's hearing on the matter of the Super Collider."

As Meena watched, she kept a different kind of inventory than the one growing on Lily's legal pad. Instead, as the speakers resumed, exchanging places at the podium, one after another, Meena noted the speakers who made sound, well-reasoned points:

"Before you scoff at the questions we ask here today," one woman urged, "take a moment to remember how many times during the past fifty years our government has asked us to trust its decisions. They say they have our best interests at heart, yet twenty years from now, when the true effects are known, all they will say is, 'We're sorry. We didn't know.' People who believe this will be safe because the federal government says so are being naïve. Those of us who oppose this project are not a lynch mob. We are mothers and fathers, grandparents, homeowners, farmers, and businesspeople who want to protect our homes, our community, our children, and our wildlife."

One supporter, who introduced himself as a technician at the Lab, pointed out that "this project is not, as many of the opposition would have you believe, 'welfare for the overeducated' or 'a toy for scientists.' It is a project deserving of our intellectual curiosity and attention."

At the other end of the spectrum, Meena noted, were the speakers whose words caused one side of the audience or the other to erupt:

"According to these maps they're showing us, this thing is going to run right underneath my daughter's school," one man said. "Now, what about electromagnetic fields? One study I read about found that children living near power lines have more than their fair share of leukemia. And this is going to be located under a school? No one in their right mind could approve such a thing!"

Another speaker, her voice full of anger, insisted, "You people can put as many charts and pages of information as you want in front of us, but it will never take away our fear of living above this experiment. We will not be turned into the next Three Mile Island or Chernobyl. You officials tell us this is safe, but so were the others, until they blew up!"

And then, following these, Meena noticed, were the frustrated, exasperated responses:

"There have been absolutely no incidents in which a collider has blown up," one of the Lab scientists responded, his voice loud and angry. "This is simply fear-mongering at its worst. What a picture we must present to our government officials here today—a bunch of uninformed yokels who, they will probably decide, don't deserve the honor and distinction of such a facility."

One speaker, temper already flaring, began, "I'm tired of hearing from you people at the Lab, who tell us we ought to sacrifice ourselves and our homes for the good of science. You think we ought to listen to you just because you have a bunch of fancy degrees. Well, I might not be a college professor, but I know horseshit when I see it, and as far as I'm concerned, you scientists can all go to hell." As he spoke, there was a growing crescendo of applause from the opposition side of the auditorium.

@

Randolph's and the villagers' running was no match for the wall of water that rushed in on them.

One moment he was running, heart pounding against his chest. The next he was lifted off his feet—buoyed up, swept past trees, houses, buildings, faster than his own feet could have carried him, and all around, the bobbing heads and limbs and panicked cries of others who had been swept up along with him. He looked frantically for something to grab hold of as the water rushed through the village, carrying him along with it.

@

Back and forth, one after another, supporters and opponents of the collider took their places at the podium. As Sarala listened, she could sense the disconnect between the careful scientific communication the supporters—especially those from the Lab—felt they needed to use, and the desire on the part of the opponents for guarantees, for absolute assurances about the safety of operating such a facility. The scientists had been trained not to think in such terms. For them, a probability of 99.9 percent was a good answer, she knew, a reasonable indication of safety, but the opponents were tortured over what that 0.1 percent chance might mean for themselves and their families. Beyond their fundamental disagreement on the issue, Sarala thought, the two groups just didn't know how to talk to one another.

The next woman paused before speaking, allowing herself a moment to smooth her cardigan over her waist in a slow and deliberate way that suggested she wasn't a person to be rushed. "You scientists tell us that this collider is going to help you understand the Big Bang and the creation of the universe, but I think many of us prefer the version of that we can read about in Genesis. You experts should remember," she continued, "that not all of us care to know what happens when protons collide with one another."

@

Rushing through the center of the village, carried along by the wild, churning water, now full of detritus, Randolph caught site of a large tree approaching. *Could he reach it? Would it stand against the water?* The ocean rushed on, sweeping him with it. He reached up, caught hold of a branch, and wrapped his arms and legs around the trunk, clinging to it as he pulled himself up slowly. He climbed, wet and shaking, into the highest branches of the tree that would bear his weight and watched, below him, the dark, feral ocean rising.

@

As the parade of state officials continued, Rose, from her seat on the opponents' side of the auditorium, was paying careful attention to each of their performances.

The director of the state Department of Agriculture had, she noted, been persuasive, arguing that construction of the collider could result in positive developments. "We see the collider as a mechanism to protect farmland from residential, commercial, and industrial encroachment," he explained.

She was concerned to hear this opinion echoed by another speaker, a man she recognized as a longtime resident of Nicolet, who asked, "Have you all considered what might become of this land if it's not acquired for the collider? Maybe we'll build more $400,000 homes that none of us can afford to live in. Maybe a couple more shopping malls. That's just wonderful. Make no mistake," he warned, "change and growth are coming. I believe the collider will give us a way to control that change."

Rose thought of what had become of the farmland of the Nicolet she remembered from her girlhood. He was right to note that not much of it remained. Not much of Nicolet looked, anymore, like the small farm town of her girlhood.

@

Next had come the Lab director, Dr. Palmer, and then Dr. Cohen— Abhijat and Dr. Cardiff exchanging wary looks as he took the podium, both of them knowing him to be short-tempered and already long past exasperated on the matter.

Missing from Dr. Cohen's speech had been any note of empathy, of sincerity, Sarala thought, listening as his tone shifted into one that might be used with a group of unruly kindergarteners. Predictably, the audience began booing, someone yelling out, "Quit patronizing us!"

"Look, I'm one of you," Dr. Cohen continued, looking back at the audience. "I'm not some evil scientist. I live in this community. I raise my family here. If I thought this accelerator would be a danger to the community, do you think I would support it?" He turned back to the panel behind their long table. "Do not be misled by the shrill voice of opposition." He turned and made his way back to his seat.

"Thank you, Dr. Cohen, and our thanks to all of you who shared your comments this morning," the moderator said, beginning to gather his papers. "At this point we will adjourn for lunch," whereupon the panel recessed, to reconvene at two o'clock that afternoon.

Many of the audience from the hearing made their way to the Cozy Café and Diner, where the restaurant's three harried waitresses scurried from table to table in an attempt to serve everyone within the two-hour recess.

Sarala had invited Lily, Rose, and Dr. Cardiff to join them, and Rose, though conscious of the potential for awkwardness, had been so hungry for a glimpse into Lily's life, having felt, since their argument about her letter, so entirely closed off from her own daughter, that, much to her own surprise, she found herself accepting the invitation.

The conversation at their table, like most of those throughout the diner, concerned how the hearing seemed to be going so far. Abhijat felt it was impossible to tell. Dr. Cardiff thought it would be important for the Lab to make a better effort to acknowledge the opposition's fears. Both felt that Dr. Cohen's comments had done them no favors, but Lily said that she didn't think it was fair to expect the Lab's representatives to be evenhanded when it seemed to her that the opposition was relying on hyperbolic scare tactics.

Perhaps, Sarala suggested gently, if they hoped to stand up against the heartfelt, emotional appeals of the opposition, the supporters might rely less on dry testimony from the directors of state agencies and a bit more on some heartfelt, emotional appeals of their own.

But wasn't that, Lily argued, precisely what Dr. Cohen had been doing?

Sarala and Rose exchanged a look, which Lily caught and found at once both perplexing and exasperating.

Sensitive to Rose's presence at the table, Sarala suggested that perhaps they should refrain from discussion of the collider over this meal among friends.

"An excellent idea," Dr. Cardiff agreed.

The waitress circled their table, setting plates before each of them, and Meena began to pick at her French fries. There was a long, awkward moment as they all tried to come up with another, more suitable topic of conversation.

"Perhaps we might talk about the girls' opportunity at the Academy," Rose suggested. "That is certainly a happy turn of events." Rose smiled, first at Lily and Meena, then at Abhijat and Sarala. She wondered why her smile seemed to be returned only by her daughter, who had, over the last few weeks, expended a considerable amount of energy in pointedly avoiding doing any such thing.

Abhijat and Sarala looked first at Rose, then at Meena, who sank down into her seat, as though willing herself to turn invisible.

Sarala spoke first. "I'm afraid we must be, as you say, out of the loop."

"The Math and Science Academy," Lily explained. She looked at Abhijat and Sarala, Abhijat's brow furrowed, Sarala still looking pleasantly expectant that soon someone would explain this to her. Then Lily turned toward Meena, her own brow furrowing.

Meena had decided that, of the limited remaining options, the best plan was to take charge of the conversation and to steer it as determinedly as she could away from the topic at hand. "We haven't had much time to discuss it yet," she explained to Rose and Lily. Then, turning to her parents, "I'll fill you in later. I didn't want to bother you with the hearing coming up."

Abhijat, still frowning, had the sense from Meena's voice that something strange was afoot. "I look forward to our discussion," he said.

Dr. Cardiff, perceptive enough to sense that something unpleasant was stirring beneath the surface of the conversation, took charge and turned toward Rose. "I understand, Mrs. Winchester, that you grew up in Nicolet when it was quite a different town?"

"Oh, yes," she said, turning her attention toward Dr. Cardiff. "I suppose it was just your typical small farm town then. Everyone knew one another." Indeed, some people still did, Rose thought to herself, as the waitress, a classmate from her school days, set a cup of coffee in front of her.

"And what was it like to return from your travels to find it so changed?" Dr. Cardiff asked.

"Well," Rose thought for a moment. "To be honest, I found it exciting. The whole place had such a sense of—" she looked up and around the diner "—such a sense of possibility."

©

Back at the high school, a crowd of participants made their way back into the auditorium. Sarala had expected that the room might thin out a little after lunch, but it seemed just as crowded as it had before the break. She, Abhijat, and Dr. Cardiff saved seats for Lily and Meena, who made their way to the restrooms before the hearing reconvened.

"You haven't even mentioned the Academy to your parents?" Lily asked, incredulous, as they walked through the empty halls of the high school. "And Mr. Boden says you still haven't asked him for a letter of recommendation. What's going on?"

Meena shrugged and rolled her eyes. "Nothing. It's just been busy and kind of stressful around our house lately. It hasn't felt like the right time to bring it up."

Lily eyed her strangely. It felt, to her, much like the conversation they'd had weeks earlier about cheerleading. But Meena seemed determined to ignore this strangeness between them. She ducked into the ladies' room, Lily following behind.

©

The moderator and the rest of the Department of Energy panel filed back onto the stage and re-took their seats behind their microphones and name placards. The moderator again leaned forward into his microphone. "Ladies and gentlemen, I now reconvene the public hearing on the matter of the super collider. We will now hear from Mr. Lawrence Callahan, mayor of Nicolet."

Rose watched with interest as the mayor stood, hiking the waistband of his dress slacks over his substantial girth, and made his way to the podium. The difference between the professionalism of Rose's campaign staff and Mayor Callahan's loose group of family and friends pitching in to help when they could, was, Rose believed, a manifestation of the difference between the old, rural Nicolet and the Nicolet of the present—a suburb that, with the arrival of the Lab, of developers, had become savvier, more sophisticated. Mayor Callahan, Rose hoped the voters would see, was a relic of the old Nicolet.

"Hello, everyone," he began. "Gentlemen. I'm awfully glad so many of our good citizens have come out today to participate in this hearing. And now if you'll bear with me, like I said, I'd like to say a few things." Here he looked down, consulting his notes.

In his comments, he came down, as Rose expected, squarely on the side of the collider's supporters, pointing out that the Lab was a good neighbor, a showplace for the arts, a cancer treatment center, and an educational institution.

Rose had also registered to speak. Her own comments were brief, largely an affirmation that she stood "in support of the safety and sanctity of our homes, schools, and farmland," and that she believed the local elected officials had "failed the citizens of Nicolet by allowing this proposal to proceed this far."

@

When they returned to the school from lunch, Sarala had taken Rose aside and asked her to explain the conversation about the Academy, so Sarala, unlike Abhijat, had a better sense of what was afoot. As the hearing continued, she began to guess, correctly as it turned out, at why Meena had not before mentioned this opportunity.

Abhijat, however, now found himself distracted, half following the hearing, and half curious to learn what it was that Rose had been referring to, what this opportunity for Meena was, and why she hadn't shared this information with her own parents.

Meena sat stiffly next to her parents as the hearing continued. Surely, the moment they found themselves in the car on the way home her father would ask her about the conversation. *And what to say?* she wondered.

After the two mayoral candidates had come a kindly old lady, who urged the panel to pray over the matter. "Please don't build this terrible machine under our homes, our schools, our beautiful farmland," she urged them. "All of us, on both sides of this auditorium, want safe homes for our families. Don't you want that, too? Then don't take that away from us."

Throughout the afternoon, the audience grew restless in their seats, and tempers grew short. Outbursts came from both sides, followed by stern reprimands from the moderator. Listening, Abhijat could feel his heart pounding. He felt afraid for the Lab and afraid for himself. Beyond his own hopes for what the collider might mean for his legacy, he had begun to worry over what would become of the Lab if they lost this bid. The Lab was the one place he had ever felt at home in the world, and the opponents seemed to be threatening its very existence. He felt Sarala's hand on his, and he looked at her, grateful for her presence.

"We will next hear from Mr. Horace Emery," the moderator announced, his voice crackling over the auditorium's speakers.

Mr. Emery approached the podium. He took off a hat with what Rose recognized as a seed-company logo on the front—her father had worn one like it—and tucked it into the back pocket of his overalls.

"My name is Horace Emery," he began. "My family roots go back to the land that is now part of the Lab, and I want to go on record as being 100 percent in support of this project. When the Lab was first proposed twenty years ago, I was opposed for many of the same reasons you folks are. But I was wrong, and you are wrong today."

At this, booing from the audience.

The moderator leaned toward his microphone. "We have all agreed we will not have that sort of outburst. Mr. Emery, please continue."

"With this new proposal, I am going to lose 189 acres of farmland, and it is probably going to destroy my way of life. I'm getting too old to go out and start all over again. But that's okay, because this is for a good cause."

Here there arose a series of shouts from the opposition's side of the auditorium.

"You folks want to yell?" he said, turning to face them. "Well, that's all right. I like those kind of discussions. Progress always involves risk. We cannot stand in opposition to progress. I know people who have been cured of cancer out at the Lab with their medical experiments, and in my mind, losing my land is worth keeping one of my neighbors alive. I wish this sort of thing existed back when my father died of cancer. He had a tumor. He went into the hospital and they cut a hole in his head and he lay there a vegetable until he died. Nowadays, I hear about people who go down there to the Lab and in a few treatments they're healed. No knife, no blood transfusion, not even a Band-Aid. I certainly hope we cut out this monkey business and get on with this thing, the sooner the better."

Mr. Emery turned from the podium and walked back to his seat, the audience, for a moment, strangely quiet.

"And now we will hear from Ms Lily Winchester," the moderator announced. Lily had told no one, not even Meena, that she had registered to speak. She had kept it to herself, and for the past several days had spent her evenings, like many of her fellow citizens, poring over her comments, timing herself so as not to exceed her allotted five minutes, refining her points down to the most salient, the most persuasive. She inched past Meena, Sarala, Abhijat, and Dr. Cardiff, who watched, as surprised as her mother on the other side of the auditorium, as she made her way down the aisle.

"Good afternoon," she said, speaking into the microphone affixed to the top of the podium. "My name is Lily Winchester. I am fifteen years old and a student at Nicolet High School.

"Many people are against this proposed project. Some because they are afraid of change and progress." Here there was shouting from the opponents' side, but now, hours into the hearing, it had begun to feel both expected and half-hearted, as did the moderator's move to quiet it. Lily continued. "But if we listened to people like that, we'd never have gone into space or done any of the other important things our country has done. By the time construction on the super collider is completed, my peers and I will be freshly out of college, and this project will open up countless opportunities for those of us pursuing careers in science. We should be honored to have the collider built here. I see the super collider as a tool, an instrument of science that has much to teach us and will help us to unlock the mysteries of our universe. It is true that the new facility will displace families. Your dreams may be affected. What, though, is wrong with another, bigger dream? Thank you."

Rose watched Lily return to her seat on the other side of the auditorium, filled with a pride she hoped did not show on her face.

The moderator spoke again into his microphone. "And finally—" at that word, signaling an end in the nearby future, it was as though the entire audience, supporters and opponents alike, sighed deeply in relief "—we will hear from Dr. Gerald Cardiff."

Dr. Cardiff rose and made his way down the row of seats, Sarala giving him an encouraging smile. Abhijat noted his friend's slow and careful pace, the grey encroaching on his few remaining dark hairs, and again Abhijat became conscious of the fact that they were, both of them, aging.

"When I was a boy, many, many decades ago," Dr. Cardiff began, "we were taught that the atom was the smallest thing in the world." He paused. "How woefully unimaginative that turned out to be. What has been revealed to us by the Lab's work and accomplishments is a magnificent world, more astounding than any of us could have imagined."

Listening to him, Sarala felt like he was explaining to her all of the things that Abhijat loved about his work but so often did not have the words for. She reached over and took Abhijat's hand in hers.

"It is my most cherished hope," Dr. Cardiff continued, "that we might work together as a community to ensure that this sort of revelation is available to the young people who join us here today, to their generation." Here he looked at Lily and at Meena beside her. "They will, I believe, discover things that today we are unable to even conceive of, but we must provide them with the tools to do so, to participate in this remarkable unveiling of the world's mysteries. The greatest gift we can bestow on future generations," Dr. Cardiff said, turning to the audience, "is to encourage their curiosity. Thank you."

The moderator leaned in to his microphone one last time.

"Ladies and gentlemen, Dr. Cardiff being our final speaker of the evening, this concludes our hearing. I, and the panelists who have joined me here today, wish to thank you for your thoughtful comments. With that, we are formally adjourned. Thank you and goodnight."

Whereupon, at 7:30 p.m., the hearing was concluded.

CHAPTER 21

Cartography of the Time

Abhijat managed to wait until he, Sarala, and Meena had gotten into the car, the doors closing, one—two—three consecutive thumps, before raising the question.

"Meena, what is this opportunity, this academy Mrs. Winchester mentioned at lunch?" he asked, turning from his place behind the steering wheel to face Meena in the back seat.

All around them doors slammed, engines started up, the cars of the other hearing participants snaking up and down the parking lot aisles toward the exit, brake lights glowing out into the dark.

Meena had been expecting this, had buckled herself grimly into her seat waiting for one of them—of course it would be her father, she realized now—to ask the question. "I didn't want to bother you," she said.

"That you have mentioned," he said. "But what is the opportunity?"

"It's a special school," Meena began haltingly, doling out as little as she could. "For science and math. You live there. Mr. Delacroix... the guidance counselor. He said Lily and I should apply."

Abhijat was quiet for a moment, taking this in. "And do you want to apply?" he asked finally.

Sarala, listening from her seat beside Abhijat, was surprised by his choice of question. It was exactly the right one.

Meena scratched at a spot on her jeans. She spoke without look-ing up. "I didn't want to bother you while all the stuff about the collider was going on."

"Yes, but it is my responsibility as your father to help you pursue opportunities," Abhijat answered. "It is not a matter of bothering me—this is my duty as your parent. And now, again the question—do you want to apply?"

Sarala turned in her seat to look at Meena, offering an encour-aging smile.

"No," Meena said, her voice small, apologetic.

"A useful piece of information," Abhijat replied, nodding. "And, may I ask, why?"

"I don't know," Meena mumbled, hoping her vagueness, her lack of enthusiasm for the conversation might deter her father from pur-suing it further.

But, like parents everywhere, Abhijat instead took this as en-couragement to forge ahead, imagining that somewhere, underneath that "I don't know" thrown aside so carelessly, she did in fact know, did in fact want to share this information. He pressed forward, and it felt to Meena a little like the evenings around the kitchen table, so long ago now, when he would gently nudge her on through the difficult terrain of a particularly tricky math problem, displaying a kind of certainty in her ability that even she did not feel.

"I just." Meena started, then stopped again, assessing the hazards of the tangled path before her. "I like my school. And I don't—" She took a deep breath, as though preparing to dive. "I'm sorry. I know this sounds mean, and I don't mean it to, but I don't want to have a life like you."

For a moment this ricocheted around the quiet of the car. Abhijat felt himself absorbing the force of it in an almost phys-ical way, as though being tackled. And then, like parents every-where who have pushed forward and learned something they are no longer sure they wanted to know, he wondered if he should have, perhaps, not pressed her. Should have let her float in the cool uncertainty of her mumbled "I don't know." Should have let himself float there, safe from knowing this. Though of course he had known it already.

After a long moment, Sarala spoke. "Meena, we have never asked or expected that you choose a life like ours."

For Abhijat, there was a moment of light in that pronoun—ours. He listened as Sarala continued. "But we do ask that you respect the choices we have made, the hard work and dedication your father has given to his work. Whether you apply to the Academy or not is of course your choice," she said. "But it seems to me that Lily was quite confident that you had applied or were planning to."

Meena looked down at her knees. She nodded.

Abhijat started the car, the noise of the engine filling the silence of the interior in a way that felt welcome to all three of the occupants. By now, the parking lot had cleared of all of the other hearing participants. Abhijat swung the car around in a graceful circle, down a row of empty parking spots to the stop sign at the exit, and headed for home.

@

Lily and Rose's car ride home had been nearly silent, Rose in the driver's seat negotiating the traffic, Lily staring determinedly out the window. Rose stopped at the mailbox to gather the day's mail before piloting the car into the garage. In the laundry room, both shed their coats, hanging them on the hooks along the wall.

Sorting through the envelopes in her hand, Rose made her way into the kitchen and turned on the television on the kitchen counter, hoping to catch the evening news.

But the regular programming had been preempted, and nearly all news channels showed maps of the Indian Ocean.

Lily turned on the larger television in the family room and sat down before it. The voice of the reporter floated out into the room. "Reports today that the Andaman and Nicobar Islands, a remote chain of islands in the Bay of Bengal, have been devastated by a tsunami that struck the island early this morning."

Lily turned to look at Rose, who held in her hands a letter from Randolph bearing the return address: Andaman Islands.

@

For two days they had no word. Lily stayed home from school and rarely moved from the couch in the family room, where she monitored the news coverage, grainy videos taken by tourists in the more populated areas of the islands, aerial images showing sixty percent of the island chain's landmass now under water.

The first night, Lily appeared in the doorway of Rose's bedroom.

"I can't sleep," she said.

"Me, either," Rose said.

"Could I stay here with you?" Lily asked.

"Of course," Rose answered, holding up the comforter and making a place for Lily beside her.

Lily slid into the spot, what would be Randolph's place were he there with them, and allowed her mother to wrap her arms around her. Rose buried her face in Lily's hair, spread out over the pillow, and gathered her daughter to her.

"Do you think he's alive?" Lily asked, her voice small and muffled by the pillow.

At the very thought of it, Rose could feel her heart beginning to race. What was best in this situation, she wondered. She could feel her careful veneer of parental authority and competence beginning to fracture, a slow spreading, like a cracked windshield.

She imagined herself saying, "I think he's probably dead." But she did not say this, for by saying it aloud, wasn't she calling that very possibility into being? She felt like a traitor for even allowing herself to think it. She was meant to be a better wife than that, a better mother, the kind who kept faith, who believed in his survival.

She imagined herself saying, "I think he's alive." But she did not say this either. It felt dangerous to admit, as though acknowledging any small chance of hope would only irritate fate into snatching him away.

Still her heart raced. *Lily would be damaged beyond repair*—the thought passed through her consciousness, and her heart beat faster. *This is your fault for allowing him to go, for permitting such a life.* Pressed against Lily's back, she wondered if her daughter could feel her heart thumping so furiously inside her. It felt as though it were trying to escape the confines of her body. Rose took a deep breath, hoping to calm her racing thoughts.

"I don't know, sweetheart," she said finally. And although—or perhaps because—it was as unsatisfying an answer as she could have given, Lily did not ask again.

Rose counted slowly to ten. She listened to Lily's breathing and tried to breathe in tandem with her, slowly, deep, long breaths. She could tell the moment Lily slipped off into sleep, and Rose thought of all of the times when Lily was a baby that she'd watched for that moment, laying her down gently in her crib, tiptoeing quietly from the room, afraid of waking her.

When she was sure Lily had fallen into sleep, Rose slid from the bed and padded downstairs to Randolph's study. In his office, she sank into the large wing chair before the bookshelves and opened the tin box of his letters—line after line of his small, cramped handwriting (economical, he would argue, she thought with a smile), sketches, here and there a memento tucked between the pages.

She had always been keenly aware of how Randolph had chafed against his overprotective parents, and in their marriage, she had taken great pride in her willingness to tolerate, her enthusiasm, even, for his wanderings, for his work.

The moonlight shone in through the windows, reflected in the glass of the display case. She thought of how it had all once seemed so thrilling, but now—now it seemed so futile, such an unnecessary risk.

And what if he didn't return? She and Lily would continue on without him. What else could they do? Break down entirely? Let their lives come to a standstill? No—Lily would go to the Academy as planned. Rose would continue on with the election. Her day-to-day life would look much the same. But, she thought, holding the tin box in her hands, she would have no more letters to add to it. She ran her fingertips over his handwriting on the page. For so long, he'd been her dearest friend, her closest confidant, her greatest love next to Lily.

@

Meena brought Lily her books and assignments from school, and in the evenings sat with her in front of the television, though Lily hardly spoke, and her schoolwork remained untouched.

Sarala prepared a large stack of casseroles and filled the Winchesters' freezer. Before she left, she put one in the oven and reminded Rose to take it out in forty minutes, but neither Rose nor Lily remembered or even thought of it until they began to smell it burning.

In the kitchen, Rose kept the radio on and tried to work, listening for each time they cycled back to the story.

"Mrs. Winchester is so calm," Meena had said to her mother. But Sarala suspected that, while on the surface the waters appeared still, below it was a rolling boil.

Lily tried to prepare herself for the worst. "He's dead," she told herself over and over again, imagining that, somehow, anticipating this possibility, preparing herself for it in advance, might offer her some sort of protection once the news arrived, might somehow make it less painful.

Then, finally, on the third day, a scratchy phone call, and, like a miracle, his voice on the other end. He would be home within a few days, courtesy of an empty seat on an NGO's return aid flight.

@

At the airport, Lily rushed for Randolph the moment she caught sight of him.

Rose stood where she was and watched him approach, afraid, almost to believe it, to believe in their good fortune. It was a trick of the world, she thought, to visit upon you such bad fortune that you were reminded every now and then of how lucky you were—a built-in guarantee that no one should ever become complacent or begin to feel entitled to one's happiness.

Back at home, Rose put a plate of food in front of him, but Randolph showed little interest in it. Lily sat with her chair pulled close to his, every now and then her hand snatching at him as though to reassure herself that he was there in the flesh. They looked exhausted, Rose thought. She bundled them both off to bed, to little protest from either, and then the house was quiet and dark.

Rose made her way downstairs to Randolph's study. Filling the bookshelves were his travel journals in which he'd recorded the details of so many places, so many ways of understanding the world, so many other ways of living. She thought of the rituals of these cultures. What was the ritual, she wondered, for overwhelming relief, for giving thanks, for burying fear? For being reminded, by almost losing something, of how important it was to you?

The moonlight shone on the framed maps that hung along the walls. She put her fingertips against the cool, smooth glass of one and a wave of grief rolled over her. There had been no preamble—just a sudden sob, as though it had broken free and escaped. She sank down onto the floor in front of the bookcases, pulled her knees to her chest as tears came. Why now? It made no sense. He was home and safe. She held her hand over her mouth to keep from waking them.

@

This time he returned with nothing. Randolph imagined his trunk, his travel journals, swallowed by the ocean and sinking, finally, to its bottom. He'd been so tired of the clothes he'd arrived in—having lived in them for nearly a week—that instead of handing them over to Rose to be laundered, he had thrown them into the garbage, happy to be rid of them and their smell of mud and sweat and dark, stagnant water.

He had survived, he explained, by climbing into a tree from which he watched possessions, entire cars, splintered pieces of wood, hunks of metal, and people being carried away by the torrent below him.

And in telling it, he is again rolling with the water, rushing toward a tree he counts himself fortunate to have caught hold of. Catching his breath, he begins to climb, pulling himself through the fragile branches he wouldn't have gambled would hold him. But it is his only hope, the water below him rising, black as charcoal and filled with the detritus of what it has already encountered, splintered boards, concrete blocks, a bicycle, a woman.

"What happened to those people?" Lily asks.

"I don't know," Randolph says—though he can still hear them calling out for help, some rushing past atop an island of debris. He'd had nothing—not even a rope to throw down to them.

Cars against cars, an ocean of steel and tin and wood filling what had once been the streets. And what to do? He had found himself praying.

"Then what?"

After a long while, the waters shifted, began to recede, returning to the sea. All around were still, shallow pools of dark water containing who knew what. He had climbed down then, out of the safety of the tree's embrace.

At the first muddy spot, he had fallen forward, palms against the wet, soft soil, touching his forehead to this solid earth, inhaling its smell.

He'd headed inland on the back of a motorcycle, hitching a ride with the local postman. Together they rode north to the airport along empty stretches of road. At one spot, the hulls of two enormous freighter ships lay across the road, the traffic—all motor-bikes—passing carefully between the two beached craft.

@

On his second night home, Randolph had come to sit beside Lily in the living room, where she sat surrounded by her schoolbooks. "Your mother told me about your speech during the hearing," he said.

For Lily, the hearing had receded from her mind, which had, instead, for so long it seemed, been full of images of rushing water.

"I'm very proud of you," Randolph continued. "It's not always easy to stand up for what you believe in, especially in the face of friends, neighbors, and family who disagree, and on matters about which passions run high. I understand from your mother that you did so articulately and with grace."

It seemed now like such a silly, inconsequential thing, Lily thought.

@

Randolph had been absent for so long that the daily rhythms of the Winchester home were entirely foreign to him, and he observed them as curiously as though watching a native people in their hab-itat. He learned the small, simple routines of the household—on what day the trash was collected, when he might expect the arrival of the newspaper.

Randolph and Rose's was a marriage that had, for years, been conducted in absence, via letter, scratchy phone connections that ran under the sea, long cables stretching from continent to continent. Now, as they each adjusted to the other's daily presence, Lily noticed the way her parents moved around each other in the kitchen in the mornings, bumping into one another as they both reached for the milk. It was as though they had to learn all over again how to live with one another.

Rose took pleasure in the routines that had sprung up among all three of them. The waking, each morning, to a warm presence in the bed beside her. The rising to prepare breakfast. The bustle of the morning routine as they all—three of them now—busied themselves preparing for the day ahead. She and Randolph, once Lily was off to school, retiring to their corners of the house to work—he to his study, she to her small desk in the kitchen, and how, now and then, they might meet in the hallway or over the teakettle. The house quiet, then coming back to life with Lily's return from school. Gathering in the kitchen to prepare their evening meal, now Lily's and Randolph's heads bent together over the last difficult bits of the crossword, here and there calling out clues for Rose. Dinners over which Lily regaled them with stories from school—then the quiet evenings in which they each withdrew to their work, Lily to her room, Rose to her small desk in the kitchen, and Randolph to his study. And then, at night, again, Randolph there beside her, and the whole lovely routine ready to spin out ahead of them once more each day.

@

There were moments when a map beckoned to him—this or that spot as yet unexplored. But for the first time in his life, Randolph did not feel excitement at the possibility of the unknown. At first he had not known what to call it—caution, a wariness, trepidation? But, he realized, with a sudden and shameful understanding, this was nothing more than fear. When he recalled his travels now, instead of thinking of them fondly as he once had, he found himself cataloguing the risks he had taken, all the tiny ways in which he'd been so lucky that he felt sure he must have used it all up. In such a new place, he thought, he wouldn't know how to save himself should the situation arise. He would not again be so fortunate. And so, each day, it felt reassuring to travel no farther than his study where, surrounded by his own memorabilia, he could recall his more adventurous days.

@

The editors of the *Nicolet Herald-Gleaner*, more than a little surprised to learn that there had been a Nicolet connection to one of the most significant natural disasters in recent decades, printed a long piece about Randolph's narrow escape. Randolph had not wanted to be interviewed, and so had asked Rose to speak to them instead.

Rose, for her part, found herself dominating the news cycle as coverage of the mayoral race began to increase. It was looking good for Rose, her campaign team assured her, though in the world of local politics, they reminded her, things could change dramatically in the months leading up to an election. And still there was the matter of the electorate's discomfort with her strange marital arrangement, her campaign advisors reminded her. Still, there was the matter of that for her to contend with. But now, even more so than before, it was a conversation she could not imagine having with Randolph.

@

Rose had begun to prepare, to steel herself against the announcement she knew would come soon enough: that he was again leaving. She knew that for the first time in their long marriage, it would be difficult for her not to ask him to stay.

She wanted him to stay. To unpack, to put away his boots and his travel guides and his journals for good. Not because of her political ambitions, not this time, but rather because she wanted the luxury of taking him for granted. The banal daily interactions over schedules and groceries had begun, to Rose, to feel almost sacred, full of meaning and intention and reverence.

She thought of the farm families she had grown up with and of her own parents, her farmer's upbringing—the notion that the harder a thing was to do, the more worth doing, the more valuable. And what, she had begun to think, could be more challenging than to go on loving someone through so many grim daily routines? To love one another not through absence and letters and joyful returns, but through snow shoveling, and meals together one after another, and bills pored over at the kitchen table. Through no longer the electric thrill of brushing against one another in the hallway or the kitchen, but instead through the possibility of growing so familiar that it sometimes felt impossible to still see one another. What love, to still love one another through that.

As Rose prepared dinner, Lily sat at the kitchen table, poring over her schoolwork, and Rose thought of how, at Lily's age, she had been just a few years from running off with Randolph, from taking flight from this farm town where she'd been raised. Now, here she was, perhaps about to become mayor of this town, though it had grown so different as to be hardly recognizable were it not for a few familiar landmarks—the granary along the railroad tracks just off Main Street, where bistros and coffee houses had begun to take up residence; here and there a silo in one of the fields that frayed off at the edges of town, not yet developed, not yet transformed into still more and more houses.

And here she was, also, quiet evenings at home with her husband, beginning to fall in love with the idea of a marriage that looked less like the grand love story she had always envisioned and more like the quiet, committed, humble marriages of the farm couples she'd grown up surrounded by and had vowed to be nothing like. Now, though, she could see the dignity in those relationships—the simple bravery of staying together through routine and hardship, through overwork and fatigue. She felt ashamed that she had ever been so dismissive. How little she'd known of life then. How little Lily knew, she thought, as she watched her daughter, bent over her schoolwork at the kitchen table.

@

And so Rose was surprised, one evening, when Randolph, home then for just over a month, made his way into the dining room where she was working on her campaign literature. "Rose," he began. "I've been thinking."

She looked up, recognizing his tone as the sort that indicates a conversation deserving of one's full attention. Here was the moment she had steeled herself for.

"I've been thinking," he said again, "that it may be time for me to take a break." Lately, he explained, he had found himself thinking about a book project—photos and text, maps of his journeys, suggested routes, helpful tips for other intrepid explorers. "I'd like to be home," he said. "For a good long while this time."

At first, Rose said nothing. She watched him for signs that he might have known what she had considered asking, that he might have known about the many unsent letters she had drafted before—

She stopped herself from thinking of it, as she always did.

"Is this because of my political aspirations?" she asked, finally.

Randolph took a seat in one of the chairs beside her at the glossy dining room table. "Not at all," he said, confused by the question. For his part, he was wondering if Rose could sense the fear that had grown in him. He hoped not. He was ashamed of it. He held his hand out to her. "Just a good time to begin a book, I think."

Rose took his hand, but rather than feeling pleased or relieved, she found herself feeling both guilty—that just like that, she'd been delivered from having to ask him something she had so thoroughly dreaded—and relieved—that he would be here with her, with Lily.

Lily, coming down the stairs in search of a snack for her study break, had found them, her mother, strangely, sitting on her father's lap like a child, their foreheads resting together, eyes only for each other.

@

"I've decided to take a bit of a respite from my travels," Randolph explained to Lily that night over dinner. Lily was slowly growing accustomed to her father's presence each evening at the table, each morning at breakfast. Rose folded her napkin and set it beside her plate, feeling certain she knew what was coming.

Lily looked across the table at her mother, suspicious. "Why?" she asked.

What to say, Randolph wondered. Would he tell her all of the ways in which he'd felt himself growing fearful?

"I almost lost you both," he said, finally, looking down at the table. "And I've been thinking about what's most important to me."

Lily looked down, too, a tear budding in the corner of her eye, which she brushed quickly away. Still, she stole another look at her mother, who, noting it, wondered whether Lily would raise the issue of the letters she'd discovered—the letters Rose had written but never sent.

She did not.

"I'm glad you'll be here," Lily said, taking her father's hand and weaving her fingers between his.

CHAPTER 22

Awaiting Decision

IN THE WEEKS FOLLOWING THE HEARING, THE LAB SEEMED STRANGELY quiet, the scientists unable to concentrate. To Sarala it felt like the whole town had grown silent and closed in, as if bracing itself for a blow.

Abhijat found himself more often than not looking out his office window toward the city in the distance. How precarious it felt to have one's professional fate in the hands of others.

At the grocery store, neighbors passed each other with curt greetings, having seen once and for all in the auditorium where everyone stood on the issue. They imagined the Department of Energy officials flying back to Washington, looking down over Nicolet from the windows of their airplane, its farmland and subdivisions growing smaller and smaller as they rose into the air and off to make their decision.

@

After the hearing, the letters began to arrive. In an office in Washington, a secretary who had been charged with collecting all correspondence on the matter of the super collider for the purposes of assembling a public record opened letter after letter from Nicolet. Some neatly typed on letterhead, others hand-lettered in nearly illegible scrawl—the shaky handwriting of elderly citizens, the large, looping handwriting of children.

Filed away with the others:

A letter from a woman who'd written *I hate the SSC,* across the bottom of the page near her signature.

Children's drawings: SSC in all caps, a circle drawn round it, a line struck through in prohibition. And their letters, asking why the collider couldn't be built on Mars instead of under people's houses. *There's lots of space up there. Then no one in our town would be fighting.*

In the rounded, decorative script of a teenage girl: *I don't really know much about this issue but our biology teacher asked us to write a letter in support of this. I hope this hasn't wasted your time. I'm getting extra credit for writing this.*

One in long, elegant cursive: *It is my testimony at the hearing that has prompted my writing. I would like to apologize to the panel members for my attitude during the hearing. While this is an emotional issue for those of us facing relocation and the loss of our community as we know it, this does not excuse my anger toward the panel members. Shortly after the hearing, the Lord reminded me that as a Christian, I had failed to represent Him in a way worthy of His name. So I ask that you please extend this apology to the gentlemen taking testimony that day in the auditorium. Please also express to them that I continue to pray for all of you for wisdom in this decision-making process.*

@

Anderson Hall rumbled with the low murmur of nervous conversation. Dr. Palmer made his way to the podium set up in the center of the stage, the auditorium seats filled with anxious Lab employees. Dr. Palmer was not a man who hid his emotions well; written across his face were the signs of fatigue and disappointment.

"Colleagues," he began. "This process has been a long and emotional journey for many of us, and I am afraid I call you together today to share with you disappointing news. After careful consideration, the Department of Energy has decided against construction of the Superconducting Super Collider here at the National Accelerator Research Lab."

There was a heavy silence in the large room. Dr. Palmer continued speaking, but Abhijat could no longer hear him, his mind racing.

Would it be built somewhere else, he wondered? Perhaps. But where? And more importantly, when? For surely it would mean more waiting, further delay, starting from scratch with studies and outreach and attempts to explain the magnitude of their work. His breath caught in his throat as all of this made itself clear to him.

Dr. Cardiff, beside him, turned at the sound.

Abhijat met his eyes, wiped a palm over a forehead now beaded with sweat.

"I know that many of us are profoundly heartbroken over this decision," Dr. Palmer finished. "I wish that I had some words of comfort to offer you all. Perhaps it is enough to remind us all that very big projects don't always have happy histories."

@

From his office window, Abhijat looked out over the charred prairie grasses.

For months now, he had been counting on the arrival of the super collider, had so freighted it with meaning, with the possibility of the great prizes, of his theories being recognized and his work remembered. He'd come to think of it as the most important thing to happen in his life, in his career. Now, though, without it? It felt as though a giant obstacle had been placed in his path. And for the first time in his life, he felt unequal to the task of determining how to circumvent it.

There would be, over the course of the next year, he realized, a slow trickle of young, ambitious physicists from the Lab. There was still work to be done, but Abhijat and Dr. Cardiff knew, as did the younger physicists, that the Lab was no longer the place from which the most groundbreaking work would emerge.

' ©

One by one the staff filtered down to the cafeteria, taking places at the long tables that lined the atrium. The sun shone in through the windows, but inside, the mood was glum. Abhijat took a seat at a table with Dr. Cardiff and Dr. Cohen. The cafeteria ladies, who knew how badly the scientists had hoped for the collider, brought over plates of cookies, which the physicists picked at halfheartedly.

"This will be the end of the Lab," Dr. Cohen said, breaking the heavy silence.

"Don't be hyperbolic, Adam," said one of their colleagues. "There's still much to be found in the lower energy levels we've got here now."

"Oh, please," Dr. Cohen answered. "That will be wrapped up in a matter of years. And then where will we be?"

"We'll be off to another lab," answered another colleague, as he took a seat.

That, they all knew, was likely true. Most would head to Europe or Japan. There were rumors of CERN trying for a super collider. Perhaps they would end up there.

Some would leave physics entirely, Dr. Cardiff thought, though he didn't say this.

"Now I'm going to have to wait until I'm fifty to understand what breaks electroweak symmetry," one of their young colleagues said, looking up from the napkin he'd torn into tiny pieces.

"If then," Dr. Cohen added. "I think this may be the death knell for our field."

"Entire fields of academic inquiry don't just die out, Adam," another colleague said.

"Of course they do."

@

Alone now in his office, Abhijat looked again, as he had so many times before, out the window and over the great prairie.

He felt tired, he realized. Tired of the constant striving that had been the focus of his attentions for as long as he could remember, the most important part of his world. Tired of attending to a professional legacy, of contributing, critiquing, keeping up, being first. But he was afraid, too, of living without those things. Who would he be without them? Was there, as his mother had always insisted, happiness in contentment with what one had?

Instead of driving home, he decided, that evening, to walk, following the paths laid out through the Lab's prairie grasses, toward town, toward his home.

He felt angry with ambition, he realized as he made his way home. It had, after all, come to nothing. Had seduced him with promises undelivered, and perhaps, he thought, undeliverable.

He had been an unwise man, he realized—no, worse, a stupid man, he decided, angry with himself.

@

For a week after the announcement, Abhijat stayed in bed, venturing out only to graze, listlessly, in the kitchen when his body reminded him to feed it. Each night when Sarala joined him, she felt his head for fever, but she knew what this was. She brought him cups of tea that grew cold on the nightstand, chicken soup at Carol's suggestion, but this, too, grew cold and gelatinous in the bowl beside his bed.

"What will this mean for his work?" Carol had asked, and Sarala realized that she didn't know.

When he emerged, finally, a week later, dressed again in a suit and tie, appearing at the breakfast table as though nothing had changed, Sarala and Meena exchanged looks. Once again he loaded his briefcase and made his way, for the first time in days, back to the Lab.

What to do now, he had asked himself. There was only going forward, letting go, embracing.

©

By the time of Randolph's return, Lily had only a few days until her application to the Academy was due. She'd turned it in just under the wire, which was unlike her, but understandable given the circumstances. Meena had ignored the deadline entirely, something she had not yet had the heart to tell Lily.

CHAPTER 23

Field Guide to the North American Household

Duane Bantam, a man who, though comfortable and successful in his role as the high school's wrestling coach, did not harbor finer academic ambitions, had, that spring, inexplicably been assigned to teach the Nicolet Public High School's Advanced Placement U.S. History class. As they neared the end of the school year, Mr. Bantam, in what was either an act of desperation or of genius— his students and colleagues had not yet decided—announced that the class would participate as reenactors during Heritage Village's annual Revolutionary War Days, a hands-on learning activity, he explained. Mrs. Schuster, the director of Heritage Village, was thrilled by the idea. She assigned each of the AP U.S. History students a character, and they had thrown themselves into their preparations, studying and designing period-appropriate costumes with the attention to detail she usually saw only in the "career" living-history buffs.

The students, the majority of whom had been Lily and Meena's classmates in the Free Learning Zone, now spent class periods poring over information on colonial-era field gear and weaponry, cookware, soap making, blacksmithing, indentured servitude, medicine, spinning, needlework, and woodworking, leaving Mr. Bantam to peruse his coaching manuals in peace.

Along with their newfound enthusiasm for reenacting, the AP students, with the zealotry of the recently converted, had also acquired a passion for the careful monitoring of accuracy above all else, and this had manifested in an awkward conversation (one Mrs. Schuster would have preferred to avoid) over Meena's participation in the reenactment.

"It's inauthentic," Tom Hebert argued. "There wouldn't be a housemaid in the period who looked like Meena."

Lily glared at him. Meena rolled her eyes, tired of her classmates' seemingly never-ending arguments over historically accurate footwear and undergarments.

Mrs. Schuster, who had not before been confronted with this issue, having dealt almost universally with the white, towheaded, and corn-fed volunteers who presented themselves to her, began to fumble. "We will do our best, Tom. You are right to note that it isn't..." Here Mrs. Schuster paused, searching for the word she wanted. "... ideal. But we will make the best of it."

"What a cretin," Lily muttered. Together, the girls sat down under a tree a little away from the rest of the class to look through one of the books Mrs. Schuster had lent them.

"Well," Meena allowed, "he does have a point." She expected that she might encounter similar sentiments, similar questions from the Revolutionary War Days audience. *Also, I drove here in a car and had Cocoa Puffs for breakfast,* she imagined replying.

☺

Sarala had offered to help the girls with their costumes. "I used to be quite skilled with a sewing machine when I was your age," she told them as she laid out snacks and Lily regaled Sarala with details about their characters, both housemaids in Heritage Village's mansion.

"For six weeks, we'll be in training, learning about the time period and creating costumes. The mansion is the most difficult assignment," Lily explained, "because there are so many rooms to interpret. You have to learn millions of details about each of them."

Meena had been relieved by Lily's interest in the project, for it meant a reduction in the steady stream of chatter regarding when they might finally receive news about whether they had been accepted at the Academy.

At some point, Meena knew, she was going to have to break the news to Lily that she hadn't applied. Until then, though, Meena negotiated these conversations with noncommittal, single-syllable responses, which Lily happily did not seem to notice amid her own growing anxiety and impatience.

@

Randolph had begun his book project with dedication and enthusiasm, but had found himself unable to make any meaningful headway. Each time he sat down at the large desk in his study, prepared to regale his imagined readers with tales of his wildest exploits, he was seized, instead, with a sense of the danger and the futility of it all. Reading through his drafts at the end of the day, he began to notice that he'd focused almost entirely on warnings: how to avoid cultural misunderstandings, the importance of preparation, the necessity of keeping one's eye on surrounding crowds.

He had asked Lily to read and comment on his work, and each night before bed, he presented her with his day's efforts. As she read, she noted helpful suggestions and asked questions, but she could see that he was struggling. What was missing from the pages was the sense of her father's enthusiasm, his curiosity, traits she had never known him to be without—indeed, traits which he had always seemed to have in abundance compared to the other adults she knew.

She had asked him one night what it was about exploration that had so appealed to him at her age, what had drawn him to his adventures. Randolph didn't know if she was asking because she was wise and hoped to remind him of what he had first fallen in love with, or because she was simply curious. In the end, though, it didn't matter. As he answered, Lily in the great chair in his office, Randolph behind his desk, he found himself thinking back to his childhood, to the books that had seemed to promise that there was still adventure to be had in the world, still unknown parts of the world left to be explored. And he began to see the way forward.

As he sat behind the polished mahogany desk from which he could survey the collection of curiosities he had acquired on his travels, he began to imagine who his audience might be, and found himself surprised that instead of writing to the intrepid adult travelers he had imagined addressing, he found himself instead remembering the nights he hid under a blanket with a flashlight, transfixed by wild tales of adventure. Perhaps a book for children might stoke that same curiosity in others, might help him remember his own curiosity rather than his fear.

@

Now that the collider had, as Rose's campaign literature noted, "been successfully defeated by our citizens standing up for their rights even when their elected officials would not," the citizens of Nicolet turned their attention to the upcoming mayoral election.

Rose had expected that the informal candidates' forum held in July at City Hall would be her time to shine, for Mayor Callahan had never been renowned for his skill at extemporaneous speaking. Her campaign staff had, of course, encouraged supporters to attend, and had even suggested a handful of question topics on which "your fellow citizens might be interested in hearing Candidate Winchester's thoughts." As they neared election day, Rose felt certain they were nearing, also, the end of Mayor Callahan's long run as mayor of Nicolet.

But as the candidates' forum progressed, the meeting room in the Nicolet Public Library packed with curious citizens, Rose had been caught off guard by one of the forum participants, who stood up to ask, "Isn't it true that your own daughter won't be attending Nicolet Public Schools? That she's being shipped off to an elite boarding school for 'exceptional' children? What sort of investment will you have in the schools here if you don't even trust them enough to educate your daughter?"

Rose, not realizing that word of Lily's application had reached the ears of the electorate, had fumbled her response, sounding as unprepared for the question as Mayor Callahan when he responded to what Rose thought were obviously questions planted by his supporters.

"Sir," she managed, finally, after many halting starts and stops, "where my daughter attends school has no bearing on my commitment to this community."

"Mrs. Winchester." Mayor Callahan stepped out from behind his podium. "I'd just like to go on record here today as agreeing with you that personal matters should be off the table when it comes to the mayor's race." He nodded, as though this was, indeed, a grave and serious matter.

Rose looked at Mayor Callahan over the top of her reading glasses, unable to decide, finally, if he was the bungling yokel she'd always pegged him for, or a far shrewder politician than she'd ever imagined.

@

Sarala had spent weeks studying the patterns and books on period-appropriate fabric Mrs. Schuster had loaned the girls. She had pulled her rarely used sewing machine from the spare bedroom closet, set it up on the dining room table, and spread the tissue-thin pattern pieces out over the living-room carpet, pinning them to the calico and cutting carefully. She wrestled with long yards of fabric that slowly, under her patient hand, transformed into petticoats and bodices.

The level of excitement in Nicolet over the upcoming Revolutionary War Days was far greater than she remembered from past years. Perhaps, Sarala considered, it was that the town felt able to breathe again now that the specter of the super collider had evaporated. Or maybe it was just that the town, fearful of the future, had chosen, instead, to take refuge in the past.

@

At the beginning of the summer, plans were announced for a large collaborative collider in Europe at CERN, and with that news it became clear that the Lab would no longer operate on the forefront of the physics community.

In July came the announcement from the Department of Energy that within the next four years they would cease to request funding to support the Lab's current accelerator. Was this some sort of punishment for not securing the collider, some of the staff wondered? Either way, it was clear that the department's priorities lay elsewhere.

The day the announcement of the defunding was made, Abhijat had taken a deep breath, gathered his energies, and began to make a list of his options. That facility, this university, yes—all of these were viable, promising possibilities, he thought, perusing the list once he had finished.

But that evening, over dinner, Meena had asked him, her voice, he noticed, halting and uncertain, "Does this mean we'll have to move?" Sarala watched him, waiting for his answer.

Abhijat looked up and across the table at his wife and daughter, taking in the lines of worry on both their faces.

He decided it then, just as he said it.

"No."

He said it again, as though to test himself.

"No. The accelerator may lose funding, but there will always be a place at the Lab for the theorists. It will just be—" he paused for a moment, imagining it "—a very different place. No longer the facility it once was."

He could picture it—the halls grown quiet, a skeletal staff of mostly emeritus-aged physicists still reading and occasionally publishing an article here and there. Abhijat thought of the rusting buildings of the linear collider and wondered how long until the old accelerator's buildings, once bustling with activity, would begin to look like that. How long until the cafeteria, once filled with chattering scientists, would be populated by one or two physicists sitting together over coffee at a too-large table.

"No," he said again, "we will not have to leave," and, watching the looks of relief that passed over his wife's and his daughter's faces, he knew he had made the right decision.

CHAPTER 24

The Road to Independence

For Revolutionary War Days, Sarala had selected for herself a red, white, and blue sweater, its front decorated with an image of a group of pigs sewing an American flag.

She had been surprised when Abhijat suggested that he join her for the event—he'd lived in Nicolet for over a decade and hadn't once visited Heritage Village.

As they walked together through the grounds, she turned now and then to point something out to him. Here were all the things she loved about Heritage Village—the blacksmith's shop, exhibits on colonial life in America, the costumed villagers—but now the grounds were full of elaborately costumed Revolutionary War reenactors from all over the country, regiments and camp followers, Redcoats who imagined they might quash this young republic.

The weekend's reenactors had set up campsites under the canopies of trees that spotted the grounds—canvas tents arranged around campfires, and from the part of the green that functioned as the day's battlefield came the sound of cannon blast, the sharp crack of muskets being fired.

Sarala thought back to the times she had brought Meena here as a child, how Meena had loved the smoke and racket of the blacksmith's shop, how this place had performed for Sarala the America she'd imagined.

Their first stop, she decided, leading Abhijat to it, would be the early frontier log house, surrounded by its split-rail fence.

A junior reenactor Sarala recognized as a classmate of Meena's was leading another group through the cabin when they arrived. It consisted of a single room—kitchen, dining room, and bedroom all at once—but the group's attention was on the ladder in the corner that reached up to a loft. "Pioneer families built the loft for two reasons," Meena's classmate, in his simple frontier costume, explained. "In the winter, heat rises, so that was the warmest place in the house to sleep. Also, you'll notice that there are no doors here—just flaps of animal hide. Well, if you were cooking something that smelled good, or your house looked toasty and warm, it wasn't uncommon for a wild animal to wander in. And when that happened, the whole family could scramble up to the loft and pull the ladder up after them. Then they'd just wait until it wandered back out again."

"Fascinating," Abhijat said, smiling. "What kind of animal?"

Sarala, surprised by his interest, turned to observe her husband.

"Oh, a raccoon maybe, or a bear," the student answered.

Sarala had not expected Abhijat's delight at the house's plank floors, the large stone fireplace. In one corner of the single room sat a wooden bed covered with a rough wool bedspread, and he pointed out to her a small, worn doll made of corncobs in a basket at the foot of the bed. Outside, he was intrigued by the children trying their hand at pioneer chores, grinding dry corn into meal using a wooden mortar and hollowed-out log as a pestle, or carrying buckets of water hung on a yoke they wore across their backs. It seemed to Sarala like an entirely new Abhijat who accompanied her through Heritage Village.

They made their way through the church, the tavern, the sawmill, the farm laborer's cottage, the tiny post office and mercantile, the smokehouse, the doctor's home office, and the brick farmhouse with its stoneware jugs and quilts, its barn full of farm tools. They looked through display cases with exhibits on local history, full of tea sets and dolls donated by elderly residents, memorabilia from businesses that had once existed in Nicolet. In one, an old photograph of a team of oxen pulling a wagonload of timber through town; in another, a city ordinance prohibiting pigs from running loose within the town limits. They made their way through the gift shop, stocked with souvenir tea sets and crockery, child-sized coonskin caps and bonnets, slates, magnets, wooden nickels, field guides to Illinois trees and wildflowers, postcards, and an old cigar store Indian whose display sign indicated that it was on "indefinite loan" to Heritage Village.

Revolutionary War Days was always Nicolet's biggest annual event, but this year it had drawn an even larger crowd than usual. During the festival, Heritage Village would be unveiling its newest building—a replica of the Custom House, site of the Boston Massacre. Mayor Callahan was scheduled to give a dedication speech followed by patriotic music by the Nicolet Community Band.

Sarala led Abhijat along the paths, following the hand-painted wooden signs. "We should see Meena and Lily give their tour of the mansion," she suggested.

The mansion stood a bit off from the rest of the village on a small swell of land, which, against the surrounding flat prairie passed for a hill. It was a tall, two-story home of dark red brick, its imposing entrance at the top of a steep limestone stairway.

Abhijat and Sarala joined a group making their way up the stairway to the front door, where they were met by Meena, in costume. She grinned at her parents. "Welcome to the mansion," she said, showing the group into the house's entrance hall. Abhijat was struck by how grown up Meena looked in her long dress, her hair pinned up.

Meena led the group through the dark foyer into the parlor, where she began to tell them about the house and the family who had once lived there, Nicolet's own founding family.

Abhijat was used to being proud of his daughter, but he felt a new kind of delight descend upon him as he watched Meena, who had not only memorized an impressive number of facts for the tour, but was also, Abhijat noted, skilled at speaking to this group of strangers, at animating her recitation with a quick smile, kneeling down to listen to the question of one of the small children. Abhijat felt like he had, for a moment, caught a fleeting glimpse of the adult Meena.

She led them through the dining room, hung with its ornate chandelier and bright wallpaper, and into the kitchen, where she explained the rigid but invisible class threshold that existed at the doorway between kitchen and dining room. Outside, she pointed out the carriage house, the stable, and the kitchen garden arranged across from the root cellar, where the family's cook had stored potatoes, turnips, and apples through the winter. From here, she led the group back to the stairs and handed them off to Lily for her tour through the bedrooms, the upstairs parlor, and the dark upstairs hall.

Lily did not have that same easy way with the crowd, Abhijat noted, though he took no pleasure in the realization. She recited the details of the house's second floor as though eager to have them out of her, closing her eyes a little as she spoke, as though willing her audience out of her sight.

In the doorway of a bedroom, one of the mothers in the group pointed to the bed warmer, which looked to Abhijat like a long-handled skillet. "You put that in your bed," the mother explained to her children, "while you were sleeping to keep you warm."

"Actually…" Lily, overhearing this from across the hall, turned to face the mother. "That's not correct. It's not like a hot-water bottle," she continued. "It was filled with red-hot coals. If you left it in your bed all night, you'd burn your feet off. You ran it over the sheets before bed."

The mother looked at Lily, halfway taken aback, halfway interested—she seemed unable to decide. "Well, thank you, young lady," she said. Then she gathered her children and herded them down the hall toward the next room.

@

Once they had seen out the last of the tour groups, Meena and Lily took seats on the limestone steps in front of the mansion to listen to the mayor's speech and watch the ribbon-cutting ceremony, their skirts spread out over their knees, feet disappearing beneath the deep folds of the fabric. The afternoon sun was bright in contrast to the oppressive, Victorian darkness of the house.

Some of their classmates from the regular classes wandered the grounds carrying large turkey legs or American flags. A pack of teenage boys passed the house and looked up at Lily and Meena. "Hey, old-time lady," one of them yelled. "You're hot."

Lily rolled her eyes. "Have you gotten your acceptance letter yet?" she asked Meena. Lily had been on a high since Thursday, when her acceptance letter from the Academy arrived. "I'm sure it's on its way," she continued before allowing Meena to respond. "Mr. Delacroix all but guaranteed you'd be accepted. I've been thinking about whether we should request to be roommates. On the one hand, we know we get along. But on the other hand, we might meet more people—"

Meena stopped her, turning to face her friend. "Look, Lily," she began. "I haven't wanted to tell you this." She still didn't, she thought to herself. Meena took a deep breath. "I didn't apply," she said, finally.

"What?" Lily asked, her brow wrinkled, eyebrows drawn together over the bridge of her nose.

"I didn't apply to the Academy."

"But why not?" Lily asked, incredulous. "It's a tremendous opportunity."

"I know it is," Meena said.

"So you've been lying to me about this?" Lily asked. "For months now?"

"Not lying," Meena corrected her. "I never said I was going to apply."

"You never said you weren't," Lily argued. "I thought we were both—" Lily thought for a moment, looking out over the paths that divided the grass into neat geometrical shapes. She shook her head. "I just…" She was unable to find her words. "I just… I can't believe you're going to throw away an opportunity like this. Do you realize how isolated you'll be?" she asked. "The most interesting person to talk to for the next three years—until college, Meena—will be Tom Hebert. Have you thought about that?"

Meena looked down at her skirt, draped over the steps of the great house. There was a long, fraught silence.

"I thought we were going together," Lily said. "Now it's just me? Just I'm going?" Her voice was small and uncertain.

Meena looked up at Lily, who was now plucking at a loose thread along the hem of her skirt. As she watched her, Meena began, slowly, to realize that this smart and confident friend of hers was afraid. Afraid of doing this alone. Meena took her friend's hand in hers.

"Lily. You're going to be fine there on your own. Better than fine. You're going to be amazing."

Lily sat in silence for a moment, considering this.

"Without you, though?"

"You don't need me," Meena said.

◎

Mayor Callahan stood at the microphone on the bandstand. Behind him, the Nicolet Community Band sat quietly in their seats, shiny brass instruments catching the gleam of the sun.

"While this community has, over the last year, found itself in conflict and disagreement over an issue of modern science," he began, "we are pleased to come together here today as friends and neighbors to unveil Heritage Village's most recent addition and to honor our country's forefathers, who, like I said, fought for an ideal they believed in."

The Custom House stood ready for its unveiling, a red ribbon across the front door. A reproduction of the Liberty Bell had been erected on its lawn.

In front of the entrance to the new building, Mayor Callahan and Mrs. Schuster, the director of Heritage Village, posed for photographers from the *Herald-Gleaner* with a pair of shiny, oversized scissors. When they had gotten the shot they needed, Mayor Callahan cut the wide red ribbon and stepped aside to welcome the citizens of Nicolet inside, the community band striking up a wobbly, uncertain version of "America the Beautiful."

Outside, beyond the wrought-iron gates of Heritage Village, the traffic hummed along Homestead Road, the growl of a plane's engine cut through the warm spring air, and the visitors tried hard to ignore the specter of the Research Tower rising up in the distance.

CHAPTER 25

Manifest Destiny

For Abhijat, there had been a slow understanding and a gradual acceptance that this was where his career would come, gracefully and respectably, if not as memorably as he had hoped, to an end. And he had surprised himself by responding to this acceptance with relief.

At first, he hadn't known what to call it, this strange feeling of lightness, of freedom that had come over him. It was as though he had set down a heavy and unwieldy burden he'd been carrying for years.

It did not leave him all at once—he thought often, still, of what might have been. Some days he wondered if it might still be possible, one of the great prizes. But he had begun to grow accustomed to this new sense of peace that had come over him, to understand that it was valuable.

Fading slowly into the background was the pressure to produce, to publish, to chase, always, after the new, and it was liberating. Instead, he found that he enjoyed his quiet office, enjoyed thinking and writing about the things that had always piqued his curiosity, enjoyed his colleagues and his family.

He had, one morning, surprised Sarala, joining her at the table where she was finishing her morning tea. "Do you know that in a few weeks we will have been married for seventeen years?" he asked.

"Yes, that's right," Sarala replied, looking up at him curiously. It was not like Abhijat to remember this sort of thing.

"We should—" Abhijat began tentatively, watching her face, attempting to decipher what it was that a husband was expected to do in this situation. "We should have—" He paused. (*Yes*, the look on his face said, *I think this is right—proceed.*) "—a cookout with friends?" His voice lifted at the end, as though attempting to protect himself by wrapping the suggestion in as much ambiguity as possible.

Meena, sitting across the table from her father, frowned, perplexed.

Abhijat looked at Sarala, who blinked and nodded slowly. "Sure. Yes," she said, nodding again. "We could do that."

Abhijat clapped his hands together. "Then it's settled! I will begin the planning," he announced, gathering his things from the table and bustling out the door to begin the day.

@

Abhijat had thrown himself into the idea of the cookout. He had prepared and sent invitations that read: "We invite you to join our family, the Mitals, to celebrate the seventeenth wedding anniversary of Sarala and Abhijat." He'd invited Carol and Bob for Sarala, the Winchesters for Meena, and Dr. Cardiff for himself.

He'd made what Sarala was fairly certain was his first-ever trip to the hardware store and had come back with the trunk of their sedan tied open, bobbing up and down as he navigated the bump at the end of the driveway as slowly as possible. He had then (for the first time ever) knocked on the front door of Carol and Bob's house and asked Bob if he might help Abhijat unload his purchase.

From out of the trunk came an enormous barbeque grill. Together, Bob and Abhijat rolled the grill behind the house and onto the patio, where Bob admired Abhijat's selection. "The Performance Series. That's a good model," he said, nodding.

"Do you think?" Abhijat asked, though he was certain he'd made a wise purchase, having first consulted numerous back issues of *Consumer Reports* at the public library before making his selection.

@

The day of the barbeque was as sunny and warm as Abhijat could have hoped.

"Your seventeenth anniversary," Rose said. "This is certainly a novel way to celebrate such an occasion."

"Is it?" Abhijat asked, his head turned a little to the side as though taking this in. "We have not, in previous years, marked the occasion."

Sarala made her way around the patio with a tray of lemonade, handing out glasses to each of their guests.

Lily stood near her parents.

"So are you packed and ready to go?" Meena asked her.

"Not yet," Lily answered, though she seemed to be looking off somewhere behind Meena's head as she spoke. Since Meena's confession, their interactions had yet to return to normal, though Meena hoped they would soon.

"And how has your campaign been going, Mrs. Winchester?" Carol asked.

"How kind of you to ask," Rose said, smiling and turning toward Carol and Bob. "We're all very hopeful."

"I imagine this business with the collider has been quite a coup," Bob said, hands in his pockets, rocking back a little on his heels.

Carol gave him a look, but he was prevented from further pursuing that line of thought by Abhijat's voice, which rang out through the small group of guests. "Please, ladies and gentlemen, may I have your attention?"

Their heads turned to regard their host, who stood in front of the sliding-glass doors. Abhijat took a note card from his back pocket and, peering down at it, realized he had forgotten his reading glasses.

He patted the pockets of his trousers and shirt as though hoping to discover them hiding there, but, finding this search unfruitful, had turned toward Rose.

"Mrs. Winchester, if I may," he asked, indicating the glasses she wore on a chain around her neck.

"You're certainly welcome to try," she said, handing the reading glasses to him, "but the prescription…" She trailed off.

"Thank you," Abhijat said, taking them from her. "I am most grateful." He held them up in front of his face and again looked down at the note card in his hand. "Yes. Now, you must all please excuse me for wearing ladies' glasses."

He cleared his throat and began in earnest.

"Thank you all for being here today for our celebration. Seventeen years ago, this beautiful woman, Sarala, was joined with me in marriage. That day made me the happiest of men."

As he spoke, Sarala looked up at her husband, holding Rose Winchester's glasses before his eyes as he peered at his note card.

"I have," he continued, "I must confess to all of you, not always been the easiest of men to be married to." Abhijat's small audience began to laugh, a strange mixture of discomfort at the truth of his statement and warmth at the idea that he'd been aware enough to realize it. "No. It is true," he insisted. "This," he gestured at Sarala, "is indeed a very patient lady.

"As many of you know, I was gravely disappointed by the turn of the events regarding the super collider, and now the Lab itself." He nodded along with his audience. "It was shocking indeed. I believed that the Lab getting the collider was the most important thing that could happen in my life, in my professional career. But I must tell you all that I was wrong. That, in fact, *not* getting the collider was the most important thing that could have happened."

Sarala stared at her husband, surprised, and in that moment, it was as though the rest of the party receded into the background. As though he spoke only to her.

He continued. "And that is because it has caused me to take note, finally—after much too long, I am afraid—of all of the blessings of my life. A beautiful, talented daughter; a loving and loyal wife; and, it is to be hoped—" He held his hand out to the assembled guests stiffly, Sarala noted, as though this was a gesture he had included on the note card, along with the text. He continued, "—new friends."

Across the patio, Abhijat's eyes met Sarala's, timidly, as though uncertain of the sentiment he might find there.

@

Later, after their guests had left, as they prepared for bed, Sarala asked Abhijat, "At the end of the party, when it was time to say goodbye to our guests, I couldn't find you."

"Yes. I was done socializing," he explained.

"Where did you go?" she asked.

"To my study to read," he answered. "Are you—" He looked at her tentatively, trying to determine if he had done something wrong. "Displeased?"

Sarala took a breath. "No," she said. She looked at him. He was different, yes—this she had noticed gradually over the last few months, a slow realization. But still, so many things would likely always be entirely the same. She took his hand in hers.

"Your speech," she said, "it was lovely."

CHAPTER 26

Reconstruction

In a collider, virtually all of the combined energy of the two particles becomes available for the creation of new matter.
—To the Heart of Matter:
The Superconducting Super Collider, 1987

The week before the new school year began, Rose and Randolph helped Lily pack, deciding which things she'd need, which things could stay, and which things they could bring to her should she change her mind, should they need an excuse to visit. They were both full of pride at their bright daughter and thrilled for her to have such an opportunity, but all three recognized this as the end of their brief period together as a family.

Rose watched Lily carefully folding clothes, stacking favorite books, and thought of all the times she'd watched Lily and Randolph performing this same ritual in preparation for one of Randolph's trips. Randolph sat in Lily's reading chair in the corner of her room, offering commentary on how she might pack more efficiently, what she might consider leaving behind.

Rose smiled. It was bittersweet. They had, that summer, grown used to a new sort of life, the three of them all together like the most conventional of families, and now that was about to change again. She wondered what the house would feel like without Lily, just her and Randolph rattling around.

@

Lily hoped that Meena was right, that she'd do well at the Academy without her. For so long, she'd counted on having Meena at her side to help smooth the interactions with peers she sometimes found so genuinely baffling. But perhaps the students at the Academy would be different. Perhaps they'd be like her.

As she emptied the drawers of her desk, sifting through stacks of paper and old schoolwork, she found the report she and Meena had done years ago for Mrs. Webster: "Lady Florence Baker: The Journey from Slavery to Exploration." She leafed through the not-insubstantial text tucked into a glossy report binder. On the cover was the map of their subject's travels that Meena had drawn, a meandering line snaking from Cairo along the Nile, all the way to Lake Albert. Lily traced it with her finger. Perhaps the Academy would feel the way things used to feel between her and Meena. Familiar, comforting, like home.

@

Sarala had planned her conversation with Abhijat carefully. Cautiously, watching for just the right moment, having given Abhijat time to adjust first to the news of the collider, then to the news of the defunding, Sarala made her announcement.

The passage from the Mary Kay biography that rang most true to Sarala was this: "The first sale a married woman needs to make is to 'sell' her husband on her new job opportunity."

It wouldn't really be a job so much as a hobby. For she knew that much of Abhijat's pride was tied up in the knowledge that he could provide his wife with a life in which she need not pursue employment. Just a few nights out a week, once she established her client base, she explained.

Abhijat had not been as surprised by Sarala's announcement as she had imagined he would be, and indeed, watching her present the opportunity to him, he had been struck by her confidence, her poise. She would be good at this, he realized, feeling proud of her. "If this is where your interest and passion lead you, then you must follow that," he told her. And so it was settled.

On the first page of her notebook, in her careful printing, Sarala wrote out "Client Histories." She looked at the lined page, imagining it full, soon, of useful and valuable information.

@

Sarala had been nervous before her first party, had prepared for hours, practicing with her flip chart and her case, enlisting Meena as her guinea pig, setting out the trays of makeup with their Styrofoam inserts, Carol looking on to critique her performance.

"Sarala," Carol pronounced when she had finished, "you are just a natural at this. I'm half afraid you're going to put me out of business," she added, smiling at her friend.

@

For Meena, the first day of school without Lily there beside her had been both strange and exciting. She found herself wondering how Lily was settling in at the Academy. The night before, on the phone, Lily had described her room in the Academy's dormitory, her impressions of some of the other students, the academic expectations. As Meena had expected, Lily sounded entirely at home there. Already she'd begun to leaf through some of her textbooks, Lily confided, wanting to get a head start. Many were college-level texts, she told Meena, excited.

The girls exchanged plans for the upcoming weekend: Meena cheering at her first soccer game of the season, Lily attending the Academy's annual Kurosawa retrospective.

"You should come to visit," Lily said before they hung up. "You'd fit right in."

@

With Sarala often busy in the evenings, Abhijat had taken over preparation of the meals, a task he enjoyed and an arrangement the whole family found they preferred.

He planned the meals carefully, retrieving Sarala's mother's box of recipes from behind the Tupperware, working his way through each one and interspersing his offerings with experiments—new dishes he discovered, reading carefully each week through "Phyllis's Fixin's," the *Nicolet Herald-Gleaner*'s cooking column.

These days, in his office in the Research Tower and at home, evenings, Abhijat found that he now read more than he wrote, that he now listened more than he spoke, and each night, he set out on a walk—a stroll through the neighborhood, hands clasped behind his back, his pace slow and measured, taking in the world that had lived and breathed around him for years. Always, he walked at dusk, leaving the house as the sun dropped behind the elementary school. Always, he walked alone, for now it was Sarala who was otherwise occupied, her evenings filled with meetings and parties over which he imagined her officiating with poise and confidence.

He enjoyed these walks, the neighborhood silent, the glimpses of the lives of his neighbors he could snatch as he walked home, their houses lit up from inside; overhead, planes making their way through the dark night sky.

At the Winchester home, Rose otherwise occupied with her campaign work and Lily now off at the Academy, Randolph, too, had begun to take an evening constitutional. It was after a week of these slow, contemplative walks that Randolph noticed another figure engaging in the same evening routine.

"Ah, Mr. Mital," Randolph said, extending his hand as he recognized Abhijat. "I see we have gotten into the same habit." The men shook hands. "I wonder," Randolph suggested, "if we might not take our constitutional together this evening."

"Yes, why not?" Abhijat answered, pleased to have the company.

◎

The night of the election, Rose, Randolph, and her campaign team gathered at one of the new restaurants on Nicolet's Main Street to watch the results coming in via the local cable channel. From her seat beside Randolph, Rose sipped a glass of white wine and kept one eye on the television.

Early indications showed Mayor Callahan in the lead, but Rose was confident.

She was certain the electorate realized that Mayor Callahan's era had come to an end and that it was time for a new type of leadership in Nicolet.

But perhaps because she had so wanted it, had so entirely expected it, Mayor Callahan's win that night—"another term for Mayor Callahan, our mayor and friend," the television announcer said, his voice carrying out into the noise of the room—took Rose completely by surprise. The restaurant had grown quiet at the announcement.

Randolph turned to watch her as she took in the news, his arm around her shoulders. He found himself searching her face, her voice, for a sign of what stirred beneath. But she was, as always, composed, unreadable.

Later, after the news had sunk in, after she'd graciously received visitors to their table sharing their condolences, their assurances that their votes had gone to Rose, she'd decided that what she wanted to do was to collect her signs, and to do it alone.

She'd dropped Randolph off at the house and now circled slowly through the neighborhoods of Nicolet. At the height of the town's division over the collider, Rose's campaign signs and those of Mayor Callahan had begun to spring up in front yards, sprinkled among the pro- and anti-collider signs, so that each yard was a mingled cacophony of political opinions.

Now Rose just wanted the signs to disappear. She couldn't bear the thought of her supporters waking in the morning to such a visual reminder that they'd bet on the wrong horse. She wanted no such public reminder of her failure.

The streets of Nicolet's neighborhoods were quiet and dark. At the first house—not far from their own, where she'd left a concerned Randolph, assuring him that yes, she wanted to do this now, and that yes, she preferred to do it alone—she'd stopped, the car idling on the smooth, dark pavement. The sign caught the light from her headlights. WINCHESTER FOR MAYOR: A NEW ERA FOR NICOLET. She pulled the thin metal frame from the soft earth of the yard, opened the car's back door, and carefully laid the sign down on the backseat. She returned to the driver's seat, put the car in gear, and drove on.

It took two hours. She drove through all the neighborhoods of Nicolet she remembered from her girlhood, through those that had sprung up in her absence, and through some newer still even than that. There was something oddly heartbreaking about the number of signs, a physical presence growing behind her as she drove on, of the votes she'd won, of how close she'd come to the thing she'd worked toward and planned for and counted on.

@

On their first walk together through the neighborhood, Randolph and Abhijat had found themselves mutually delighted by one another, Randolph fascinated by the latest theory Abhijat was puzzling his way through, and Abhijat by Randolph's thrilling stories of adventure.

Soon, their evening constitutionals were, by habit, taken together, Randolph opening Abhijat's eyes to the larger world, and Abhijat opening Randolph's to the smaller.

"I was sorry, for Mrs. Winchester, to hear the results of the election," Abhijat said as the sun began to set in the damp evening heat.

"Yes," Randolph nodded as he walked, hands clasped behind his back. "It's been quite a disappointment to her. Quite a shock, as well, I think."

"And what goal will she now pursue?" Abhijat asked.

Randolph looked up into the sky, where the light of the day was fading. "Do you know," he said, looking back at Abhijat, "I haven't got any idea. And I'm not sure she has either."

They walked for a while in companionable quiet.

Abhijat felt, sometimes, as though he were awakening to his own life. He'd begun to notice the details of their home. The decorations Sarala had accumulated and arranged so carefully suddenly struck him with their beauty, all the more acute knowing that for years he had failed to notice their presence.

"It can be liberating," Randolph noted, when Abhijat shared these thoughts with his new friend, "to let go of hopes that chain one to unhappiness, dissatisfaction."

"And you?" Abhijat asked. "How go your memoirs, my friend?"

"Quite well, thank you," Randolph said. "Now, at any rate. As a book for adults, I wasn't able to find my way, but this—" He was writing now for the kind of curious child he had been, the kind both of their daughters had been. "This way feels, I think, like the right path to take."

They made their way past the small man-made lake around which some of the more sought-after homes of the Eagle's Crest subdivision had been constructed, pausing in their conversation to listen to the low gurgle of frogs.

"Today I revisited the Nile Delta, a place of much beauty and intrigue," Randolph continued.

"Should you need another set of eyes on the manuscript as you work," Abhijat ventured, "I would be honored to read it."

Randolph smiled at him, clapping him on the back. "Just the thing, my friend. I'd be honored to have you."

Their walk coming to an end at the Winchester house, Randolph took his leave of Abhijat, who continued on the few blocks to his own home.

The sun had set, and as Abhijat walked, he looked up into the lit-up windows of the houses he passed, as he had done in the early days of his marriage, just before Sarala had arrived in the States, searching those lit-up rooms for a hint of the lives that might stretch out before them.

☺

Now, with Lily away at school, the Winchester house felt less lively. Rose missed coming in to find Lily and Meena at the kitchen table, heads bent over their schoolwork, chattering back and forth.

Randolph and Rose adjusted to the new quiet of their lives, of their home. On the happy days when letters from Lily arrived, they opened and read them together, Rose thinking of the many evenings she and Lily had sat together over dinner reading aloud from Randolph's letters the latest news of his adventures.

How like her own parents, too, Rose imagined, picturing them together at the kitchen table poring over one of her own letters describing her and her new husband's strange adventures.

"She's liking her roommate a bit more than she did initially," Randolph reported, skimming the page as Rose set the table for their evening meal. "Though she's still cautious. I confess to not being terribly surprised about that," he added, smiling at Rose. "And here, darling, listen to this."

Rose could hear Lily's voice tangling with Randolph's as he read.

I know, Mom, that we didn't agree on many of the issues, but I'm sorry that you didn't win the election. I really am. I know how hard you worked and how important this was to you. I hope you'll be able to find something else to work toward.

The truth was, Rose had so expected to win that she had in no way prepared herself for the possibility that she wouldn't. Once the collider had been defeated, it had seemed so certain that she would take Mayor Callahan's place. That this would be the beginning of a new era in Nicolet.

Now what? she'd found herself wondering the day after the results. It was the first time in her adult life that she'd been without a plan.

Before, Rose would have wondered whether she and Randolph might not again take up their adventures together—Lily off at school and there being nothing to tie them to Nicolet. But just now Randolph seemed so happy there at home, content in a way she had never seen when he was not traveling. No, she realized, those days were in the past.

She wondered, though, her thoughts drifting back to her political ambitions, if she had perhaps not set her sights too low. If her loss was in fact best seen as a nudge toward something larger, as an opportunity.

She called a meeting of her campaign team.

@

Abhijat, who had never permitted himself much time for pleasure reading, had allowed himself to sink happily into Randolph's drafts, finding himself captivated by the world Randolph had conjured. Often, Abhijat would sit down in one of the comfortable living room chairs to read and would find, upon looking up at the end of a section, that hours had crept by and that it was now long since past time for him to begin preparing dinner.

He had begun assembling his own box of recipes—something he planned to give Meena one day. He'd bought a new wooden box, this one decorated with a wreath of hand-painted flowers, and a set of cream-colored index cards on which he kept track of the meals that became their favorites:

For when you have forgotten to see the loveliness around you, he wrote. And here his recipe for a simple dal.

For when one must be reminded of one's own good fortune. Then Meena's favorite—chicken prepared on their new barbecue.

For when you wish to thank the world for your happiness. And here, Sarala's favorites—Kraft Dinner, Rice-A-Roni, green bean casserole.

©

Sarala made her way home from the evening's party. She'd done well that night. Indeed, she'd been surprised by how easy it seemed, how effortless, how fun. She wondered if this was how Abhijat had felt among his theories and equations. At home. Where he belonged.

Now, she often passed her neighbors, returning from work just as she was setting out. She thought of this as her reverse commute, and she waved to those she recognized. Her first night, she'd felt as though she were setting off on a great adventure.

It was almost always dark when she returned home, and Sarala loved peeking into the houses with the curtains left open as she drove, loved catching glimpses of families in the midst of their evening rituals.

In front of the elementary school, she slowed for the stop sign. There on the corner was her home, light glowing out from the kitchen windows where she could make out her own family inside, Abhijat preparing a late dinner so they might all share their meal together, Meena at the table, bent over her schoolwork.

Postscript

The Superconducting Super Collider (SSC) was a real project. Those readers who remember the SSC will recall that, unlike in this novel, it was not a matter of whether it would be built, but of where. For the purposes of this story I have simplified this, making Nicolet the only site under consideration, but the conflict illustrated in this novel played out in many locations around the country. The Department of Energy conducted studies of a number of potential sites, finally settling on Waxahachie, Texas. There, construction of the super collider began, but the project was canceled before it was ever completed, the site abandoned for years.

Notes

The idea for Abhijat's chart in chapter one comes from *The Strangest Man: The Hidden Life of Paul Dirac, Mystic of the Atom* by Graham Farmelo.

For the sections on Randolph's expeditions, I'm indebted to the following books for inspiration: *I Married Adventure* by Osa Johnson, *The Remarkable Life of William Beebe: Explorer and Naturalist* by Carol Grant Gould, and *Safari: A Chronicle of Adventure* by Bartle Bull.

The quote from the farmer's letter in chapter two comes from *Fermilab: Physics, the Frontier, and Megascience* by Lillian Hoddeson, Adrienne W. Kolb, and Catherine Westfall.

The captions and quotes from *The Secret Museum of Mankind* in chapters two and ten come from *The Secret Album of Oceana* and *The Secret Album of Africa*.

The blessing in chapter three comes from *The Hindu Woman* by Margaret Cormack.

The mosquito analogy in chapter four is paraphrased from *To the Heart of Matter: The Superconducting Super Collider*, 1987, Universities Research Association.

The title of chapter seven comes from a quote by Francesca Nessi-Tedaldi in an article titled "Crystal Gazing," hosted on the CERN website.

For the details of Lily and Meena's report and presentation in chapter eight, I'm indebted to Pat Shipman's *To the Heart of the Nile: Lady Florence Baker and the Exploration of Central Africa*.

The quote Sarala remembers from her schoolbook in chapter nine comes from *Women and Society in India* by Neera Desai and Maithreyi Krishnaraj. The quote in chapter nine about turning coffee into papers comes from a personal interview with Adrienne Kolb, Fermilab, 2010. The list of questions Sarala finds on Abhijat's desk in chapter nine comes from *Fermilab: Physics, the Frontier, and Megascience* by Lillian Hoddeson, Adrienne Kolb, and Catherine Westfall.

Quotes from the glossy reports produced by the Lab come from *Siting the Superconducting Super Collider in Illinois: A Report to Governor James R. Thompson and members of the 84th General Assembly, 1985* and from *To the Heart of Matter: The Superconducting Super Collider,* 1985 and 1987, Universities Research Association.

The title of chapter fourteen comes from a letter from W. E. Gladstone to Roderick Murchison regarding Lady Florence Baker.

In preparing the chapters on the letters to the editor and the public hearing, I drew heavily on the Environmental Impact Statement and the records of the public hearings held in response to the Draft Environmental Impact Statement in Illinois in October 1988, in some cases reproducing bits of text verbatim. Much of the text of the public hearing comes from direct quotes from transcripts of the Superconducting Super Collider hearing held in October 1988 at Waubonsie Valley High School. Names and descriptions of the speakers in the hearing are fictional.

The quote from chapter twenty-two: "Very big projects don't always have happy histories," is from a personal interview with John Peoples, former director of Fermilab, 2010. The quote from the same chapter: "Now I'm going to have to wait until I'm fifty to understand what breaks electroweak symmetry," comes from a personal interview with Andreas Kronfeld, Fermilab, 2010.

About Fermilab, the Inspiration
for the National Accelerator
Research Lab

Much like the novel's National Accelerator Research Lab, Fermilab is a particle physics laboratory located in the Chicago suburbs. The lab focuses on research into one of the most enduring mysteries of science: what is our universe made of and how did it come to exist? Named after renowned Italian physicist Enrico Fermi, Fermilab houses the Tevatron, which ceased operation in 2011 but was for a time the world's highest energy proton-antiproton collider. Its technology has since been outpaced by the Large Hadron Collider (LHC) at CERN in Switzerland, where scientists recently confirmed discovery of the Higgs boson and a new class of particle called pentaquarks. CERN has also been the subject of numerous conspiracies and much speculation about the creation of black holes, time travel, etc.

The story of the founding of Fermilab is fascinating. The campus is located on land that was once the town of Weston, Illinois, a town that no longer exists. Weston was annexed in the 1960s to allow for the construction of the Fermilab campus. As in the novel, many of the former town's homes are still in use today as offices and to house visiting scientists and their families.

When Fermilab arrived, the area was still very much a small, rural community. Suddenly, this small farming community found itself home to a number of internationally renowned scientists. Over the years, this, as well as other forces and changing land-use patterns, have been at the root of the area's transformation into a busy suburban community. For more information about the founding of Fermilab, I recommend *Fermilab: Physics, the Frontier, and Megascience*, which was invaluable to me in my research.

In the late 1980s, Fermilab was one of the sites under consideration to house the proposed Superconducting Super Collider (SSC), a project eventually begun in Waxahachie, Texas. Today, Fermilab is still considered by many to be the premier laboratory for particle physics in the United States. In recent years, Fermilab scientists have focused on experiments on dark matter, dark energy, and some really interesting projects, including an experiment called MINOS in which beams of neutrinos were sent underground all the way from Batavia, Illinois, to the Soudan Mine in northern Minnesota to help provide scientists with a better understanding of neutrino oscillations.

About the Superconducting Super Collider

The Superconducting Super Collider (SSC) was a real project under consideration at a number of locations around the United States. Scientists believed the collider would help them understand more about the matter that makes up the universe, and as such, would help them understand the circumstances under which the universe came to exist.

For many years, the United States stood at the forefront of physics research, and many proponents of the SSC believed its construction would help the United States retain that position. But this was the era of Chernobyl, of Three Mile Island; mistrust of the government was strong, and questions about the safety of scientific facilities were on the minds of many citizens.

Much like in the novel, physicists hoped the SSC would help to prove or disprove many of the theories about particle physics that were under consideration at the time. In the 1980s, the Department of Energy began the process of searching for an appropriate location for the collider. One of the locations under consideration was Fermilab and the surrounding communities. At the end of a long process that included environmental impact studies and public hearings, Waxahachie, Texas, was selected as the site of the future SSC.

Construction of the SSC began in 1991, but by 1993, with increasing costs, the U.S. government pulled the funding, having already spent $2 billion on the project. The Waxahachie location, where construction had already begun on tunnels and buildings, was abandoned. For many years, the partially completed site of the SSC stood empty, vandalized and filling with rainwater. (You can find some really interesting photographs of the abandoned site taken by urban explorers.) Recently, though, the site has been acquired by a company that uses it as a chemical blending facility and that has, in an interesting twist, preserved the initialism SSC, which now stands for the "Specialty Services Complex."

Had it been completed, the SSC would have been the most powerful accelerator ever constructed, three times as powerful as the LHC, currently the world's largest and most powerful particle collider. Many scientists believe that had the SSC project gone forward as planned, discoveries such as the Higgs boson (frequently referred to as the "God particle") would have happened earlier and would have been made in the United States.

The story of the SSC has much to say about American attitudes toward science and the challenges scientists and science writers face when communicating such complex research to lay audiences.

About the Academy

The Academy is based on the Illinois Math and Science Academy (IMSA), a residential high school for gifted and talented students founded in 1985. Leon Lederman, Nobel prize–winning physicist and director of Fermilab at the time, was one of IMSA's founders.

Acknowledgments

Love and gratitude to my partner in crime, Brook Miller, for his support, encouragement, time, feedback, and pep talks along the way.

A thousand thank-yous to agent extraordinaire Eleanor Jackson for fiercely believing in this book, for working tirelessly to find it a good home, and whose suggestions at every step made it better.

To the good people of Dzanc, for bringing this book into the world, especially Michelle Dotter and Mary Gillis, for their wise, careful edits; Guy Intoci for his impressive schedule juggling and oversight of the whole shebang; Steven Seighman for his design expertise and patience; Gina Frangello, Rhonda Hughes, Meaghan Corwin, and the entire Dzanc publicity team for all of their hard work and enthusiasm.

To Sheryl Johnston—wise, reassuring, and incredibly hardworking guide through the process of getting this book into the hands of readers.

To Adam McOmber and Christine Sneed, my writer support system, for years of encouragement, guidance, and understanding.

To the many early readers who participated in the Feedback and Serialization Project, especially Holly Witt, Katy Sirovatka, Nancy Barbour, Tom Noel, LeAnn Deane (also for her mad librarian skills!), Karen Cusey, Lindsey Fierros, Julie Eckerle, Ann DuHamel, Linda Kolaya, Helen Bergman, Vicki Wilmer, Katie Beach, Carter Beach, Pete Wyckoff, Sara Harding Lou, Aaron King, P.B. Carden, and Kevin Fenton. Forgive me if I've inadvertently left anyone off this long list.

To Gail Kearns for the name "Yankee Noodle Dandy." To Wendy Gross for letting me observe and take notes during her Mary Kay event. To Pallavi Dixit for her help with Sarala's mother's recipes. To Jennifer Bridge for her living-history facility expertise. To the Anderson Center, where I wrote the first chapter, and fellow resident Kora Manheimer, who came up with the name "Heritage Village." To the good people of Fermilab, especially Adrienne Kolb, John Peoples, and Andreas Kronfeld.

To the Jerome Foundation for funding to support research. To the Lake Region Arts Council and the Arts and Cultural Heritage Fund for writing time.

To Jennifer Goodnough, Troy Goodnough, and Jennifer Rothchild for helping me survive the weekend of the great book emergency.

To my family and friends for cheering me on and celebrating each small step along the way.

And with love, always, for P and E.

Discussion Questions

1. What do the chapter titles and the epigraphs at the start of many of the chapters suggest to you about the ideas at work in the book?

2. What is your initial response to the Winchesters' unconventional family arrangement? What does Rose see as the connection between their arrangement and her certainty that hers and Randolph's will be "one of the world's great love stories"?

3. Early in the novel, Sarala reflects on Abhijat's ambitions, noting that "each time he achieved one of the many goals he set for himself, he responded not with celebration and satisfaction at his own accomplishment, but by thinking, Yes, but there is more to be done." In what ways might Abhijat's attitude be useful? In what ways might it be detrimental?

4. Books are important to many of the novel's characters—for Randolph and Meena it's The Secret Museum of Mankind; for Lily and Meena it's their love of encyclopedias; for Sarala, her self-improvement books. In what ways do these books reveal interesting or important information about each of the characters? Which books have been important to you as a reader in this way?

5. Early on in the novel, Abhijat notes that curiosity is the most important human quality. In what ways is curiosity important to each of the characters?

6. The novel explores the ways in which land use in Nicolet changes— from prairie to farmland to suburb—with the arrival of the Lab.

How does this history of changing land use and the arrival of the Lab affect the community?

7. How do you respond to Abhijat's mother's advice that "one could best find success by first finding peace and contentment"?

8. Lily argues that "sometimes letters are a better way to know someone than all of the silly, inconsequential interactions of daily life." Why do you think she feels this way? Do you agree?

9. If you were a resident of Nicolet, where do you think you'd come down on the issue of the Superconducting Super Collider?

10. Where in the book do you encounter characters struggling to communicate successfully? How does this manifest? Is this resolved? If so, how? If not, why?

11. How does the use of physical space in each of the homes convey ideas about the characters? For example, are there rooms that seem to "belong" to certain characters? What do these rooms say about their owners? Are there ways in which these spaces reveal something about the social structures in each of the families?

12. The idea of feeling "at home" is a central focus of the book. Where do each of the characters feel most at home? Why?

13. Do you think Sarala ever really considers leaving Abhijat? If not, why? If so, what do you think changes her mind?

14. In what ways are the two families different at the end of the book than when we meet them at the beginning?

15. What are each of the characters most hoping for throughout the novel? Which of them get what they're hoping for? How do these outcomes affect each of the characters? Do you agree with Randolph's opinion at the end of the book that "it can be liberating to let go of hopes that chain one to unhappiness, dissatisfaction"?

16. What do you find likeable about each of the characters? What do you find unlikeable about them?

17. What do you imagine the future has in store for each of these characters?